THRESHOLD

Susan Feathers

THRESHOLD by Susan Feathers

Copyright © 2016 Susan Feathers

Cover design by Christine Horner

Interior design by Jacqueline Cook

Map illustration by Nathan George and Elizabeth Colrick George

"The Maze, or Se-eh-ha's House" and "A Potsherd Speaks" from *Pima Indian Legends* by Anna Moore Shaw. © 1968 The Arizona Board of Regents. Reprinted by permission of the University of Arizona Press.

ISBN: 978-1-61179-369-7 (Paperback)
ISBN: 978-1-61179-370-3 (e-book)

10 9 8 7 6 5 4 3 2 1

BISAC Subject Headings:
FIC000000 FICTION / General
FIC002000 FICTION / Action & Adventure
FIC048000 FICTION / Urban

Address all correspondence to:
Fireship Press, LLC
P.O. Box 68412
Tucson, AZ 85737

Visit our website at:
www.fireshippress.com

For Tom and Heather

A Note to Readers

This story is my way of saying, "It's time." I intend to sound the trumpets, to get your attention, in a story about love, community, and beauty. To remind you of what is at stake.

Earth's biological systems, which allowed forms beautiful and unending to evolve with time, are unraveling under the pressure of over seven billion human beings in need of resources to live and thrive. We are at the edge of human history at a watershed moment when collectively we must find ways to renew and sustain the biological systems that maintain life on Earth and make it worth living. In finding these ways, we will usher in a new age.

While it is a perilous time, the potential to innovate, and to "bend the moral arc of justice" as we do so, has never been greater. It will take all of us at all levels of power, knowledge, and skill.

In *Threshold* you will follow individuals who are coming to terms with climate change. They are like you and me: raising their families, going to work or school, falling in love, wondering about their future. Teachers, entrepreneurs, scientists, policemen, parents, grandparents and kids—these are the heroes and heroines of my story because it is we who will ultimately find solutions and guide our leaders to help make them happen.

Use this book as a starting point for discussion among your friends, family, colleagues, book clubs and church groups. You will find questions at the back of the book to guide your discussions.

Acknowledgments

In writing this novel, I am grateful to the Frank Waters Foundation for giving me the time, place, and inspiration for first drafting the story, and to Mark Rossi for continuing the important work of Frank and Barbara Waters of nourishing the creative spirit.

Thank you to the Tucson Festival of Books for selection of *Threshold* as a finalist in the 2015 Literary Awards, and to the University of Arizona Press for permission to reprint two Pima legends from Anna Moore Shaw's *Pima Stories*.

To Madeline Kiser and Oscar Beita, Mikaela Quinn and Jim Ricker, Annemie and Don Baker for room and board, wise counsel, and enduring friendships; to Helen Gutierrez, fellow bibliophile, friend, and guide to Tucson's cultural roots; and to fellow writers Diane Skelton, Judy Fawley, Victoria Franks, Anne Howard, and Jeannie Zokan—members of the Portfolio Society of the West Florida Literary Federation—you have my devotion.

To Rick Brusca, Wendy Moore, Debra Colodner, Barbara Warren, Valerie Rauluk, Bruce Plenk, Bill O'Malley, Roger Pfeuffer, Raul Ramirez, Jesus Garcia, Grace and Ed Beltran, Leza Carter, and Tres English, I am grateful for the time you gave me as I gathered current information for the book.

To colleagues and docents at the Arizona-Sonora Desert Museum, my thanks for the important work you do with such joy and panache. My gratitude also for the vision of Bill Carr and Arthur

Pak, founders of the Desert Museum—a vision that has engendered love and appreciation of the Sonoran Desert in local residents and visitors from all over the world. I am grateful, continuously inspired, and dedicated to following that path.

To Mary Monahan, Fireship Press Publisher, for taking a chance on my novel, and to Betty and Bill Falter who made it possible, thank you. To able editors Anna Mirocha and Marguerite Wainio, thank you for making this a better book. Special thanks to Marge Pellegrino, an early reader: your advice was golden.

To Marylyn Valencia, Program Director, and the students of Changemaker High School in Tucson, I thank you for the inspiration of your leadership and vision. You give me hope.

To the visionaries at Sustainable Tucson and 350 Pensacola: you are the torchbearers.

To my sisters, Barbara Feathers and Kathryn Johansen, thanks for being the ever present Muses. To my nephew, Nathan George, and his wife, Elizabeth Colrick George, I am grateful to you for creating the Map of Threshold.

Thanks to my parents, Mildred and Edward Feathers, for giving us kids an adventurous life in the US Air Force and for introducing me in 1947 to Tucson, where I impaled myself on a prickly pear and with a blood offering sealed my fate as a future desert rat.

To two women without whom this book would be mere imagination: Annemie Baker and Betty Christensen, friends for life.

To Tom and Heather, my dear children, your love is my inspiration for continuing to write and to speak the truth as I see it. I am grateful for your love, support, and example. This book is for you.

Cast of Characters

Duma – a jaguar born in the Sky Islands of Northern Mexico

Luis Munoz – Director of Living Collections at the Natural History Museum

Kim Turner – Veterinarian at the Natural History Museum
Henry Waxman – Director of the Natural History Museum
Harold Lieberman – Senior Docent at the Natural History Museum
Rich Downey – U.S. Fish and Wildlife biologist
Ron Butler – Director of Wildlife Rehabilitation Center

Dr. Carla Connor – Climate Scientist at the University of Arizona
Jim Mullins – Casual Intimate Partner and Colleague of Carla Connor
Ed Flanagan – Operations Director at the Community Food Bank and Climate Change Denier

Daniel Flanagan – Ed Flanagan's son and Junior Docent at the Natural History Museum

Betty Golden – Director of the Community Food Bank

Sal Castillo – Mission Garden Ethnologist

Dolores Olivarez – Teacher at Mission Viejo Middle School and Community Leader

Roberto Olivarez – South Tucson Policeman, Drug Trafficking Team
Enrique Santos – Troubled teen just out of Juvenile Detention for a purported drug offense

Diego Santos – Enrique's brother, in jail for selling drugs
Camilla Santos – Enrique's grandmother
Mrs. Carrillo – The Santos' family's neighbor and friend
Esmeralda Martinez – Enrique's dream girl and daughter of a prominent South Tucson family

Sonya Morales – Border Patrol Official in charge of child and family immigration

Samantha Garcia – Sonya's childhood friend and compatriot in fighting drugs and crime

Albert Pope – Former Tribal Sheriff and lead investigator on the Morales kidnapping

Bob Minor – Mayor of Nogales, Arizona and Sonya's close colleague

Luna Lopez – Tohono O'odham youth and aspiring basket-maker
Mr. and Mrs. Lopez – Luna's parents
Flora Romero – Tohono O'odham elder and master basket maker; Luna's mentor

George Romero – Tohono O'odham elder who teaches traditional practices to tribal youth

Lou Taylor – Embattled Mayor of Tucson in search of solutions to the water crisis

Rudolfo Ramirez – Arizona Congressman representing Tucson and the region

The ideas which determine our character and life are implanted in mysterious fashion. When we are leaving childhood behind us they begin to shoot out. When we are seized by youth's enthusiasm for the good and true, they burst into flower, and the fruit begins to set.

Grow into your ideals so that life can never rob you of them. If all of us could become what we were at fourteen, what a different place this world would be.

—Albert Schweitzer

THRESHOLD

Susan Feathers

Cortero
An imprint of
Fireship Press

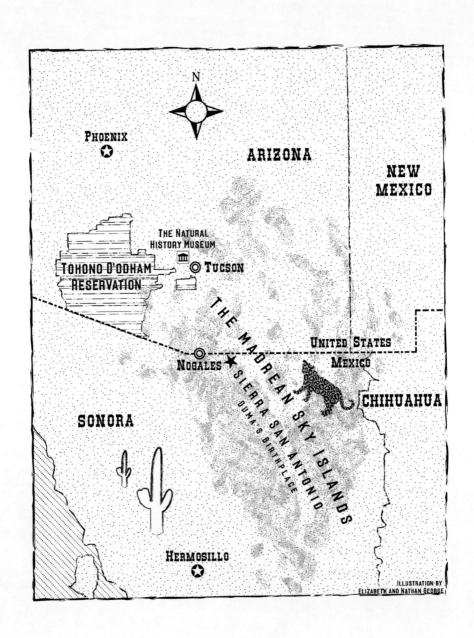

N

PHOENIX

ARIZONA

NEW MEXICO

THE NATURAL HISTORY MUSEUM

TOHONO O'ODHAM RESERVATION

TUCSON

THE MADREAN SKY ISLANDS

SIERRA SAN ANTONIO

OUMA'S BIRTHPLACE

UNITED STATES
MEXICO

NOGALES

CHIHUAHUA

SONORA

HERMOSILLO

PROLOGUE

Sky Islands
Sonora, Mexico

The jaguar made her way down a jagged escarpment on the Sierra Madre plateau. Her ebony and tan flanks rippled through the pale green of manzanita and scrub oak. Falling pebbles, pushed from their earthen beds by her great paws, scattered noisily down the slope ahead of her.

Her mate roused from an afternoon nap in a tree above her. They had been together for many sunrises and sunsets. Soon he would leave her, and she would return to a solitary life and give birth to their cubs. The pair ambled along the path to a rock-lined bowl in the stream for a refreshing swim. Later they lingered by the water's edge, where a nearby deer quivered in the brush, caught unaware by their silent arrival yet saved by being upwind.

This season brought more frequent rain—a blessing. The oak woodlands teemed with prey, which meant ample milk for the jaguar's four kittens. Among these kittens, a white cub startled her. Following her instincts, she ignored him and gave the cub little access to her milk until her other cubs had drunk their fill.

The pale cub was weaned early and began foraging to survive. He learned to imitate his mother's low growls and grunts, though his youthful attempts were more like yips and squeaks. This furry ball loped over rocky terrain, following his mother and siblings through the scrubby wooded forests and pouncing on the prey his mother wrestled to the ground. He ate what was left behind long after the others in his family had satisfied their hunger.

Duma left his family early and traveled far and wide.

PART I

CITY IN THE DESERT

1

Tucson, Arizona
In the Near Future

In his fifth year of life, Duma wandered from the Sierra San Antonio Mountains where he had been born. The high ranges, separated by a sea of desert and grassland, formed an archipelago of mountains, some spanning the US-Mexico border. Oblivious to human borders, he'd found egress where humans had breached the wall near Nogales. He devoured what deer and small game he could find along the way until he discovered a ranch and some small farms where cattle and horses lured him into dangerous liaisons.

One clear night, Duma trotted across some fields irrigated by a canal. He crossed a road into rows of tall corn. Lately his prowls were confined to nocturnal activity since the ranchers and homeowners were on the lookout for the white jaguar, named the "Ghost Cat" by locals. Duma and his kind were crepuscular creatures, active at dawn and dusk, but Duma's pale pelt afforded little camouflage at night. So the big cat struggled as the human stalkers drove him into hiding. He had to be faster, stronger, and more cunning to survive as sightings of the white jaguar roaming the fields sparked colorful legends among the two-leggeds. His large tracks aroused fear in farmhands who worked the same fields during the day.

Now it had been many days without meat and Duma felt weakness slowly spreading through his large limbs. Then he detected the scent of something new and stopped in his tracks. It was not the smell of the two-leggeds . . . but what? Duma crept closer in the direction of its source. In a low crouch he advanced without a sound. Another smell—of death—was unmistakable. His nose led him closer to the road than he liked. At its edge he paused and stretched out his long white neck, peering through the corn stalks. Every fiber of his being was on alert, and his round ears drew forward to catch the slightest sound. The Ghost Cat's glassy pink eyes opened wide to catch any movement. He held himself completely still, absorbing every possible clue as to what this prey might be and calculating what it would take to bring it down.

Finally the animal came into view. It was squatting on its tail and it smelled strange. Duma's full-grown jaguar body demanded flesh and blood, and now he felt the gnawing ache of hunger, so he continued to investigate. The strange animal stood up and walked toward something ahead of itself. Duma understood with his nose that, whatever that thing was, it was dead.

The jaguar sniffed the air again, breathing in its chemical language. An acrid scent of urine and scat pierced his nostrils. He crept slowly toward the prey, sensing no imminent danger. The creature turned. Duma let a series of low grunts roll from his powerful throat onto the warm night air. The animal seemed unafraid. Perhaps it was more of a threat than he realized. Duma paused, bringing himself more upright. He cocked his intelligent head, straining to understand what he'd encountered. Then he crouched, waiting to see what this strange beast would do. It approached him, walking, then falling down and righting itself. Was it injured?

Duma stood and walked forward with more curiosity. The moonlight lit up the white jaguar. Silence.

The child extended her hands and said, "*Ven, gatito,*" calling Duma as she would a kitty.

What a strange sound, high-pitched like a rabbit's. The creature held its paws out toward him. Duma reflexively swiped them away, knocking the child down. It began to wail. Its smell was foul. Duma realized it was an infant two-legged, not prey. Just as he made that determination a noise cut the sky and sunlight shot down the road. The jaguar bounded out of sight. Behind him, the child shrieked. Duma looked back. It was the sky beast he'd seen many times. It filled him with terror. Now it dropped from the sky with wings swirling and fire breathing from its mouth. Duma had never seen anything like this animal, many times his size. He leapt into the air and soared over the tall corn, white flanks streaming through the dark field toward a line of cottonwood trees. He stopped for a moment and looked back, expecting to see the beast take its prey. But instead of devouring the child, it turned toward him. Its deafening roar and flapping wings came rushing at greater speed than Duma could maintain. He lost traction in the muddy soil along the canal, so he raced toward the harder surface of the open road. That's when the creature threw its light on him. He heard a two-legged shouting from above. Ripping heat tore into his flank. He crumpled to the ground, pushing up a cloud of dust. His three-hundred-pound body came to rest in a heap of muscle, fang, and claw.

2

The natural history museum sat low and snug in the gentle curve of the desert. At night, in the moon tide, big brown bats swooped over its lush vegetation, snapping up insects that hovered over the beaver pond. Bobcats and coyotes stalked small prey gathering seed under the white moonlight. Rattlesnakes moved silently on their belly scoots, reigning over their nocturnal kingdoms. But at daybreak the night stalkers and their prey disappeared, confined to subterranean caves in the heat of the day. The cactus wren, the hummingbird, and the human each took their place in the sun tide of the desert sea.

Dr. Luis Muñoz surveyed the grounds with a furrowed brow. Sustained high temperatures stressed the animals under his care. He stopped to wipe the sweat from his face with a bright blue bandana. At 6 a.m. an already arduous day dawned. The oppressive heat stirred old memories of cooler temperatures in the Sky Islands of northwest Mexico, where he had grown up. There he'd spent his youth exploring the pine-oak forests, tracking the mountain lion and its prey the mule deer. Once he had encountered *el tigre*, the elusive jaguar. Those woods, filled with a rich diversity of life, had provided the young boy with his first real education. Each animal and plant had had its own spirit, unique and discernible to Luis. He had begun to see how all the life around him fit together into a whole, with each species providing something for another.

Luis rambled down the path to a spot where two Mexican gray wolves paced open-mouthed from the heat. He stopped to observe them, checking for signs of dehydration. The desire to protect the species on the one hand, and the need to educate and inspire the public on the other, bore down on the staff and caretakers charged with the welfare of these animals. As director of Living Collections, Luis held the most responsibility for their fate.

The sun breached the mountains and poured across the valley from the east. Luis picked up his pace, returning to the visitor entrance. The lush botanical displays of Sonoran Desert flora on the museum's grounds contrasted sharply with the condition of the desert he'd observed on his drive to work that morning. The mega-drought, now in its twentieth year, had shriveled the saguaros to the point of death, disrupting natural cycles. The museum had increasingly become an oasis for creatures seeking refuge. It was not uncommon for Luis to discover signs of a wild bobcat or mountain lion that had roamed the grounds during the night in search of water.

The purr of an electric motor drew his attention. Kim whizzed down the path in a golf cart. Luis's mood lifted when he saw her smiling face and curly blond hair aglow in the intense sunlight. A gifted veterinarian, Kim Turner shared Luis's love of wildlife. A special bond had formed between the two of them over the years. They had ministered to injured animals, attended the births of young born in captivity, and guarded the lives entrusted to them like good shepherds.

"*Hola!*" Kim said.

"*Buenos días, amiga. ¿Cómo estás?*"

"Great, as long as Henry doesn't think up some new scheme for the public."

Luis chuckled as he plopped onto the cool shaded seat of Kim's covered go-cart. She was still fuming over the museum director's idea to string "zoo lights" over the grounds to attract more visitors in the cool evenings.

"How can an educated person, the director no less, be so thoughtless?" she complained. "They're nocturnal animals!"

Luis had learned to let Kim's storms blow over. He pulled his museum cap down as the cart wobbled its way along a sun-blanched path to a grove of tall cottonwoods that provided delicious shade. More staff members arrived and began tending the animals.

"I've got a surprise for you," Kim said, stopping the cart in the shade.

The riparian exhibit was a favorite among visitors due to its water, shade, and frisky otters. Overhead, the furry faces of coatimundi peered down from tall palms. Deer and wild turkeys strutted nearby.

"I think I know what the surprise is. At least, I hope I do," Luis said as they passed a burbling stream flowing into a pond where a flat-tailed beaver glided under willows.

Kim unlocked the chain-link fence at the rear of the exhibit. Before they could step inside the enclosure, a row of black-and-white furballs waddled toward Kim. Each sniffed her familiar scent with its long, upturned nose. She handed a baby coati to Luis, who knelt to reassure the mother. The infant sniffed the air, squinting up at Luis with onyx eyes.

"What a fine little fellow you are! Time for breakfast, *mi'jo*," Luis said.

Kim cupped another baby in her hand and stroked it with one finger. Sometimes captivity interrupted the natural behavior of animals, but it looked as if this mother and her cubs were thriving.

"How much longer will you seclude them?" Luis asked. The announcement of new babies always brought a flurry of visitors.

"Probably a couple of weeks. I want the mother-baby bond strong before putting them on exhibit."

Luis admired Kim. Under her care, the museum's living collections were so far weathering the region's climate change. Increasing desire from the public to see the "real desert" made their work challenging.

3

Dr. Carla Connor studied the incoming data from the NASA satellite-imaging system, G.R.A.C.E. It monitored land ice and the amount of water in aquifers across the world.

Rajiv Ramachandran, Carla's lead lab tech, read in silence over her shoulder as she retraced the data. The two turned in unison, reading from monitors around the room. There could be no mistake. Earth's land ice was shrinking faster than anyone had predicted. Other monitors showed significant decreases in groundwater.

Unlike other labs at the university, Carla's spanned the whole upper floor of the Science Center, and it included a chamber whose central area was taken up by semi-circular tables with swivel chairs. Advanced communication capability allowed scientific teams to connect with each other across the planet. Carla's lab hosted policymakers and international science teams several times a year.

Carla rubbed her eyes and let out a long sigh.

"I'm fried. I'm supposed to give a presentation to the city's emergency responders in the morning. Think you can keep going alone?" she asked Rajiv. "At least until Karen gets here? I need sleep."

She swept back thick waves of red hair from her shoulders. Beads of sweat had formed on her upper lip and in the wells under her green eyes. She surveyed her desk—a storm of papers, reports, sticky notes, and half-eaten meals.

"God help me!" She looked at Rajiv with a pleading expression. "Could you or Karen just . . . just stack this mess into some semblance of order so I can pretend I know what I'm doing tomorrow?"

Rajiv grinned, revealing a row of white teeth made dazzling against his dark skin.

"Sure," he said. "But you'll never find a thing again."

Carla laughed. Her students and colleagues were continually amazed at how she could put her finger on just the right document among a tsunami of paper.

She adjusted her wide-brimmed hat, threw her backpack over one shoulder, and disappeared through the maze of offices that constituted the rest of her lab.

As she made her way down the long row of steps from the portico of the Climate Center and out onto the university mall, her head throbbed with tension. Inhaling the scent of warm loam from the green lawn, she felt her focus shift from her mind to her body. This was wonderful and long overdue.

Then a deep male voice called her name. She turned to see her colleague Jim Mullins jogging across the mall. Her mood altered instantly as she considered the possibilities.

"Doing anything tonight?" Jim huffed, rubbing up against her shoulder.

"What do you have in mind?" Carla attempted naiveté, but she could tell from Jim's look that he wasn't buying it. She laughed and slipped her arm around his waist. They strolled together toward their bikes.

Rajiv was looking out at the mall from the window above. For a while he studied the two scientists. Then he turned back toward the monitors.

Jim and Carla undressed each other on their way to her bedroom, leaving a trail of garments. Hungry for release from intellectual duels, writing under deadlines, and the constant pressure to be relevant in her field, Carla sought deliverance in Jim's deep kisses and groping hands. He knew how to please her, and she rode each tidal wave of sensation with abandon until exhaustion rendered them a sweaty heap and deep slumber overtook them.

Later, in the evening, Jim woke and dressed. For a moment he stood over Carla, enjoying her nakedness and watching storms rage across her flickering eyelids, then he left for his own home.

As Carla lay in bed, a recurring dream kept her tossing and turning:

In a white world, a frantic polar bear struggled to pull herself onto a melting ice floe to join her onlooking cubs. The mother clawed at the edges of the melting ice but failed to gain traction. The figure of the white bear drifted down into a dark abyss, her cubs left behind.

In her dream world Carla was transfixed by the frightened eyes of the drowning mother that stared up at her. She awakened in a sweat, her hair matted in damp clumps. In her shower, under the slow dribble, she faced the fact that her dream held more reality than even she wanted to accept. Jim's embrace faded, replaced by her deep concerns.

On her living room couch, curled up with a glass of single-malt whiskey—the golden gift of her Irish clansmen—she combed through the library of facts and figures that kept her company day in and day out, while letting the libation work its magic.

The Southwest had been identified as a "global hotspot" for climate change in the large-scale models developed by scientific teams across the world. The latest models suggested that average temperatures in the Southwest would probably increase by an additional 3–6°C by the end of the twenty-first century. Carla realized that few Americans even knew how to convert Celsius to Fahrenheit, and they certainly were not paying attention to what plants and animals were telling them about the changing conditions.

A recent study had traced the elevation of plant communities on Mt. Lemmon in the Catalina Mountains near Tucson. They'd found that over a six-decade period (1949 to 2011), the upper and lower ranges of plants had shifted dramatically to higher elevations. Average temperatures had increased and precipitation decreased.

Areas that previously supported trees were now scrub or grasslands.

Only through such long-term research could scientists and citizens understand the large-scale changes occurring in the land communities around them. But these studies took time. Carla thought about the old tale in which a frog happily boils in a pail of gradually heated water. To Carla it seemed that something similar was happening in her home town.

She sank further into the plush leather of her couch. Climate changes were happening all over the planet. Droughts and flooding were more common than ever, and shorter summers in the north had decreased the production of crops that Americans depended upon.

Fear gripped her again and like air hissing out of a balloon, she felt a deep unraveling in the core of her body. Carla understood that failure to act *at sufficient levels* of coordination among governments and nations would mean failure to mitigate these changes.

Day dawned over the Tucson Mountains—black silhouettes against the pink sky. Carla trudged to the kitchen where she made coffee, groping around in the semi-darkness. Beginning a day when she faced the city fathers and the water director required mental alertness. She must stoke her inner fire so that she'd be able to outline the scientific data rationally and comprehensively. Carla threw back her shoulders and surveyed the contents of her fridge. She would make a she-man's breakfast: eggs, bacon, toast, potatoes—the whole works.

Later she chose an emerald linen suit with a short skirt and a white silk blouse that revealed the fullness of her breasts. Piling her flaming locks up on her head, she surveyed the results before a mirror. *Not bad for a lab rat*, she thought.

Before leaving, she remembered the locket her mother had given her as a girl with the Celtic goddess Epona etched on its surface. It cradled the photos of her maternal grandparents on the Emerald Isle. Carla put it on ceremoniously.

As she crossed the threshold from her bedroom, Carla recalled her father's voice and the phrase he had used whenever her mother entered a room.

"Now *there's* a fine doorful of a woman."

4

Kim burst into Luis's office with the news that Arizona Game & Fish had captured an albino jaguar near Nogales, Arizona. A lock of curly blond hair hung over one eye, increasing her look of incredulity. Luis laughed.

"And I lassoed a pink bobcat on the trail this morning," he quipped.

"No," Kim insisted as she sat down in front of his desk. "No, Luis. This is for real. It was brought down by a Border Patrol helicopter near some undocumented immigrants who had entered the city at night. The mother is dead, but her baby survived. They think the cat may have been stalking the kid."

Luis sat in stunned silence, taking it in. For starters, what was a jaguar doing in Nogales, Arizona, and second—did she say a *white* jaguar?

"The US Fish and Wildlife Service wants a specialist to examine the cat and assist in the investigation."

"Investigation?" Luis said, pushing back his chair.

"Well, yes. The animal's fate is uncertain," Kim said. "If indeed it was stalking the child, it will have to be destroyed."

"But how can that be determined?" Luis asked. They were silent, thinking. Then Luis said, "The whole thing is weird. Jaguars don't stalk humans, and normally they don't roam around agricultural fields. It must have come across the border from Mexico," he surmised, mentally tracing the physical terrain of the land near Nogales, the spine of mountains in the Sky Islands that spanned the border. That must be where the jaguar wandered from, he thought to himself.

"I bet it drifted in near the cattle ranches," he said—more to himself than to Kim, who sat in front of him, studying his reactions. "But why would it leave the mountains, its natural habitat?"

Suddenly Luis jumped up and donned his hat.

"This is one for the books. Let's go discuss this with Henry."

Luis and Kim disappeared down a covered walkway and across a stone patio where a mesquite tree was heavy with seed pods. Their boots crunched on dried pods, leaving a trail below the canopy.

They found the museum director standing on a small ladder looking for something on the tall shelves that lined his office. Fashioned out of mesquite wood by one of the original artisans on the staff, the shelves held photos, books, pottery, and taxidermy animals and birds—relics from past directors over the museum's fifty years of operation.

Henry Waxman lowered his rotund body down the library ladder with audible breath. Seven decades of outdoor scientific work and the strains of leadership showed in physical wear and tear, but Luis and Kim admired his dignity, which shone like oiled leather.

Behind his back, Kim sent Luis a questioning look that asked, "Should we even bother him with this?"

Luis answered by addressing Henry. "Henry, sit down. We've got a story for you."

"Uh-oh," Henry said intuitively.

Duma lay sedated in a steel and concrete enclosure kept by the Border Patrol in Nogales. The building sat long and squat, a cement structure built for multiple purposes, from receiving rabid animals to sequestering dangerous (human) criminals. A few warlords from Mexican drug cartels had been stashed there, but the albino jaguar was by far the most dramatic resident yet. While the cat lay unconscious a steady stream of Border Patrol officers frequented his cell, aghast at Duma's size and white coat. They'd heard the tales about the Ghost Cat too, but here it was. Duma's presence could be felt throughout the building like a contained menace.

The jaguar swam in a misty landscape where two-leggeds could be sensed but not clearly seen. He felt pain in his flank. When he tried to move his heavy limbs, they would not obey his command. He drifted in a strange world. Duma remembered the sky monster well, and the awful-smelling prey. But the great cat's nostrils failed to twitch when he strained to lift his heavy head to read the chemical language through which he understood his world. Taken down in violence, he lay in a pale heap in an utterly alien and cold world.

Kim gently lifted one of Duma's flaccid eyelids and peered into his bloodshot eye. She had remained inside the enclosure with the big cat after expertly repairing his torn muscle where the pellet had exploded on impact. Kim had seen her fill of animals permanently impaired by unskilled agency personnel called in to take down wildlife when Game & Fish could not respond. The men who had botched this job appeared to have believed they were on a big-game hunt.

Luis joined her and began taking measurements for the record. This white giant was the largest jaguar either of them had seen: eight feet long from nose to tail tip, and paws ten inches wide. The four-inch curved claws shone white as bone. Clearly this was an expert hunter that had probably never known the bitter taste of defeat—until now.

Sonya Morales stood at the cage door, mesmerized by Kim's skill and courage but keeping a hand on her revolver in case the jaguar roused. Tanned and trim in her Border Patrol uniform, Sonya's body appeared incongruous with her clunky boots and the thick leather holster around her waist. She was shapely with warm brown eyes and a jet-black ponytail glistening under a green campaign hat.

Sonya remained at a fixed distance from the cage, not entirely thrilled to be in such close proximity to the jaguar. Watching the white cat's ribs rise and fall in even breath and anticipating the monster's revival made her weak-kneed.

How could such a tiny woman be so close to those murderous claws, and even act with empathy toward a passionless predator? she wondered.

Then her mind's eye flashed to the image of the dead woman lying in the moonlight between the irrigation canals, trenches that Sonya regarded as highways of tribulation and death.

El Norte is no El Dorado, she thought bitterly, *but you can never convince people of that when they're coming from more dire conditions.*

Sonya's thoughts turned to the fate of the child found wandering in the field. She would be the one to make the decisions that would alter that child's life course.

Sonya's cell phone vibrated.

"Lieutenant Morales here." It was Bob Minor, the mayor of Nogales, Arizona. "Another migrant death, I'm afraid," Sonya explained, moving away from the cage. "This one is particularly heartbreaking," she said in a muted voice. "The woman must have been with a group. Why would they leave her behind when inside the city limits? It makes no sense to me unless they were hiding nearby when the chopper scanned the field. They must have known about the child."

"Their own lives were in great danger too," Bob said. "Desperation makes people do desperate deeds." Then as an afterthought he asked, "Hey, is it true that the jaguar is albino?"

"Yes. Why?"

She heard a long sigh and a chuckle. "I thought I was going crazy," he explained. "The other night after dinner I checked the perimeter around our house and thought I saw a big white cat disappear behind a tall prickly pear. I had my gun with me and almost took it down, but then I thought I must be seeing things!"

The mayor's new habit of carrying a rifle with him after his home had been ransacked by desperate immigrants seeking water and food left Sonya cold. Encountering this mother and child had brought the tragedy of the border starkly into focus for her. *How can politicians and the general public be so insensitive to human suffering?* The mayor asked her to come down to his office. He said he had much bigger problems to discuss with her. *What could be more dramatic than this?* Sonya wondered for a brief moment, but then she accepted that given the life she led, nothing should really surprise her anymore. She turned away from Kim, Luis, and the great cat, instructing another patrolman to take over guarding the scientists. At the exit of the veterinary center she repositioned her stiff hat for more shade, put on her agency-issued Oakley M sunglasses, and strode into a curtain of intense sunlight.

5

Ed Flanagan waited until the end of the day to respond to the mayor's request. Only a few staff remained in the cave of the food bank warehouse. He nodded to each as he made his way into the dimmest part of the building. At the entrance to the walk-in cooler, Ed hesitated. A tall, powerful man, he spent his time ensuring there would be enough food for any contingency that could confront the region. Ed dealt well with certainties.

As he stepped over the threshold into the cooler, pulling a metal tape dispenser from the pouch on his belt, he felt the first of many uncertainties the future would hold for him. The chill of the air felt wonderful, but he began to feel dizzy as he measured along one wall, calculating how a body bag might stack against it. He was engrossed in averaging the sizes of bodies and considering the pros and cons of potential containers for them when a voice made him jump.

"Hey, boss. What are you doing?" his warehouse manager asked. For a second Ed stared blankly, the mental calculations still running in his head.

"Uh . . ." He cleared his throat, winding up the tape. "I couldn't remember the actual capacity of the cooler. I think we may be getting a large shipment of beef from Chicago," he lied.

"That's weird," Frank said. "I thought they were low on beef. Besides, you know the cooler's capacity by heart. What's up?" He grinned, expecting Ed to reveal a joke.

Although Ed trusted Frank with his life, he declined to share the mayor's concerns with his employee. To voice it would make something real that Ed still couldn't accept. He changed the subject as he left the cooler, distracting Frank by asking him to check on an unrelated issue. Then he headed straight for his office where he slumped over his desk.

The mayor's request had stunned him.

Was Lou Taylor, the long-time mayor everyone trusted, overreacting? *Or*, Ed wondered, *am I out of touch with reality?*

The fair-haired man considered this for a moment, then sat erect and drew back his shoulders, filling his green food-bank polo shirt with his muscular chest. Besides wanting morgue space, the mayor had arranged with Ed's boss to have him placed on the Emergency Response Task Force, another loss of control that had made Ed fume when he'd learned about it from the food bank director.

"No. I don't have time for that kind of bureaucratic crap!" Ed had asserted. "Besides, I don't believe this nonsense about climate change. It's just hooey, Betty. I can't believe the mayor has fallen for it."

Betty Golden had stood firm. Ed had been able to see her gathering her forces. He knew he was a stubborn bastard, but he liked that reputation. Still, he and Betty had worked shoulder to shoulder in the five years of her directorship at the food bank. He had grown to respect her and considered her a friend. Since Bonnie had died, Betty served as a confidante on occasion. Ed recognized that he had grown brittle in his grief and from the mounting pressures on him at the food bank, but he didn't know how to change that.

Ed headed home early. It was his night to cook anyway. With just Ed and Daniel batching it, dinner often came from food bank cans— more than he liked to admit. Once a refuge, their house now seemed a relic of another life. His wife Bonnie had spoiled her husband and son with her artful cooking and abiding sense of humor. Not until her death did either realize just how much they had depended on her.

In the spacious kitchen he'd designed for his wife, Ed flipped opened a cold beer and began to rustle up a pan of Texas hash. Bonnie had called it comfort food. Tonight he hoped it might ward off his increasing anxiety. He heard the screen door bang and Daniel's familiar whistle.

"How was school?" Ed asked as his son flung down his school bag. Sweat rolled down the teen's tanned cheeks and stained the underarms of his T-shirt. He'd biked home.

"Mr. Reagan brought in a roadrunner today," Daniel began.

"Fool," Ed said, swigging the beer with one hand and frying onions with the other.

"Yeah," Daniel said. "It escaped and charged around the classroom, hopping over desks. The girls were screaming before Mr. Reagan recaptured it."

Daniel's tale drew a big grin from Ed. He added the ground meat to the pan and looked around at his son. Daniel's brown eyes sparkled. Ed loved to see that.

Later, as they wolfed down the hash with warm tortillas, the conversation predictably dwindled. What could Ed share of his day with Daniel? Body bags?

Ed's vacant face mirrored Daniel's as they settled into another night alone without the woman who'd made their lives worth living. Only after the kitchen went silent did Ed become aware that his son had departed.

Upstairs Daniel plopped onto his bed, pulling a heavy book toward him. He propped it open on his stomach and flipped the pages to a section on small desert mammals. Since graduating as a junior docent at the museum, Daniel had studied these unique creatures with more intensity than ever. How did the kangaroo rat thrive without a drink of water? How was that possible?

After his mother's death, Daniel had turned to nature for refuge from his pain. With his father distant and preoccupied, he had unconsciously extended his family to include the docents and staff at the museum. Daniel mistakenly believed that, while he felt uncertain about almost everything, his father never questioned anything. He felt he lacked something important that his father possessed. He yearned for his mother's presence. She'd served as interpreter between father and son, the one person who understood Daniel's strength as being different from what Ed held as the mark of a "true man."

On this lonely night, Daniel read on into the evening until gradually the lids over his eyes closed, and he fell into the deep sleep of the young.

When Ed later noticed the light in Daniel's room, he stopped at the door and listened. Hearing only the lonely hoot of the barn owl outside Daniel's window, Ed opened the door and crept toward the sleeping boy, removed the book from his hands, and gently swept aside a shiny brown lock of hair from his forehead.

Ed studied the fine-looking teen, his long limbs burnished by the desert sun, the outlines of a man visible just beneath the skin. Tears filled Ed's eyes as he painfully realized how little he knew about being a parent, another of life's arenas in which he felt powerless to change circumstances.

That evening the June moon ascended high above the hills, illuminating the house and tall saguaros in the yard. Datura blossoms unfurled into white trumpets with yellow throats. A hawk moth took flight, following the sweet fragrance of the blossoms' perfume that floated on the warm desert air. While Ed and Daniel slept, the desert awakened around them.

6

The Tucson Emergency Response Task Force operated with little public awareness, though its meeting schedule and agendas were posted on a public website. Formed after 9/11, the Task Force protected the region's safety as an integrated team. Within it, subgroups met separately to facilitate lateral decision making. Only twice a year did the entire group convene.

Mayor Taylor had paid particular attention to the members of this group. He strived to bring the best minds and diverse perspectives to the challenges at hand. He requested representatives from South Tucson's Hispanic leadership and representatives from the Tohono O'odham—a populous nation spanning an area a hundred miles to the west of Tucson—and the Pascua Yaqui in the heart of the city. Together these groups held the longest memory of the region.

Widescreen monitors streamed news and weather, helping the staff keep the daily pulse of the nation. As more disturbing data poured into local governments about the state of the planet, terrorism, and the food supply, the ability to sort through the data increasingly challenged Tucson's leaders.

By 9 a.m. on the morning of the first annual All Task Force Meeting, most of the team members had assembled. The morning's agenda included a climate-change expert from UA who had come at the invitation of the mayor. Ronald Smith, the city manager, was briefing the mayor when Ed arrived. He scanned the room and sat down behind the mayor to eavesdrop on the conversation.

"I've heard this woman is passionate about the data, and you can expect she'll deliver one rousing case for action," Smith advised. He had cautioned the mayor about inviting her, but Lou Taylor was a man who would rather know bad news than dwell in denial, and in this way he provided the city a failsafe. The fact that commerce often trumped caution, he rationalized, was more a result of the inertia of government systems than of his own ineptitude.

Just then Dr. Carla Connor entered the room. Her peaches-and-cream complexion was flushed from her having run to make the meeting on time. The crowd turned toward her as she approached the mayor and introduced herself with aplomb.

The room went silent.

Ed stared at Carla. She was definitely not what he had expected. The ground shifted, then firmed. His senses awakened.

As Carla loaded her presentation onto the agency laptop, the mayor leaned toward the city manager and said under his breath, "Where did this woman come from? She's charismatic."

Ed thought it funny that two powerful men could be so easily upset by a sexy redhead. Then he realized, shamefully, that he was too.

"Ladies and gentlemen," she began, "what I will present is the latest data for our region. This will include projected temperature rise over time, estimates of precipitation, and predicted climate scenarios. Let me start with this: The region faces serious impacts from advancing climate change. Business as usual is no longer an option."

The room remained hushed.

Dr. Connor updated the task force on the recommendations of the Colorado River Council, a body of independent climatologists and water experts from universities across the seven states of the Colorado River Compact.

Focusing a laser light on a chart that showed Lake Mead reservoir levels since 1939, she indicated the spot that showed when the 1,075-foot level had been breached in 2016, an event that had triggered a state of water emergency.

Ed's mind was more engaged in roaming Carla's body than the data she was presenting. They all knew that California was getting priority grabs on the water and that Arizona was drawing down its CAP allotment. That was nothing new. She was in really great shape, he thought, noticing her firm calves.

"We are midway through the second decade of the drought. With temperatures higher than average, and thirty percent less precipitation than we had 20 years ago, the city will have to do more than draw down the CAP water stored in the aquifer. The city simply cannot continue to grow while the water supply is shrinking. Climate changes should be considered permanent—at least, for the foreseeable future."

Ed noticed the mayor squirming in his chair. The scientist pressed on: "Normal ocean and air currents have shifted due to increased absorption of solar energy caused by the loss of snow and ice cover on the planet. We have seen an increase in methane as tundra thaws. Methane is more effective than carbon dioxide at heat trapping. We are now in a full-scale heating of the planet.

"In my work with NASA we are documenting worldwide depletion of aquifers, many of which supply major food-producing regions. The human community is drawing down its aquifers faster than precipitation and snow melt can replenish them."

So, Ed groaned inwardly, another the-sky-is-falling routine. He was ready to bolt. The tree-ring research Dr. Connor described seemed far-fetched too. His mind spun as he listened. He noted the woman's confidence, her skill at presenting, and her spectacular good looks. He vacillated between attraction and repulsion. Her assumption that data equaled fact put him off. Ed did not take information at face value. He did his homework, making important decisions slowly. In his mind there was a lot of room for variability in matters of nature and climate. Clearly Dr. Connor's emotions had affected her objectivity.

"And so, we can expect as much as a seven-degree Fahrenheit

average increase over the next thirty years, as the North Pacific high remains stable over our region, and with that will come a deepening of the drought, further reduction in snow melt, and consequently a sharper decrease in Colorado River flow. The monsoon will continue to weaken and may even be absent during the worst years. Mayor Taylor, this region is in ecological transition."

The previous quiet in the room had dissipated and given way to a new tension. Hands shot up in the air and a few people left the room.

Carla sat down on the edge of the projection table and crossed her legs as she pointed to the first person with her hand up—a city water planner.

"Are your figures based on new predictions of increased evaporation?"

"Yes. That is why I believe that we should use no more stored water than we are using today. That means that if the city is to grow, it can only do so by using less water. Innovation and changes in how we live here will be necessary."

Ed could contain his frustration no longer. He stood up to address Dr. Connor and the room as well.

"With all due respect, Dr. Connor," he began, "isn't there some room for error in this data? We all know that water is an issue, but to call this an *extreme crisis* seems to overstate the case. All I've read assures us we have a stable water supply, probably for the next one hundred years."

The audience affirmed Ed's statement in a wave that rippled across the room then went silent again. Ed noticed Dr. Connor's face turn a deeper shade of red as she turned to answer him. But the mayor interrupted before she could respond.

"Dr. Connor, thank you for this detailed report. Of course it concerns me greatly. Mr. Flanagan brings up a point that I want to discuss. Our hydrologists tell us we have decades of reliable groundwater even at current projected growth rates." He gestured to the people around the table, representatives of the water department and business sector, offering them an opportunity to comment.

Ed watched Carla's eyes sparkling with intensity as she tried to make her case. While he strongly disagreed with her, he admired her ability to stand up for her beliefs, but dismissed her conclusions as rather hysterical.

"The issue is this: Current projections assume unchanging conditions in climate. Yet the evidence shows that even without climate change, we've overestimated the amount of Colorado River water we'll be able to harvest over the next one hundred years.

"What I am telling you is that in addition to that fact, the climate will . . ." She hesitated. "No, the climate *has* changed. It's too risky to assume that these are normal seasonal variations. You have to look across the region and the globe to understand the emerging patterns. To ignore this information is to imperil this community."

Now she had their attention.

Carla paused and softened her voice.

"In a situation like this, it's best to *err on the side of caution.* The public depends on our ability to sort through difficult, often conflicting, data. We traditionally act on ideas without proper consideration of long-term impacts, like overharvesting water in a desert. Well, we can no longer afford to make mistakes. We are at a crossroads as a community."

The representatives of the tribal nations were quiet, unmoved. They had seen this coming long before the science had confirmed it: the newcomers had overharvested a precious resource that the original inhabitants had learned to conserve. For now, they would let the scientist battle it out with the powers that be. It was entertaining.

Carla paused briefly, pondering what she would say next. She looked directly at the mayor as if they were the only two people in the room, and said, "Mayor Taylor, lives depend on this."

The mayor reared up in his chair at that comment. Ed watched the dramatic exchange. She had penetrated the mayor's armor of denial.

The city manager spoke last. "Dr. Connor, you surely aren't accusing the mayor or any of us here of not having the community's best interest in mind, are you?"

Ed watched Carla's shimmering green eyes framed by soft arching brows. He could tell she was pondering her response. Finally she stood up, straightened her shoulders underneath the green tailored suit, and took a deep breath.

"Of course not. However, I do believe that the information you're currently using to plan for the future is wrong."

And with that, the meeting adjourned.

At the food bank Ed settled into the hard leather seat of the forklift. After the disturbing meeting he was ready to seek solace in physical work. While he loaded, lifted, and stacked heavy pallets of food amid the hustle and bustle of staff and volunteers, Ed pondered why he'd reacted so viscerally to the scientist's presentation. His blood had boiled at her haughty assurance.

Academics can be so full of themselves, he thought. *And weather—nothing more unpredictable*. But, as he continued to mull it over, the realities he was facing at the food bank seeped through the fissures the scientist had opened in his confidant assumptions. As hard as he fought it, Dr. Connor had made him think twice. Could they truly be in a *crisis*?

"Boss!" Frank's voice bellowed above the high-pitched whine of the forklift. Ed jerked around just in time to avoid a collision with a high column of stacked pallets. A group of warehouse employees looked on as Frank waved him down to prevent his toppling a ton of canned food, which would have threatened injury to volunteers and staff alike.

I've never done that before! Ed thought, admonishing himself. He saw Frank grinning and looking at him incredulously. *Divine justice*, he thought with more than a little chagrin. Ed had zero tolerance for incompetence in his staff. Now he'd gotten a dose of his own medicine.

"Happens to the best of us," Frank said.

Ed ignored the comment. He let Frank take over and retreated to his office, closing the door behind him.

"Perfect end to a perfect day," he muttered under his breath.

From his desk a yellow notepad with the mayor's grim statistics on it loomed up at him. He tore the page off the pad, crushed it between his hands, and flung it across the office. It landed without a sound and rolled to a stop. Ed stared the crumpled paper. He felt a sudden jab of grief, like a bolt of lightning come out of nowhere. A tear brimmed on his eyelid. He dabbed it away with his finger, turning away from the office window and hoping that no one had observed him.

7

It was Dolores Olivarez's monthly habit to hike to the top of Sentinel Peak—otherwise known as "A" Mountain. University of Arizona students had placed a huge letter "A" near its top, and it had soon become *A Mountain* to locals.

Now in her mid-thirties, she felt determined not only to stay fit but also to continue demonstrating the faith instilled in her by her mother and grandmother. Combining these two undertakings became her signature blend, which on this hot summer's day presented a significant challenge. This was not the season most hikers chose to ascend A Mountain or its eastern neighbor, Tumamoc Hill.

Both mountains—favorites among hikers—had been formed of lava flows from ancient volcanic eruptions that had also created the Tucson Mountains. These twin hills had been home to Tucson's earliest inhabitants.

For Dolores, a woman respectful of ancestors, the steps up A Mountain were sacred and intentional. Today she parked her car in front of her aunt Consuela's house, with its tiny front yard and *Virgen de Guadalupe* statue. Bunches of miniature yellow roses tumbled alongside the rusting wrought-iron fence, basking in the dry, warm air. It was quiet at 6 a.m. Not even the slumbering desert bees that loved these roses were awake.

Dolores imagined her plump auntie snuggled in bed and smiled.

Tightening the drawstring of her desert hat, she set off on her pilgrimage and began her recitation of the Rosary, starting with the Apostles' Creed, one "Our Father," three Hail Marys, and a "Glory Be." Dolores would complete a simple Rosary, reciting a prayer followed by ten Hail Marys, as she held each tiny bead on her Carmelite rosary—a gift from her grandmother—all the while trekking up the spiraling mountain road.

A covey of quail scurried across the road in front of her, surprised by her presence. Leading the family, the male bellowed a warning from his rufous chest, a slim top-knot of black feathers waving distraction. Behind him a dozen diminutive copies ran like windup toys across the road, followed by a plump brown female.

The modest adobe homes, once gaily painted and maintained with love and pride, were pale remnants of a more vibrant time. Old mesquites cast meager shadows of their once-full canopies.

Not far from there, Barrio Sonombre—Tucson's first barrio—held fast at the base of Sentinel Peak. Dolores paid homage to the original Mexican *colonia* who had brought modern-day Tucson into being. The early business leaders from Sonora, Mexico, had brought the traditions of Mexican and Spanish culture to Spain's northernmost outpost on the Santa Cruz River. The early founders had continued tenaciously to develop the city long after the Gadsden Purchase had ceded the land to *los Estados Unidos*. Up through 1920, Tucson had remained a Mexican city.

Beginning at the base of the mountain, where the Santa Cruz River had once flowed, Dolores traced the city's history with her eyes and mind with each twist and turn of the road.

She passed the places on Sentinel Peak where Tucson's first African-American community had lived in the mid-nineteenth century. Around the next bend she passed a few ranch-style homes from the era of large-scale farming that had begun when the Colorado River was diverted for irrigation of industrial-sized farming operations. The little Mexican *milpas*—small plots of corn that sustained whole families—had gradually disappeared in the competition for water rights.

Dolores paced on through the 1950s and 60s.

By now she was really feeling the sun's intense heat. Stopping under the shade of a lacy-leafed palo verde tree, she drank some water and prayed: "Hail Mary, full of grace, the Lord is with thee. Blessed art thou among women, and blessed is the fruit of thy womb, Jesus. Holy Mary, Mother of God, pray for us sinners, now and at the hour of our death. Amen."

She poured a little water onto her bandana, an act that felt like a sacrament. Water, the precious blood. Then she tied the wet scarf around her neck, feeling the refreshing cool as heat wicked away from her body into the cloth. She set off up the road toward the end of the "twentieth century." This tier of the mountain showcased a few modern condos designed for maximum cooling and passive solar heating. Electric cars (among the more common SUVs) filled the garages of some of the professionals and artists who worked in the nearby downtown area. Walking up the mountain to this point was an exercise in the memory of origins. Dolores recited another verse, this time in her native language.

"*Dios te salve, María, llena eres de gracia. El Señor es contigo. Bendita tú eres entre todas las mujeres, y bendito es el fruto de tu vientre, Sal. Santa María, Madre de Dios, ruega por nosotros, pecadores, ahora y en la hora de nuestra muerte. Amén.*"

Eight Hail Marys left to go. After a long swig of water, Dolores pressed on. Heat and exertion were causing her to sweat profusely. Again and again she paused to drink water and cool her face and neck with her bandana. In her left hand the delicate rosary exuded the scent of pressed roses, refreshing her in her commitment to make it to the summit.

The road snaked sharply upward, giving her various viewpoints: the Catalina Mountains to the north, the Rincons to the east, and the Santa Ritas to her south. She paid silent homage to Baboquivari Peak in the southwest, the sacred home of I'itoi, the mythical creator of the ancient Hohokam people—ancestors of the modern Tohono O'odham Nation.

On her first glimpse of the cityscape, the strain of the hike became accompanied by doubt. For the first time Dolores questioned the wisdom of her habitual climb. By now her white blouse was soaked. Perspiration poured down her cheeks, neck, and back. She opened a packet of mineral salts and poured it into her other water bottle to replace the electrolytes lost with her sweat.

The road ahead gave way to pebbly soil dotted with barrel and cholla cacti. Black volcanic stones appeared as she ascended the last few hundred yards. At the mountain's summit, with no intervening trees or houses to block the sound, the drone of traffic from the immense city below reached her ears, shattering the morning's solitude. The sun was now fully over the horizon. Finding a shady ramada under which to rest, she studied the metropolis before her. Sentinel Peak and Tumamoc Hill were now surrounded by traffic and human habitation, both of which flowed like surf along the rocky shores at their bases. She tried to imagine the scene when there had been only the blue ribbon of the Santa Cruz River cutting through a sea of green below.

In Dolores's heart, on this morning, she felt more distant than ever from the past. As far as her eyes could see, every inch of the Tucson valley was covered with homes, golf courses, pools, highways, industry, and downtown high-rises.

Dolores dropped her head with closed eyes and finished her morning's devotional prayer. For a while she rested, mindless, listening to the pounding of her heart and letting the sweat cool her body. From this spot high above Tucson's sprawling limbs, Dolores sought to reconnect with the soul of the city of her birth.

8

When Duma came to, he raised his head, sniffed the strong two-legged scent in the air, and rolled to his feet. At first his vision was blurry, but slowly things came into focus. On the other side of the bars of his enclosure, a man sat with his back to Duma. The cat crouched instinctively, letting a low growl roll from his throat. The man jumped with a terrified look as he turned to face the huge cat. Then he shrank away, emboldening Duma to lunge and bang against the metal bars with extended claws and bared fangs.

The lunge drained Duma's strength. He felt strangely agitated. The man had left his field of view, but Duma could still hear and smell him. He returned to the darkened corner of the cage.

Several other men scuffled into the area of the cage. One pointed a gun at Duma, which the cat had learned meant danger. His flank hurt and he was baffled by the strange surroundings. He became aware of gnawing hunger and thirst. When he rose, the men backed away. He noticed water in a strange little pond. He drank all of it. It was foul-tasting, like the water in the fields where he hunted. He stood for a moment near the bars, then returned to the corner and sank down on his legs to rest and plan.

Sonya Morales sat in front of the mayor's desk, listening to his description of a recent conversation with a senior official at the US

Department of Homeland Security.

"The feds have picked up a pattern of emails and phone calls that are centered in Nogales," said the mayor. "They may be related to a terrorist group they're monitoring. I've already alerted the Nogales Police Department's Security Division. What other connections could there be?"

In the ensuing silence, Bob added, "As if I didn't have enough to worry about."

Sonya considered this new information. "This all might be hinting at a coming act of terrorism related somehow to the cartels, but how and why?"

"That's why I asked you here. To get you thinking."

Bob's phone rang. Sonya studied him as he listened to the caller. Bob was a happily married man with two kids, a dog, and a longtime Hispanic maid who it was rumored ran the household, and that included Bob.

"Well, take care of it!" he exclaimed into the phone. "I can't be worrying about a jaguar. I've got bigger fish to fry!"

Bob stood up, adjusting his crumpled slacks under his ample belly. She tried not to look.

"Okay, Sonya, think with me. Why would a terrorist group be active in Nogales other than the obvious reasons?"

"Explosives, aircraft, information . . . drugs, and money," Sonya ran down the usual list, hoping it might evoke something new.

"Yeah, that's the obvious stuff."

"What do the feds think is going on?" Sonya was intrigued now. Her mind began ticking.

Bob stood at the window with his back to her, looking out on the parking lot.

"Okay, this is completely classified." He turned toward her. "They think this may be an attempt to destabilize the power grid."

"Grid?" That was a new one, she thought. "But why Nogales?"

"Lake Powell, Lake Mead, and CAP," he said.

"That makes no sense unless they plan to . . ." Sonya looked up. "The turbines?"

Bob raised his eyebrows. "Take out the big turbines and the Central Arizona Project canals and you take down three major cities, two ports of entry, and border crossings with them. With the grid down there'd be no security on the border." Then thinking out loud he added, "This could also be part of a water deal. See what you can find out for me."

Sonya had wondered when it might come to this. Water wars. Would that now be added to the drug wars, sex trafficking, and the mafia wars?

Sonya and Bob often worked together informally, both being out-of-the-box thinkers who were frustrated with the social-political paralysis that drug cartels had caused through fear and violence. Their town lived an attenuated life as a result of it. Gripped by fear. It infuriated Sonya.

Deep in thought, she left the mayor. She would have to ponder an approach. Her network of spies and confidants provided her with reliable information. She had grown a web of informants throughout her years in Border Patrol work, but its true origins had begun with her father's work as a circuit court judge. Through her father Sonya had learned about the underworld of Nogales, a city through which billions of dollars' worth of illicit drugs flowed and where corrupt politicians and land barons ruled a parallel universe distinct from the nondescript, dusty border town that people knew.

But Sonya loved Nogales. It was home to four generations of her family, many of them leaders and business owners. She had relatives on both sides of Nogales—in Arizona and in Sonora, Mexico. For decades her extended family had regularly met up at La Roca, a popular restaurant on the US side of the border where families rendezvoused for Sunday brunch. But recently the border had become so congested that it took an hour to get into the States from the Mexico side. Shops had closed too. These changes put life as it had been known on hold.

Sonya was the odd bird in her family. Her mother could not understand her daughter's love of law enforcement. It was a man's world, her mother and grandmother had railed. They feared for her safety. Yet her father encouraged her. He knew his daughter: her keen intelligence, good judgment, and strong sense of justice. He knew that her work was her special way of making the world safer.

Sonya's specialty in family immigration law brought her into contact with "coyotes," outlaws who smuggled people across the desolate no-man's land along the international border. She dealt with the families that had managed to survive the passage. Many of the newly arrived were children who'd lost one or both parents and spoke no English. They'd previously known only a world of abject poverty, violence, and insecurity. As bad as their present circumstances might appear to the average American looking on, a bed, an indoor toilet, and water flowing from a faucet constituted Wonderland to Sonya's small charges. Her staff received them as ragamuffins. But after a few days, they were beautiful children, eyes gleaming with hope. It was Sonya's department that made life-and-death decisions about who could stay in the United States and who they would have to return to a desolate life in Mexico.

Sonya returned to her office in a low, stucco building at the official border crossing. Dark purple blossoms danced around the head of a barrel cactus in a side garden near the entrance. She paused to gaze at its beauty as an antidote to her dark concerns.

Inside, her staff greeted her, but she was preoccupied and only waved before barricading herself in her office. Sonya's assistant poured her a mug of coffee, added two sugars and lots of cream—just the way his boss liked it. He knocked on her door. When she didn't answer he entered the office, set the mug down on Sonya's desk without a word, and quietly closed the door behind him.

Sonya sipped her coffee and thought about where to begin. *From what part of my network can I shake out a spider—an underworld creature who expertly weaves a web of subterfuge?*

She needed someone to give her insider information. Only one person came to mind who could possibly lead her to an outside group with intentions other than human trafficking or drugs. Webs of conspiracy were treacherous. One wrong move could mean death.

9

Sunset glistened on the faces of the women converging at the home of Dolores Olivarez and her husband Roberto. Most of the women were young, though several silvered-haired elders were escorted by their daughters, arm in arm. The bright colors of their blouses, skirts, scarves, and jewelry created a palette of color not unlike the real garden they stopped to admire outside the young couple's new home. A living "fence" of ocotillos, aflame with crimson flowerets, surrounded a garden of yellow sunflowers, red chiles, and rows of green tepary beans. On the side of the house, sturdy citrus promised golden fruit in winter. Dolores and Roberto greeted each guest warmly. Since moving back to South Tucson, the place of their births, she and Roberto had nurtured this dream of returning home. They sought to help rebuild a community that had once nourished them and their families but was now racked by crime.

As the circle of women formed in their living room, Roberto went to stir a pot of menudo simmering in the kitchen. The elders nodded approvingly at his action, which pleased Dolores. She glanced over at her mother, who sat nearby.

"*Gracias por venir*," Dolores greeted them in Spanish, thanking them for coming. "*Comenzaremos con algunas introducciones.* We'll get started with introductions. Please fill up a plate. We can eat around the table, or however you wish."

The adobe was laid out in the old pueblo style, with its dining and living spaces conjoined. The adjacent kitchen was open to allow guests to flow in and out for food or drink, while others talked at the dining table or gabbed on the couches and chairs that peppered the room. This arrangement made Dolores and Roberto's home perfect for holding meetings.

"Please make plates for our grandmothers," Dolores said, encouraging the younger women in this so the elders could remain seated. Her mother Graciela had terrible arthritis. Roberto served her a generous bowl of menudo along with some warm corn tortillas slathered with butter.

Roberto, a short man, teased the others as they lined up at the counter. "I've been cooking this menudo since yesterday afternoon. You better come back for seconds." His warm smile lit up his youthful face. Everyone found his bubbly personality irresistible, especially Dolores.

Light in her touch, Dolores was a natural leader, respectful and a good listener. These were attributes she'd developed as a public school teacher. Her simple attire—a flowing white cotton dress and comfortable sandals—reflected a certain clarity of character. Shiny dark hair curled in ringlets around her face. Over her shoulders she wore a blue *rebozo,* a traditional shawl handed down through generations, mother to daughter.

"Not all of you know about the neighborhood watch program," she began. "First, let me tell you briefly how Roberto and I became involved. We grew up in this barrio when it was a real community. We knew everyone. There were a lot of local businesses, places you go where people know you and your family. There were festivals, birthday parties, and other celebrations that everyone attended. It was a good place to grow up."

The grandmothers were nodding their heads. Reflecting, Dolores's mother said, "There was little crime because we all knew each other and there were a lot of eyes around watching!"

That drew a ripple of laughter, as many there had experienced being under the "matrilineal thumb"—a form of cultural glue that consisted of mothers and that had served to keep children safe.

"Roberto and I left to find good jobs, and to see the world," Dolores continued. "We didn't think the neighborhood would change. When our parents began to write about gangs coming into the pueblo, we were concerned."

The women nodded and a few shared their own stories. Dolores listened patiently, then brought the conversation back to her purpose.

"Roberto worked for the LA Police Department, so he had access to reports from Tucson. One night he came home with news that a drug-related murder had happened in this neighborhood. That was it for us! We came home and built this house on the land where my grandparents' adobe once stood, next door to Mom."

Dolores looked lovingly at Graciela, whose placid face masked her pride, as was the tradition.

"This land is part of the old family *rancho*, more than 150 years old," Dolores said.

Other families in attendance that night had been there as long or longer, and many of their relatives had grown up with Dolores's and Roberto's families. The collective memory in the room spanned all the changes over time that Dolores had just witnessed on her pilgrimage up A Mountain.

"Now Roberto works in the neighborhood watch program for the South Tucson Police Department with a special unit assigned to gangs and drug-related crime. And I'm starting to teach at Mission Viejo Middle School. We hope that a neighborhood watch program can create a safety net for this community. That's why we invited you here tonight. We need your help."

Dolores watched the faces of the circle of neighbors, friends, and young professionals. She knew that affiliation with the program could be a risk.

Adelita Escobar, in her deep contralto voice, spoke first.

"*Mi hija*, it is good what you and Roberto are doing. I want to be a part of it . . . but I am a little scared for my family . . . for all of us. Only yesterday," she turned around to point across the street, "I think I saw a drug exchange in open daylight."

A young teen in their neighborhood had exchanged money for a package from a member of a gang, she explained. Adelita's long silvery hair hung heavily over her broad shoulders and ample chest. Her face bore the lines of a hard life, but also had the soft patina of one who had lived well.

A few women chimed in while others remained quiet. Dolores and some of the other professional women there that night explained that the neighborhood association had started a community garden and an afterschool tutoring program, and that soon it would host a health fair. A healthcare worker explained that obesity and diabetes were now more prevalent among youth. They were bringing back gardening to help families grow some of their own nutritious food.

However, reporting suspicious behavior was another matter. South Tucson's drug-related crime rate exceeded the national rate. Powerful gangs were involved. They had infiltrated the neighborhoods and recruited vulnerable youth who needed money.

Dolores invited Marilyn, who worked with at-risk teens, to speak. She was striking in her colorful long skirt and with her fluent command of Spanish. A poet, Marilyn had developed a writing program for teens in detention. Most of the youths were there for minor drug-related offenses. However, just being incarcerated set off a chain reaction that often put them more at risk.

"These kids are vulnerable to drug dealers because their lives are without any true security. They are poor or from broken homes. Their families and communities failed them. They have little hope of a future. This makes them more vulnerable to the predators that prowl their neighborhoods looking to recruit them. What you are doing in this neighborhood association is touching on the solutions that only a unified community can arrive at." She paused to think and then said, "These kids understand, you know? They see through all the adult rhetoric to the injustices in their lives."

"It's true what Marilyn is saying," Dolores added. "In my classroom I see the kids who are lost. I try to reach them by finding time to sit and talk, to connect them to the community. But then they go home and a sibling is showing off fast money he made by selling marijuana. There is usually no adult at home, and if there is, that person may not have a vision of where his or her child might go with an education. Drugs look promising as a way out of poverty."

There was a pause during which everyone thought and tried to judge whether what they had just heard resonated with their own experience. Finally a consensus formed that yes, maybe a unified community would make a difference for their children. Just how far would each person be willing to go to make that happen? No one knew that night. All would go home to discuss it with their families, to come to some determination about whether they were willing to put themselves more at risk. There were no guarantees. However, together they might do something important. Together they might get their neighborhood back.

That same night Dolores lay awake in bed long after Roberto had fallen asleep next to her. She mulled over the meeting and the women who had come. Dolores had grown up among strong women whose family members orbited like planets held in check by their matriarchs' gravitational pulls. Another strong woman popped up in her thoughts: Sonya Morales. Dolores recalled how they'd met at the University of Arizona in an introductory criminal justice course. They'd each possessed a strong sense of justice and deep family roots in the region. Dolores fondly remembered how that had provided the context for a great friendship. They'd often joked that their mutual conviction that wrongs could be righted had resulted in their both being bull-headed. To them the work had formed a bond of sisterhood. They would each apply their mothering spirit to shape outcomes for the people they loved.

Dolores made a mental note to call Sonya now that she and Roberto were settled.

10

It fell to Hector to feed the Ghost Cat. His previous experience at the Phoenix Zoo as an animal keeper made him the obvious choice for the job. No one was sure when the cat had last eaten prior to capture. For all Hector knew, it might be starving, not a good situation for the one feeding the predator. Arizona Game & Fish recommended ten pounds of slab beef, meat on bones, and fat five days a week for this species of cat.

Hector prepared a steel pan with big cuts of beef, liver, and vitamins. One of his buddies would accompany him with an air gun and tranquilizer dart. As they left the food-prep area and moved toward the holding pen, Hector's heart beat faster. He would try hard not to be included in that meal.

As the two officers neared the cage, the scent of blood and meat reached the jaguar. An unexpected, blood-curdling groan reverberated through the building.

"Mother of God!" Hector exclaimed. They stopped, and then crept on.

When the jaguar came into view, it lunged at Hector, straining the steel bars with its 300-pound body. The enclosure shook. The cat grunted and growled, then went quiet, staring with its pink eyes and unnerving the men.

The enclosure was designed with a single lock that opened into a caretaker area set into the animal enclosure but protected by bars. Turned one way, the lock opened the gate to the caretaker area; turned the other it opened the animal pen. Hector relied on Pepe to open the lock while he held the heavy pan of bloody meat that was sending the cat into a frenzy of predator behavior. The animal grunted, crouched near them with half-open mouth, and lunged at the bars.

Distracted by the fear so often set loose in the hearts of frail men and by the presence of a supreme predator, Pepe turned the lock the wrong way. The gate gave way and the animal raced out, then turned back toward them. Hector grabbed Pepe in time to pull him into the caretaker's space. He heaved the pan of meat as far down the hallway as he could just as another patrolman opened the outside door to investigate the racket.

Later he would report that all he'd seen was an oncoming menace of jaguar and that he'd acted intuitively by opening the door and flattening himself behind it. In just a few seconds the cat was racing across the yard, lifting huge scoops of desert sand under its paws and bounding in great leaps out of the two-leggeds' strange world.

At the edge of the property he leapt into a culvert and then entered the scrub, heading toward the surrounding foothills.

11

Carla listened to the low, woody call of a mourning dove and studied the light streaming through her blinds. She slipped out from under her sheet, tiptoed out the patio door, and stretched under a pale blue sky. Jim lay snoring, entwined in sheets. His presence annoyed her. She felt a brief twinge of guilt about how she had used him for her physical needs. But she reasoned that he had used her too, and dismissed her guilt.

Carla's mind roamed while she breathed in the fragrance of roses from the garden. A pair of gray Inca doves perched on her feeder, rubbing their bills together and fluffing their down. Following an impulse, she released the ties of her nightgown, letting it drop to her feet. The cool morning breeze felt delicious on her skin. The landscaping gave her a modicum of privacy from neighbors. She walked through the garden, stopping to breathe various fragrances and to check on the tomatoes and eggplants growing robustly on wooden frames.

Ed Flanagan's image popped into her mind—the food bank manager, a regular intruder now. She scooped up her nightgown and returned to the bedroom, where she dressed skimpily. The temperature was forecast to rise to over one hundred degrees again. She piled her hair up in a French knot to keep her neck cool.

She settled into a comfortable chair in the den to read the paper.

A feature article about rising deaths from hyperthermia shattered her tentative calm. Whenever Carla craved relief from the constant burden of her scientific knowledge, she thought of leaving Tucson.

Just let the town figure it out on its own!

The thought brought relief. But her family's roots lay partly in this region. A distant relative had led the Spanish army in the building of a presidio meant to fortify the nascent community. It struck her as ironic that five hundred years later she was essentially trying to do the same thing for the Old Pueblo.

She tossed the paper onto the coffee table, left Jim a note, and jumped on her bike for a good long ride. Carla was a competent athlete when she put her mind to it. But lately she'd grown soft from sitting in the lab in front of a computer screen. What she needed was a good workout. Sweat always produced tangible evidence of something accomplished.

And she sweated plenty as she biked through the foothills of the Tucson Mountains and up Gate's Pass, the highest point, from which a steep winding road snaked sharply downward. The workout temporarily cleared her mind. She concentrated on her breathing as she felt the cry of her quads for more oxygen. She stopped at a viewpoint and guzzled water, letting it run down her chin and chest, while she gazed out over an ocean of pale green saguaros and lacy trees nestled in the mountains' encircling arms.

In no other place do saguaros grow. The Sonoran Desert is a one-of-a-kind habitat. What will it be like here in a hundred years? Will there even be a town, or will a sojourner find only the silent, dusty streets and buildings of an abandoned city? Where will all the people have gone?

She caught herself before these complex thoughts could ruin her ride, jumped back on her bike, and enjoyed the plunge down the steep road into the caldera's green plain, riding with gusto past mile after mile of silent, stately saguaros. A red-tailed hawk rode the thermals high above her, while ahead she saw a long snake slither across the pavement. She turned onto Kinney Road and headed for the natural history museum. She hadn't been there in years.

As she rode up to the patio at the entrance, she felt like a little child with a fluttering heart of excitement. There were Mark Rossi's famous brass sculptures of a javelina family—desert versions of small wild boars in hairy overcoats—and there were the expected kids climbing on them. What a tradition this place keeps alive, Carla thought as she wiped her brow, drank more water, and prepared to explore the grounds with the early Sunday crowd.

She had just made a mental note to come more often when she saw the large sign notifying the public that the museum would be closing for the summer. The notice said it would reopen in the fall, but Carla suspected they were letting the public down gently. The heat would not let up. She knew the drought was here to stay.

Carla let the notice seep into her consciousness as she started down the path. The gardens were a riot of color with butterflies flitting among the flowers. She noticed a monarch imbibing nectar from a blossom, its delicate proboscis unfurled to function as a straw. Then her heart sank with the sudden realization that she was witnessing the end of something so beautiful it still defied description.

My God, all this beauty will vanish. Tears welled in her eyes.

A docent was explaining the reason for the closure to a family nearby, but Carla did not want to listen. She headed instead for her favorite areas—the hummingbird pavilion, the aviary, and finally the riparian exhibit. She was aware that she was rambling in a state of shock, feeling the effect of everything weighing down on her, and that this was made worse by the intense heat. She found a shady spot under a sycamore tree and sat down. The thought that she wasn't as young as she used to be only added another blue note to the day. As she calmed herself in the shade of the towering tree, she noticed a young man interpreting to a group of visitors. His voice captivated her attention. She joined the group to get a better look at him.

Daniel held up a glossy diagram, asking the crowd, "Which of these mammal groups do the coatis most closely resemble?"

A little girl with curly black locks raised her hand, jumping up and down.

"Pearl," the docent said and nodded in her direction.

"It's like a raccoon!"

As Carla listened she studied the confident young man. There was something familiar about him, but she couldn't identify what. He was a charming boy, about five-foot-six, with a finely etched face and a trace of facial hair on his upper lip. He must be about fourteen or fifteen, Carla surmised. *Isn't it wonderful to see a youth with so much knowledge about the environment?* It did her heart good.

Carla watched the coatis climbing a date palm, and then visited the beaver pond, where a humpback chub glided in the green waters below her. She followed the crowd that was exclaiming and pointing at the nearby bighorn sheep exhibit. A new lamb leaned against its mother on the high cliff of the enclosure. Holding its knobby head aloft while prancing, the baby possessed the majestic stance of her kind.

Carla spent the rest of the afternoon at the museum combing through books and jewelry on sale in the gift shop, and viewing art in the gallery. Later she lounged in the Ironwood Grill with a glass of prickly-pear tea and a sandwich. The magic of the place kept fear momentarily at bay.

She prolonged her stay for two practical reasons: cooler evening temps for the long ride back, and the hopeful exodus of Jim Mullins from her bedroom by the time she returned. She decided to end that relationship, such as it was. It had served its purpose for both of them, but now she realized she needed more.

How can I stop being concerned when a freight train is bearing down on the people and place that I love, and few heed the signs?

With that thought, Carla sat bolt upright and resolved not to be deterred from what she knew she must do. No, she would persist in her quest to wake the community to action—even if it killed her.

Riding back home, she recommitted herself to convincing the Emergency Response Task Force and the mayor of the wisdom of the precautionary principle. As officials appointed to guard the welfare of the community, surely they could understand *that*. She would convince the mayor, and maybe even that thick-skulled food bank manager, to come to their senses. Her muscles burned with resolve as she sped back toward the city.

12

Mayor Lou Taylor put on his signature panama hat, stepping into the hot afternoon sun as he emerged from the Tucson City Water Department headquarters. He'd just spent two frustrating hours with the city's "water czar" and had received little new understanding of the region's complex water system. Now increased evaporation caused by the high temperatures had to be factored into the existing conundrum of water laws—a knot of previous decades' priorities and political maneuverings.

Exasperated, he let out a long sigh as he plodded along the city plaza to the parking garage below City Hall. His worst nightmare had been confirmed by the chief engineer.

"Lou, I hate to tell you this, but all indicators show that the region's water supply has been overestimated, and even without the drought factored in, we've been drawing down our groundwater and using up reservoir water we should have been banking," he'd said.

"How could that happen? I depend on you and this department to give me the right information."

Lou felt anger coursing hot through his face and chest. But he managed to contain it in the realization that he was also guilty of perpetuating the myth of water security to keep business confidence high. The city's plan to restrict business and residential water consumption last, after using the CAP aquifer surplus and reducing water allocated to farms and tribal communities, had obfuscated the truth of their situation: Tucson was about to become a ghost town.

The contention that the city could promise a hundred years of water security seems stupid now. That campaign to attract new business was plastered on billboards, in print, and broadcast on public media. It makes me and the rest of the city and county leaders look ridiculous. Worse: incompetent . . . or, still worse, negligent!

As Lou fumed while striding along downtown's streets, he reluctantly waved at a restaurant owner who was knocking on a front window, a big smile on his face. That friendly greeting deepened his anxiety. *People trust me. How will they feel when they learn I led them down the wrong path?*

The economy has always been the driving force behind water policy, Lou thought. *Cheap, abundant water is the basis for the economy, but when water is cheap, no one values it. We made water invisible.*

Stopping underneath the cool, broad canopy of an old mesquite, his heavy frame sagged as he watched traffic streaming past City Hall. A group of kids, just let out of school, crossed the street, skipping along, chattering among themselves. At that moment, Lou longed to be a boy again, for those carefree days when he had depended on the adults around him to run the world while he was busy growing up. Now he was running part of that world for these kids.

The mayor straightened his shoulders and strode with greater determination down into the garage. In his car he flipped on a local news station for the drive home. An interview with John Weston, an international water expert, got his attention. By chance Weston was in Tucson to deliver a lecture at the invitation of local conservation groups. Lou listened to Weston describe solutions other desert cities were implementing to manage water supply: "soft-path" solutions like making conservation efforts, using water where it counted, and harvesting it from the skies.

Lou immediately picked up his phone and called his secretary to invite Weston to meet with his staff before the man left town. "Clear my calendar if you have to," he ordered.

Suddenly Lou remembered Brent Lawrence, Tucson's leading water-harvesting expert. He admitted that Brent's ideas had fallen on deaf ears when the young man presented the ancient technology to the City Council. Neither Lou nor his colleagues had recognized the simple wisdom of collecting rain from the sky. Lou regarded rainwater harvesting as impractical on a municipal scale, not as credible as traditional methods of water management. But it might work on a small scale, like in a neighborhood.

I missed the boat, Lou admitted to himself.

"Shit, I missed the river!" he said out loud, sending the echo of his voice around the interior of his SUV.

13

The Ghost Cat roamed in desperation for meat.

Not long after his escape from his enclosure, the firebirds were in the air chasing him. He staggered under an arched bulwark in a place where water flowed in a blue canal. He drank his fill of it, then retreated into the shade of the cement structure. He lay panting, occasionally batting at the flies that nagged him.

Ever alert for the slightest movement that could mean a meal, he noticed a coiled snake not far from where he lay. The reptile was totally still, staring straight at him with obsidian eyes and a flashing tongue that sensed the situation. Both animals had sought shade and cool earth on a scorching day. Desperate for food, his mouth dripping saliva, Duma contemplated eating the fat snake. He weighed the possible danger, calculating how he might spring and where he would bite. He recognized the diamond-shaped head and knew the risk. One bite could kill him. But the alternative was starvation.

The cat quickened his muscles, digging his claws in beneath him to grasp the sandy soil, rising slowly. The snake curled tighter, ready to spring, and warned Duma with a loud rattling. They met in mid-air. Duma's right paw batted the snake against the bulwark's wall, and his jaws snapped behind its head as he pinned his prey to the ground and devoured all but the head in a couple of gulps. He could feel his body dissolve the animal into his blood. It barely relieved his hunger, but it gave him a little needed energy.

It was then that he became aware of numbness rising in his right paw. He'd been struck. He hissed in protest and in grim recognition of what lay ahead. Once before when he was much younger he had been bitten. That was an old snake with little venom, so he'd survived and recovered the use of his leg. The snake he'd just attacked was young, full of trigger itch and venom, all of which caused his front leg to swell with shooting pain. Duma staggered to the shady spot where he had lain before, and collapsed to ride it out or die.

14

"I see it!" the officer called. He was secured to an observation platform outside a Border Patrol helicopter, looking through binoculars. His companion carried a tranquilizer gun.

"He's under the bulwark on the CAP canal," he shouted through the copter's roar. The pilot dropped lower, approaching the bulwark carefully, and hovered there. The cat was lying inside and appeared not to move.

"Damn," the gunner said, "he's too far under to shoot from here. We'll have to approach on foot."

The pilot called in the location to the pilot of the Ranger that would transport the jaguar to a Game & Fish facility. He alerted the CAP authorities and Border Patrol officials in the vicinity.

Once their team had assembled on the ground, patrol officers with Game & Fish and experts from the jaguar conservation team moved toward the animal. One was ready with an air gun whose dart contained a maximum dose of sedative. Approaching the culvert, they spotted the jaguar lying inert on its side. It appeared to be dead; however, a biologist warned that he could detect movement in the chest of the cat. He viewed Duma through high-powered binoculars.

Even when they were within yards of him, Duma could not raise his head due to delirium. When they stood near him, his swollen leg was grotesque. It was obvious what had happened. A thin beaded section of the tail was found near Duma. They sedated him after consulting a veterinarian by cell phone. Because of his snakebite wound, the routine procedure and dosage would need to be adjusted.

While they were waiting for it to take effect, a patrolman shouted "Look!" and pointed to the arch of the concrete bulwark above them. Secured to the structure appeared to be a bomb. An antenna stuck out from its wrappings.

"Remote detonation," another said, also pointing.

"Get me Homeland Security," the lead officer commanded his assistant.

"This appears to be an attempt to disrupt the water supply," he said into his cell phone a moment later.

He listened to the person on the line while observing the effort to save the cat.

"You mean there could be others?" he said, raising his eyebrows as his men gathered closer to listen.

"Yes, sir," he said, completing the call. He addressed the men around him. "This might be part of a larger operation," he said, wondering how much he should share of what he'd just learned from the Department of Homeland Security. Then he called in a bomb squad.

The men moved Duma into a box cage in which he would be transported, nearly dead, to a special facility. The snake's venom pulsed through the cat's limp body as it rose beneath the chopper into a royal blue sky. The officers paid silent tribute to the white cat. In its struggle to survive, it may have averted a human catastrophe.

Authorities in the Southwest knew about the vulnerability of the grid and water supply, yet little investment had been made at the most vulnerable points along the grid or canal systems. Both were open to sabotage with the most meager effort on the part of terrorists.

The Southwest was a tinderbox for saboteurs. What the Border Patrol agent learned was that numerous terrorist attempts had been foiled up and down the Colorado in recent years. The agency and federal officials believed that the mafia and cartels were involved and were providing vectors for entry across the border at a considerable profit.

Arizona's border cities of Yuma and Nogales were ports of entry for food and products as well as drugs. While the city fathers in Tucson and Phoenix worried about over harvesting water from their aquifers and their share of Colorado River water, other authorities were more concerned with sabotage of the grid and the network of canals. Most citizens knew nothing about these vulnerabilities.

15

It was the time of the saguaro harvest on the traditional lands of the Tohono O'odham people. Throughout the hot, rainless month of May, white-winged doves visited each saguaro's headdress of creamy white blossoms and, moving from top to top, spread sticky yellow pollen that would cause fruit to form. Now in late June, even as the trunks of the saguaros withered from drought, succulent red fruit emerged at their crowns and at the tips of their "arms," having grown in size and become ripe for the present harvest time. Birds, coyotes, and humans alike feasted on the sweet fruit, imbibing moisture and spreading the tiny seeds. The harvest heralded the season of monsoon rains, when all life in the desert drank the precious liquid in thanksgiving.

George and Flora Romero, Tohono O'odham elders, preserved their culture through storytelling, songs, and art. They were respected tribal members, a devoted couple who'd raised five children throughout a successful marriage. It had not been an easy life. They'd had their share of personal tragedies, but through all their years together they'd relied on their traditions to see them through. George had served as chairman of the Tribal Council twice, and Flora had helped establish a cultural arts center on the reservation. She was a well-known basket artist whose designs were unique and highly valued. Her art had supported the couple through many hard times. Two of their kids had graduated from college, two worked with their hands, and one son had tragically died in childhood from a snake bite.

On a blistering June day the Romeros stood before a modest gathering of teens who were out of school for the summer. Surrounding them, saguaros with thick arms gestured this way and that. A white Stetson cast a deep shadow over George's lined face. His tight jeans and fancy cowboy boots gave him a youthful appearance in spite of his seven decades. A man of medium height and solidly built, he had weathered hands that gave testimony to a life of manual labor.

Flora Romero, a demure woman, wore a long skirt cinched by an ornate concho belt. She wore her white hair pulled back with silver clasps of inlaid turquoise and coral stones. Flora's skin was smooth and tawny and showed only a few wrinkles around her eyes.

"We have occupied this land for thousands of years," George began. "Today we honor the saguaro, which brings delicious fruit in the hot, dry season. In the past this was the first real fruit after many months of dry, hot weather."

One boy in an oversized baseball jersey said, "You can make alcohol from it," and grinned at the other kids.

"Yes," said George, "but it's not for drinking like beer. Saguaro wine is made for sacred ceremonies." A few teens shuffled their feet and rolled their eyes, clearly bored. Flora was glad when George continued, undaunted.

"Monsoon rains come after the saguaro bears its fruit. It is part of the rhythm of this land and sky. For many thousands of years, when the people lived by these rhythms, things made sense." He paused to let the teens reflect.

A slim girl raised her hand and asked, "But Mr. Romero, that is changing now, isn't it?"

George looked up at the cloudless blue sky. "That's where our prayers and ceremonies come in." He looked intently into the faces of the teenagers, who were more engaged now with the question just asked by Luna Lopez, who was popular among them.

Flora nodded approval and took over.

"Our people once followed the moon and stars, the seasons of plants and trees, and closely observed the behavior of animals. In this way we were attuned to the land. We knew when to hunt, when to plant and harvest, when to rest, and when to travel. Who among you knows what we call this time on the T.O. calendar?" she asked.

"The moon of the Saguaro Harvest?" Luna answered.

"That's right," Flora said, looking at Luna. "Your families—your grandparents and their parents—celebrated this month by harvesting the fruit of the saguaro, making wine, and then participating in ceremonies to bring the rains."

George led the teens over to an area where they could see Avra Valley sprawled between mountain ranges. Billowing white clouds were gathering over the southern ranges.

"During this month our people pray in thanksgiving for the earth's abundance, for the rain that will make our crops grow. In the old way, our people grew crops in shallow basins down in the valley there. Some families still do it. The Tohono O'odham come together to dance and sing, and to call on Brother Wind to bring clouds from the great ocean, clouds full of life-giving water. Who knows which ocean gives us our rains?"

No one answered, so George told them it was the Pacific Ocean.

"Pacific?" Luna said. "I thought the rain was from the Sea of Cortez." Flora noted that Luna seemed well informed about her tribal traditions. But the teen was wrong on this point.

"The winds change at the time of the monsoon, and breezes from the Pacific Ocean go southward and east into and across Mexico, and then they flow up north into our valley. The change only lasts for a few months, but it has always brought the monsoon rains here."

They were on the traditional saguaro harvesting grounds of the tribal community. Flora carefully observed Luna, who seemed to still be thinking about this information. The elder could tell that her questions had not been completely answered.

Flora handed George a long saguaro "rib." He said, "We take apart the long inner skeleton to make harvesting sticks." George stood in the shadow of a fifty-foot giant. He demonstrated how to hook the end of his stick around a saguaro bud. He grinned back over his shoulder at the group.

"Stand by with your buckets to catch the fruit as it falls from the top." The kids seemed more engaged than ever now, and though many may have tried harvesting before, some had not.

With the help of two young girls, Flora laid out a sheet beneath the saguaro. She explained, "This will catch any fruit that misses our buckets."

When the first red orb fell to bounce and roll on the sheet, the children laughed at the kid who'd missed catching it. George ignored them and started handing out harvesting sticks.

"In the old way, women wove baskets from willow," Flora explained. She stepped in front of them holding a huge grass bowl. Several girls moved closer to look and touch the fibers.

"See how tight the weave is? That way, seeds of the fruit may be strained out of the juice."

George cautioned that the saguaro, like many other desert plants, runs its roots close to the surface of the ground to capture rainwater quickly and efficiently. He asked everyone to tread softly and respectfully to avoid stepping on any roots they might see.

"When it rains, do they ever topple over?" The question came from a lanky teenage boy.

"Good question!" George said. "Sometimes that happens when the rains are heavy and the desert pavement floods. But the roots on one can run out a long way, like those on this grandfather. Seventy-five feet out. So it does not happen often."

The group gazed more respectfully at the tall saguaro with its curved, fluted arms reaching skyward. Flora watched them and said, "This one is several hundred years old."

Flora nodded to George and smiled. He continued, "When we have collected enough fruit, we will strain the juice and boil it into syrup. But before we start, it is our way to offer a prayer to this land and to the saguaro and the Great Spirit.

"When we look out over this desert, dotted with saguaros, we see how the Great Spirit provides us with nourishment and encourages us to live our lives with courage, gratitude, and humility. We hope you will know the abundance that surrounds you in this, our desert home. The Desert People have been living here for thousands of years, and for all those years we lived in harmony with the earth. This is your tradition. We are the First People of this land."

In this manner the Romeros nurtured respect for the traditions of the Nation and—they hoped—gave the youth principles to live by and skills to help them thrive in life. George and Flora's work was incremental, youth by youth. Both felt it was vital for the future of their people.

Among the youth who made saguaro syrup with the Romeros that hot June day, Luna Lopez stood out for Flora. The twelve-year-old girl showed that special dignity that arises from high self-esteem tempered by humility. Flora could see the fruits of good parenting, which could be translated into true leadership for their community.

"Mrs. Romero, can you teach me to weave the grass baskets?" Luna had asked Flora after the elder had shown the girl her own beautiful basket.

"You have to give it time and devotion. Can you do that? You have to spend time learning about the plants, when to harvest the leaves, how to strip the fiber. It can cut your hands and it takes a long time to learn. To become a basket weaver, you have to have patience. Can you do that?" Flora anticipated Luna's reply.

"My mother taught me how to bead and to make fry bread. Both take a lot of practice. I want to learn the old ways before my generation forgets."

A few of the other girls were listening intently to this exchange between Luna and Mrs. Romero. Luna's reply was music to the older woman. Flora studied her more closely. Luna dressed like her peers, in tight jeans and a tank top, and she wore a little makeup (but not gaudily as some of the other girls wore it). Flora observed that she was not outside her social group, which was another indication of balance that Flora found refreshing and hopeful.

"We can talk with your parents to see if they support your

learning. Remember that it takes a lot of time, and once you start you have to see the process through a whole season—from collecting the plants to finishing the basket. It takes one year to learn just the basics."

"Can I join in too?" another girl asked and stood by Luna. Flora glowed.

July and August are the months when southern clouds gather into dark towering masses over the mountains that span the US-Mexico border near Tucson. Faces turn up to the heavens in expectation of the monsoon rains, which come as a cooling balm, but which are also terrifying electrical storms. The rains are essential to flora and fauna that are shrunken or have lain dormant since the long hot drought of the foresummer, the desert's fifth season.

Luna loved both summer seasons: the hot dry time from May through June, and the wet humid season from July to mid-September. Like clockwork, right after the Fourth of July, the rain clouds appeared over the Santa Rita Mountains. Luna anticipated the cold dollops of summer rain, the torrents of water running in the washes, and the scent of the creosote bushes after the storms. She loved to be inside when the giant cloud beings grumbled and heaved their lightning swords onto the earth.

But in this twelfth year of her life, the elders were perceiving a change in the pattern—a pattern that had governed life on desert lands for thousands of years. The monsoon was late. July stayed dry. Rains came, but they were often more like those of the other rainy season, the gentle, steady winter rains. The people who gardened in the old ways, letting basins fill with summer storm water, noticed first.

16

Dolores considered teaching a practice of heart, mind, and spirit. The opening of the school year was as much a ritual as her spiritual practice; in fact, she considered them one and the same. She had accepted a full-time position at Mission Viejo Middle School in the same spirit with which she'd entered her marriage vows: with her heart full and her feet planted solidly on the ground.

Purposefully she arranged the desks in her classroom in a theater style to begin the year. Posters and quotes from Native American, Chicano, and American civil rights leaders filled the walls of her classroom. Among them, Cesar Chavez, Dolores Huerta, Martin Luther King, Jr., and Vine Deloria, Jr. would have a presence in her arena of learning. As a final element Dolores placed a vase containing flowers from her garden. The young teacher prepared for the first day of the school year knowing it established the tone, restraint, and vision for the rest of the year.

The bell rang. Her heart pounded in anticipation. She moved toward the open door and waited. Her first student arrived.

"*¡Buenos días, Señora Olivarez!*"

It was Pepe, a kid from her barrio. Dolores knew his mother and grandmother. He chose a seat after scanning the room. Next a triplet of giggling girls marched in tandem through the portal. They greeted their teacher in chorus, voices echoing in the nearly vacant room, and found three seats in the middle of a row. They were followed by a stream of boys and girls of every height, weight, shape, and personality—the contours of early adolescence on parade. Some were dressed well, out of respect for the teacher and the school. The boys wore cologne, probably for the first time, and the girls wore their hair back, or down, or curled on top—evidence that someone at home had seen to it that their middle-school child appeared scrubbed, fluffed, and well-behaved.

The South Tucson culture still observed the old traditions of respect for elders, especially for the local schoolteacher, whom they considered above many other community members in importance. A few kids came in disarray, obviously disoriented and unprepared.

Dolores noted it all, greeting each youth in Spanish and English. Just as she was closing the door of the classroom a straggler pushed it open, passing by her without acknowledgement.

This boy stopped in his tracks when he saw there were no back seats. He shook his head, muttering under his breath, trudged to the farthest seat in one row, and threw his backpack on the desk with a *thwack*. His demeanor was familiar to Dolores. A kid full of anger, expecting another let-down, resentful and defensive. Dolores ignored his challenge.

Students gawked at the boy, then turned to observe what *Señora* Olivarez would do. The student glowered at his classmates, then studied Dolores for opportunities to disrupt her day. She noted the body language of students prone to align with him.

Dolores said, "Welcome. This is home base for the year." She moved around the room as she spoke. "Today we begin a journey together. I hope it will be fun, but it will also be hard work. Each of you will learn new things about yourself, about your classmates, and about me. We will grow together; we will explore things of interest to you and to me . . . and finally, what the State Board of Education says we have to learn." She made a funny face at the latter and some of the kids laughed with her.

"*¡Ay, Chihuahua!* It's gonna be a joyride!" The straggler boy said mockingly and rolled his eyes. A few students laughed, but most were silent. Again Dolores made mental notes about each student, gathering information needed for the approach she took to building a classroom community.

Dolores consulted her roster and guessed that the sullen student was Enrique Santos. She walked toward him with a smile and said, "That's right, Enrique. My job is to make this classroom a place that you will love to come to. *It will be an oasis from the storm.*"

This last phrase she said dramatically and with compassion, looking directly into Enrique's brown eyes. He looked down at his desk, unable to hold her gaze, baffled.

Dolores noted that Enrique had the beginning of a beard on his heart-shaped chin. He was slender in stature, muscular, and had tattoos. As she turned, Dolores scanned for gang insignia. *Was that a swastika just under his sleeve? Bloods Southwest*? She hoped not, and that she might be in time to prevent him from joining a gang. He was definitely a boy screaming, *Help!*

"What do you think of the way I arranged the chairs?" she asked the class, addressing another student. "Please tell me your name when you first speak."

A skinny girl with braces raised her hand. "Hi, I'm Helen. I think it looks like a way we can see each other. I like it! It's different."

"It's kinda weird though," a plump boy added. "Oh, my name is Juan." His cheeks were flushed pink, incongruous with his Al Capone haircut. Probably Dad's idea, Dolores surmised.

"What's weird about it?" Dolores turned to the other students for an answer.

"Most classrooms have desks in rows," answered one of the triplets. "I'm Miranda."

"Yes," answered Dolores. "The way we sit can make a big difference. Let's try this for a few weeks, and then we can vote on how you think it should be."

The students began listening more carefully then, knowing they would have a say in how their classroom functioned. Dolores introduced the classroom rules and schedule. She was very mindful of laying firm boundaries for the first few weeks. Once everyone followed them, then she could let up a little. She knew from experience that this firmness made each student feel safe. Predictability was a rare commodity in a teenager's world. Thus, *Senõra* Olivarez created a safe place where everyone knew the rules. As the homeroom hour proceeded, she continued to study the students with whom she'd share her work life that year.

During the remainder of her day Dolores organized her mathematics classes and one life science class that focused on health. She did not have Enrique in any of her other classes, but she would see about that. She would like to have him with her at least two classes a day.

After school Dolores joined her colleagues in the teachers' lounge, where everyone was waiting for the start of a short meeting with the principal. Dolores half listened to the chatter about kids who needed extra support. A few colleagues shared funny moments, like when a starry-eyed girl had told her brand-new male teacher, "You are the best teacher I've never had."

Dolores asked the school social worker, Mel Hernandez, about Enrique Santos.

"He's in your classroom?" she asked, and seeing her expression Dolores knew the information she was about to receive would not be good.

"Oh, do I *know* him," the social worker announced. "He's just out of juvenile detention."

"Why juvenile detention?" Dolores asked, her face rigid with concern for her class.

"His brother was caught selling marijuana. Enrique was with him. He claimed he hadn't known his brother was selling drugs, but he was implicated with him anyway."

"How long was he in detention?" Dolores knew how police responded to kids like Enrique. Rather than working with underage kids by focusing on their vulnerability to crime, police typically arrested them. As minors they went to JD and were inducted into the criminal justice system. A kid like Enrique had little chance of finishing an education unless someone intervened.

"One year. Dolores, you be careful. These dealers can be aggressive if you get between their young peddlers and their sales. I'll talk to the parole officer. The three of us can work together."

Dolores thanked her. It disturbed her that the social worker hadn't known that Enrique was back in school. How could that happen? Well, she'd been around long enough to know that public schools were understaffed for handling the social problems kids brought to school with them. The paperwork hadn't caught up with him yet.

She was tired but had a long night ahead of her in preparation for the next day. She decided to stop at Starbucks for a double shot of espresso, *her* drug. At the pickup window she was thinking that Roberto could find out more about Enrique.

But do I want to know? I would rather know him for myself, first, apart from his difficult world, apart from his official police record. I just want to know the boy, the young man that he's becoming.

At home she flung off her shoes, put down her large satchel of papers, and fell onto the comfy sofa, sinking into it as into an embrace. Roberto would be working all night. She breathed deeply, and suddenly became aware of her throbbing feet.

Then her phone rang. It was her mother. She was bringing enchiladas.

Enrique left school and headed home on foot. He stuck to the public sidewalks near traffic, avoiding any backstreets where the Bloods might be waiting for *burros* like him. After traveling a circuitous route, he arrived at his family's adobe home. He emptied the mailbox, looking askance over his shoulders to make sure no one had followed him.

The Santos family had lived in the barrio neighborhood for generations, in an adobe house that had been passed down through relatives. It adjoined a row of other adobes that spanned the entire block. Each family had painted its adobe a bright color. Since

Enrique's father had left his family, their home's gold exterior had not been repaired or painted. It had faded, and green mold edged the chipped adobe where it met the sidewalk and door well. An azure-colored front door bore the marks of age and neglect. Two very old prickly pear cacti adorned the sides of the cement front step, one blocking the light of a window. Enrique's grandmother insisted they remain. When she could get around, she harvested the pads and prepared *nopales* in many traditional dishes. But that had been long ago.

Inside, his *abuela* snoozed in her easy chair, looking like a shrunken doll wrapped in her yellow *rebozo*. When Enrique roused her, his grandmother's chest shook with a gurgling cough. He handed her a tissue into which she spit the fluid that filled her lungs.

"*Mi nieto, cómo te quiero,*" she intoned, showing her affection. My grandson, how I love you. Her words made Enrique smile as he kissed her soft wrinkled cheek.

"*¿Cómo estuvo la escuela?*" she asked. How was school? Enrique's brow furrowed, but he said it had been okay.

"I will get us a snack," he said. "But first, let me help you to the bathroom."

Enrique lifted his grandmother, thinking that she felt even lighter than last time and that she was like a ghost in his arms. But he felt blood coursing in her legs and heard the rasping sound in her chest. She was barely able to sit by herself on the commode.

In the kitchen he opened the cabinets and refrigerator, surveying the contents to see what he could scrape together for a snack and what his mother had cooked for dinner. Refried beans and rice, a package of tortillas. He'd hoped for a fresh tomato or onions, but the vegetable bins were empty. It was close to payday for his mother.

"Enrique?" his neighbor's voice called through the screen door.

Mrs. Carrillo held a hot dish in a towel. "I brought you all some burritos."

His stomach growled as he opened the screen door to let her in. She heard it and laughed. "Boys are always hungry," she said with the same grace with which she did most things. She knew what kind of hunger Enrique really experienced.

Enrique thanked her and followed Mrs. Carrillo into the kitchen, where she set the dish on the counter, looking around. She turned to Enrique and said, "Be sure to leave some for your mother, and refrigerate these after you and granny eat, okay?" she touched his arm with affection.

Enrique smiled shyly. Mrs. Carrillo noticed his long eyelashes. Then she eyed his tattoos. His gaze followed hers. He looked up and she said, "Why do you kids ruin your bodies with these marks?"

He shrugged and smiled, "I dunno."

Enrique brought his grandmother back to the living room. Mrs. Carrillo tucked the *rebozo* around Camilla and perched on the arm of her easy chair.

"So, how was school, Ricky?" She addressed Enrique with the familial nickname.

"So-so," he answered. He had thrown himself on the couch and hung his legs over one end. Then he added, "I have a cool teacher in homeroom."

"Who is she?"

"Mrs. Olivarez?" he said, wondering if Mrs. Carrillo knew her.

"*Sí*, she is a great teacher, young and very smart. I know her mother." She looked down, then back at Enrique. "You know," she teased, "a great teacher is a gift, but they expect a lot of work from their students."

His grandmother spoke up. "Ricky, you do your homework now. We can eat later on."

Denise Carrillo observed that Enrique seemed preoccupied.

So little support at home and too much responsibility. But what else could his mother do? No man around, and Diego in jail.

"You call me anytime, okay?" she said as she left.

Enrique brought his homework to the couch and spread it out on the coffee table. Math, English, science, and something from homeroom—a form and a questionnaire. He decided to start with the last two.

First, a government form that would qualify him for free breakfast and lunch and that asked for his address, his parents' names, the number of his siblings, his ethnicity, and how much money his family made. He fell into despair. He put aside the form and started on the questionnaire:

1. *What makes you happy?*
2. *Is there one person in your family or your life you want to be like? Why?*
3. *How important are friends? What do you like about them?*
4. *What do you hope for?*
5. *Do you think about going to college?*
6. *What would you like to learn to do this year?*
7. *Where would you like to travel or visit this year?*
8. *What do you dream about? What do you wish for?*

Reading each question with his pencil poised to answer, Enrique paused to think about each of them, then moved on to the next without writing anything. Finally he put down his pencil. *These are questions for kids with a normal life. How can I answer these? By writing that nobody is home but my abuelita? That my mother is gone when I'm here? That my father is a drunk and left us? How about that my brother is in jail? That we live in poverty? Dreams?*

Enrique crumpled up the survey and threw it across the room, more depressed than ever. School made him painfully aware that the life he lived wasn't like other kids' lives.

He stood quietly so as to not awaken his grandmother. On the back stoop in the alleyway he lit a cigarette, drawing deeply, breathing out a cloud, letting the afternoon sun warm his chest and arms. His thoughts turned to friends who had joined Bloods Southwest. He decided to talk to Pepe tomorrow at school. Then he went back inside to do his math homework. At least he could work numbers with no problem. He liked that math was governed by rules that never changed, and when he sought answers, he could always work them out.

Luna lived with Aunt Sophie and Uncle Henry during the week so she could attend middle school in the city.

She took math with Mrs. Olivarez, but struggled with the subject. After Mrs. Olivarez discovered Enrique Santos's natural abilities in math, she paired them up so that Luna could improve her math skills while Enrique would gain social equilibrium in the classroom. Her instincts were sound, and the two youths became friends through this arrangement.

"Okay, Luna, think of it this way," Enrique said patiently one day in class. They were sitting at a table at the back of the classroom working on basic algebra.

"Whatever you have on this side of the equation has got to be equal to whatever you have on this side. That is the most important thing to remember, right?"

Luna nodded. "But how does that explain why you multiplied that side of the equation by 12? How did you know to do that?"

"Well, if both sides have to be equal, whatever you do to one side you have to do to the other side to keep them balanced, or equal, right? Let's look at $2x = 36$. We want to know what x equals, right?" Enrique looked into Luna's big brown eyes and at her wrinkled brow. He wanted to laugh but held it back.

"How can we get rid of $2x$ to just have x?"

"Divide by 2?" Luna said.

"Right! But if you divide one side by 2, then what do you have to do to the other side?"

"Divide by 2 also."

"So, what does x equal?"

Enrique drew a dividing line under "$2x$," drew a line through the "2" on both sides of the equation, and added another "2" under "36."

As soon as he'd done this, Luna said, "18! $x = 18$!"

They high-fived, drawing attention from Dolores. She smiled and joined them to see how the two were faring.

Enrique said, "Luna's getting it," holding back his natural humor. He was still reserved around an authority figure.

"Why is math so hard for me?" Luna asked, laughing at herself. "I have no problems with anything else in school. It's . . . it's another language, almost."

"*Exactamente*, Luna," said Dolores. "Math *is* another language—a universal language. People from countries all over the world use it to share their research and ideas."

Luna thought about that. *Speaking in math?* She could not imagine it.

"Try some word problems next, and then write an equation for that problem."

Dolores studied Enrique and felt glad she'd assigned him this tutoring. He was more engaged and comfortable in the classroom than he'd been before. Again, she scanned the tattoos that were more visible with the sleeveless tee Enrique wore that hot September day. She was sure that he did not have the Bloods Southwest insignia—not anywhere visible, at least.

17

Unaware of the reason for the all-docent/staff meeting, Daniel meandered through the gallery and hallways that adjoined the Education Center. He explored the paintings and sculpture in the Art Institute, works created by artists inspired by the Sonoran Desert. Stopping in front of a bobcat drawn with charcoal and colored pencil, Daniel studied the lifelike quality captured by an expert hand. It was stunning: grey, white, and black-mottled fur; smart, tufted ears; and luminous eyes.

A stream of docents and staff walking nearby caught his attention. He joined them in the Education Center, which was filled nearly to capacity. Daniel found a seat next to his mentor Harold Lieberman. Luis and Kim were up front with the director, Henry Waxman. Daniel estimated that there were at least a hundred people in the room. He listened to the voices of adults he had grown to admire and trust. He noticed a few other junior docents across the room and waved.

The director took the podium, and the room went silent. Daniel sensed tension among the adults. What was up? Daniel's brow knit as he anticipated what the director might say.

"I don't have to tell you that we have entered a time of great stress on the animals and plants, and indeed on us humans." Henry looked around the room. "In our region it is predicted that the extreme drought will continue, probably worsen, and could remain for some time."

Henry paused, giving the reality due consideration.

"Many of you attended the lecture at the University of Arizona last week with speakers from the Colorado River Council. Periods of prolonged, severe drought are not uncommon in this region, but what is important is that in all the recorded history of the region, the last hundred years have been the coolest and wettest period." Henry paused to let that sink in.

"Regional planning for growth and water supply assumed that the current pattern was the normal pattern. Now we know that is not the true condition of this region, as is shown by the tree-ring research.

"The Colorado River Council is calling for water conservation and efficiency measures to be increased, and . . ." He paused. ". . . that the city and region *use no more water than is currently being utilized.*"

Again, silence marked the riveting realization settling over the room of educators and scientists. Daniel understood that this was serious, but was not prepared for Henry's next statement.

"If these trends continue, we may have to close the museum to the public."

After a period of stunned silence, hands went up, and some people began to shed tears. Passion for the desert and the museum ran high. Henry raised his big, thick hands to quiet them. Over the decades of his leadership he had proven a capable leader. This made his announcement all the more devastating. If Henry said it was so, then it must be so.

"We are now closed to the general public during the hottest months, meaning from May 1st to September 30th. While we will not be open during the daytime until the weather moderates, we *are* keeping Saturday Summer Nights going, extending them into October." The room breathed a collective sigh of relief.

Daniel observed Henry's brow darken as he looked down in thought. Then Henry said, "We all love this desert and this exceptional institution. That makes these changes all the harder. But ultimately, what good is it to pretend that we can go on here as usual when our role has always been to lead the community—to tell the truth about the state of this unique ecosystem?"

A dropped pin would have sounded like an explosion in the quiet room as the truth of the moment seeped into each person's consciousness. Daniel began to understand: this was the beginning of an end.

"But it seems to me that we all need to be thinking and planning for what may become a new role for us in these times. I will be looking to docents, to staff, and to the public to advise me and the board about how the museum might assist this community in a time of ecosystem change and potentially unlivable climate conditions down the road."

To Luis's surprise, Henry then stepped from the podium and walked out of the room. Usually Henry entertained questions in a lively exchange with the people who were the voice of the museum on the grounds, in schools, and at public events. It dawned on Luis that Henry had been too emotional to remain among all of them.

Henry had previously met with his staff to start them thinking about the new role of the museum in helping the region cope with climate change. He asked the museum scientists to give him an updated report and recommendations for managing the museum's living collections under the circumstances. But his recent presentation of all this new information was the first time the docents had heard him speak of the future, and naturally it had upset many in the room.

Daniel had taken in the news by trying to reconcile it with his long-held assumption that the museum would always be there unchanged. Suddenly he felt the earth itself move under his feet. Emotions coursed through him.

Luis noticed Daniel's demeanor. "Kim," he whispered, "Daniel is here. Look at him."

Kim made a gesture to Harold toward Daniel, and the elderly man intuitively leaned toward the younger, putting his arm on the back of the boy's chair.

Daniel looked at Harold and said, "Maybe I can help."

"That's a real possibility. Our roles will change, that's all,"

Harold reassured him.

But for many of the older docents, this would be the end of an era. The museum was a cultural icon, the region's unconscious assurance that the desert would always be protected and cherished. An unspoken trust in the institution on the part of families and the government had spurred the museum staff to cultivate a regional consciousness that would hold the desert and its wildlife in good stead. Now human habitation in the area was in doubt.

Luis looked at the somber faces before him. There was nothing further to say. Henry had been in counsel with his staff and the board of directors for months. Their first responsibility was to the animals under their care. The natural history center had installed water-efficient systems, but increased evaporation and more frequent blackouts challenged the staff to keep the generators working. While the museum had developed its own grey-water harvesting system, power was required to keep the water flowing. These factors worked against them, plus it was uncertain whether the staff and docents would be able to withstand the extreme conditions. The latter was probably a more limiting factor than anything else. Highs of 120 degrees were predicted to occur more frequently as the Earth continued to heat up.

At some point in the near future the museum would have to place its large animals in more stable regions or in facilities that could take them. This would mean returning some animals to the surrounding desert or to similar habitats and leaving them to make it on their own.

Luis remained calm and reassuring to the docents who gathered around him after Henry's abrupt departure. But his heart was broken. He was also terrified at the thought of what might be ahead for his daughter Pearl and youths like Daniel. What would their future hold? For Luis, life had been good. He'd been blessed by years of living in the beauty of nature, inspired by its wonders. He didn't think he had the fortitude to stick around to witness its unraveling.

After everyone had left the meeting, Luis went to Henry's office. It was about 4 p.m. A crumpled figure behind his desk, Henry sat reading a document.

Luis sat down in a chair near the desk. He smiled, and Henry managed a wan grin.

"Come home with me," Luis said. "I just talked to Penny. She's expecting you for dinner, already banging the pans around the kitchen."

His big-boned boss leaned back in his leather chair and smiled at Luis. "You know, that sounds great!"

Luis studied Henry for a moment. He appeared to have aged since the meeting ended. Deep lines around his eyes and mouth testified to the weight of his concerns.

"I just wish there was a precedent for what we may have to do here. Has anyone ever closed a major zoo because the climate changed?"

Luis thought for a moment. "Not that I know of."

"Well, we've often been first to set precedents in the zoo world. Guess this is no exception!"

The two men rose together and went to their separate vehicles. Luis had already asked Kim to join them for dinner too. He drove the winding road home with the windows down, his mind roaming the contours of the present moment. Despite the afternoon temperature, he could feel the quickening of the land as the sun withdrew its daggers of heat and light. Ahead a tortoise lumbered across the road's blacktop. He stopped to watch the animal's slow progress over the simmering pavement until it disappeared beneath the spiky leaves of a cholla cactus on the other side. Up in front of the car he noticed a group of male tarantulas also crossing to safety. It was nearing the end of the mating time for these hairy creatures. Most of the ten- to twelve-year-old male spiders would die soon after finding females, depositing their sperm, and hopefully avoiding being devoured by their mates.

As Luis pulled his car away, he felt the movements of the nocturnal desert pageant taking stage again in what had once seemed an endless cycle of life.

18

"Daddy!" Pearl squealed with upheld arms. Luis picked her up and twirled her around like a rag doll. Her curly black hair shone in the sunlight. She felt warm, like a heating pad, and more solid than ever. She was his chubby girl whom he loved to squeeze.

Penny joined them, embracing both in a group hug.

"Momma, Daddy's home!" Pearl exclaimed with a lot of energy.

"Yes, I can see that!" Penny said. Laughing at Pearl's observation, she and Luis kissed.

Henry pulled up in the driveway, followed by Kim. Pearl wiggled out of Luis's arms to greet them too with a hug. Henry knelt down to receive it. Luis saw his face brighten as he closed his eyes, the little girl's arms around his neck.

Kim opened her driver's side window and peered down at Pearl.

"Hmm, what kind of desert critter that can be?" she teased. "What have you been up to, Little Sister?" Kim said.

Pearl didn't answer; it was just their code for "hello." They strolled together into the house.

Inside, Henry was already relaxed in the space kept naturally cool by the home's adobe walls and soft lighting, surrounded by furniture that invited him to put up his feet and sink back into soft cushions. His heavy six-foot frame completely filled the mission-style chair and ottoman he'd chosen. Penny placed a frozen margarita in his hand.

"You are an angel!" he said, looking up at her sunny face.

"Hardly," Penny said matter-of-factly. She stood over him for a minute. "I'm glad you came, Henry. You need a little fluffing!"

He paused and drank from his salt-encrusted glass. "Yes, I need fluffing."

They grinned at each other in mutual understanding. When Henry's wife had exited the city for cooler climes on the East Coast, she had left him an ultimatum: if he didn't follow her within a year, she would ask for a divorce.

"Fran never 'got' the desert, you know, Penny?"

"Well, if you ask me, there were a lot of things Fran never got!" Penny excused herself and went to the kitchen. Henry loved Penny's loyal spirit.

Kim and Pearl joined Henry, sitting down across from him on a couch. Pearl began assembling an entourage of toy animals on the cushion between her and Kim. Henry chuckled.

"Maybe we should invite Pearl to help us formulate our exit plans!"

Kim leaned back into the cushions and tucked her legs up under herself, letting her sandals fall to the floor with a *thud, thud,* and rubbed the soles of her feet. Penny brought her a cold beer and disappeared back into the kitchen.

The aroma of fajitas frying in hot oil flowed into the living room, eliciting anticipation in Penny's guests. Tonight they needed her soul food more than she could realize.

"We really are in a tough place, aren't we, Henry?" Kim said, staring over at her director. She knew it, and she knew he knew it. They couldn't risk the death of animals by confining them to enclosures. And most of these creatures were so habituated to humans that they couldn't be released into their native habitats.

Henry stared back at Kim.

"It's the same conundrum they're facing down in Nogales with the Ghost Cat," Kim said.

Henry nodded. Kim and Luis had kept the director up to date on the jaguar's story.

Luis entered the room, carrying a tray with bowls of salsa, guacamole, and chips to the coffee table. He'd overheard the exchange and said, "Cattlemen and the mayor are for destroying the cat, but the Mexican government wants to return it to the mountains of its birth. Jaguars are revered in Sonora. For people in Mexico, it's as much a spiritual matter as it is about human affairs."

"But jaguars are still as much a trophy in Mexico as they would be here without U.S. laws to protect them," Kim said.

They all leaned forward and helped themselves to appetizers from the coffee table. Pearl took a chip and munched thoughtfully, a curious tilt to her head. "Why is everybody sad?" she asked.

The adults paused, looking at each other and waiting for someone to reply. Finally Luis said, "We are not sad, Pearl. We are worried. That's all."

Kim was still thinking about Pearl's question when she said, "We could do with a little more of the spiritual in our considerations here."

Henry looked at her hard. "No one cares more about our animals than I do, Kim." He paused. "But we can never forget that the animals we care for, at least the large cats, are first and foremost predators."

"And we have invaded their territory." Kim pressed her lips together in conviction—for her, humans were the culprits in just about any "animal problem."

Luis motioned for Pearl to sit next to him. She did so and brought her menagerie along with her.

"What are the animals doing?" he asked to divert her attention from the tense exchange between Kim and Henry.

"They are getting ready to move away," Pearl said.

Henry's left eyebrow lifted, and Kim rolled her eyes.

"Why do you think so, Pearl?" Luis asked.

"'Cause there's no water. It's all gone," she said. With her tiny hands she picked up each of her toy animals and gently placed them all in a shoe box. The adults just watched, dumbfounded.

Penny called from the kitchen. Kim took Pearl's little hand, and they went to the dining room together. Luis came with them and helped Pearl onto a chair while Kim went to the kitchen to help Penny bring the main course to the table. Henry sat across from Pearl. Luis sat at the head of the table, his daughter next to him.

"Pearl," Luis whispered, "How did you get that idea about no water?"

She had just stuffed a wedge of warm tortilla into her mouth.

"On the radio and TV . . . and from you and Mommy," she said. As soon as she'd swallowed she added, "Everybody knows there's no water left!"

She took another big bite, prompting her father to caution her not to fill up on tortilla. He pointed to the water in her glass. Pearl drank some, then set it down.

"*That* water is from the store," Pearl said, referring to her beverage. "It's not real water." She looked at Luis.

"What do you mean?" He watched his daughter intently.

Penny and Kim came in carrying large platters and bowls that exuded delectable aromas, and set these on the table.

"The real water is in the ground," Pearl said.

Then she lost interest. She surveyed the new food and glanced at her mother. A look came over her, and she stuck a thumb in her mouth and reached toward her mother as an infant would. Penny motioned for her to sit on her lap, and from there she proceeded to point to the food she wanted from her mother's plate. Dinner ensued with adult talk. Pearl said nothing further.

After the meal, once Penny had taken Pearl for a bath and to bed, the friends reassembled on the deck to gaze at the stars.

Henry spoke first about Pearl's observations. "You know, it's like Pearl has some kind of super-vision. Or is it that she's just so darn smart?"

Kim spoke up. "She's always been that way—right, Penny?"

"Yep," Penny affirmed. She'd never told anyone about the visions and dreams Pearl's *father* had. They were simply not understood by most people. Now Pearl was showing signs that she possessed some kind of special insight as well.

"Well," Henry said, "She has a gift, that's for sure. And she's right in two ways. First, animals *are* migrating with the ecosystem changes. We see it clearly with wild insects and birds right now. And then we see it right in the museum, where animals in captivity are stressed beyond their physical limits. If freed, they would be migrating up into the Sky Islands—"

Kim interjected, "The jaguar really should be relocated there."

Her director thought about it. They were both aware of the complex social and political conditions that frustrated the efforts of officials in the National Office of Wildlife in Mexico to enforce laws protecting wild animals.

"I believe the current efforts of nonprofits working with government and conservation teams to create jaguar reserves are going to move things in the right direction soon," Henry reflected. Then he sat up and said with more authority, "Folks, we are facing the fact that we'll be sending many of our animals to other zoos or preserves in the not-too-distant future."

Kim's mood darkened. Her chest filled with dread. A great horned owl hooted softly from a cottonwood in the arroyo below the house. It was barely audible, but when Kim heard it she thought its call prophetic.

"How could we have all been so deluded?" she said. "Did we think it could just go on forever?"

No one answered at first. Then out of the dark, Henry said, "I thought it might."

After everyone had left his house, Luis remained for a long time watching the night sky. His thoughts turned gloomy. At no other time in his life could he remember having felt that the future was no future at all.

How can people live without hope? Luis wondered, and then he realized: *We can't.*

Ahead lay a process of deconstructing the museum, animal by animal. The image of the ice-blue stare of the resident Mexican gray wolf burned through his thoughts. Gradually he fell into a trance and entered another dimension.

He was high above the Earth and observed land that had been green just a moment before turning a stark brown. A huddle of men, women, and children caravanned along an old highway with no vehicular traffic. It was eerily quiet. He felt his skin burning under a bright, relentless sun. Then he was speeding across the desert, finally reaching a spot where he saw a thin, blue river running below him. A town was forming in fast-forward along its shores while he watched. People streamed into the town from all directions. Now he understood where the caravan was traveling: they were coming to this place. The people looked tired and ragged. Luis felt the power being drained from the land as he felt power drain from his limbs—a fierce paralysis.

Ghostly forms now passed by him, disappearing into the clouds. To his right, a white jaguar plodded along. He called to it, "Great One, tell me, what place is this?"

The jaguar appeared instantly in front of him. Around its muscular neck hung a beaded medallion divided into quadrants. In the center was a large red rose and around the perimeter flew iridescent dragonflies. Luis watched the blue river turn red.

When Penny found Luis in this dreamlike state, she wasn't surprised. Over the years she had learned to accept her husband's tendency to drift into eerie trances, usually when he was stressed. It had been hard at first. For a while she'd thought he might be mentally disturbed, but nothing else she knew about him indicated that this might be the case. In fact, Luis generally made a lot of sense. Yet his dark moods and these dreams made part of him inaccessible to her, and that was alienating. She had consulted a *curandera*, a folk healer, early in their marriage. This woman had taught Penny to respect Luis's way of knowing. She'd said it was often inherited in Yaqui families, and Luis had distant relatives among the Yaqui.

Skeptical at first, Penny had eventually accepted her husband's eccentricities as another of life's mysteries. She leaned back in her cushioned chair and breathed in the soft air. The night lay quiet over the Old Pueblo as Penny dozed off, one hand resting on her husband's armchair.

Luis understood the jaguar from two cultural perspectives. The jaguar, *Panthera onca*, had once roamed southern Arizona as well as the high mountains in northern Mexico, but habitat loss and poaching had decimated the population of jaguars in the US. In Mexico the jaguar had been revered in Olmec society in the early development of its founding cultures. The jaguar's power, stealth, preference for nighttime activity, solitary nature, and dramatic markings implied spiritual powers that had become imbedded in local religions and spiritual practices.

The jaguar of Luis's recent dream he accepted as a spiritual messenger. If only he could decipher its meaning or message. It might symbolize life itself—captive, fate uncertain. Or it might be a guide, a way. He'd felt great power exuding from Duma when he first encountered him, not muscular power, but power in another form. From his essence, his soul. He hadn't shared that with Kim or anyone.

Science was the tool of his profession and of government for understanding the world. Luis found the scientific method useful but the spiritual way of knowing essential, perhaps because he'd known that way first.

What he suddenly understood about himself was that he'd been struggling to reconcile those ways of knowing ever since he'd arrived in El Norte, all through his education and into his professional career. It came to him that the melding of these two great human traditions might be a necessary approach in these hard times.

19

"Hello, Ed?" A female voice quavered on the other end of the phone.

"Yes." Ed would recognize that voice anywhere. Carla Connor. What was she doing calling him at the food bank? He was instantly on guard.

"I want . . . thought that it would be good to meet unofficially to discuss our different points of view. I—"

"I don't think that's necessary, Dr. Connor," Ed interrupted.

There was a brief silence before Carla countered, "Perhaps you'll reconsider. I know I can be a very passionate person when it comes to climate change."

"Really?"

"I thought you might help me understand bett—"

Again Ed interrupted, feeling tension growing in his stomach. "It's not *how* you presented it. It's that a lot of us simply don't agree with your conclusions."

Even as he said it, a voice in his head asked why he fought to accept what he could plainly see happening. He guessed that he simply still believed that conditions would moderate.

Ed listened carefully now to the silence. He thought he could hear her breathing. Then she quipped, "I guess this means we won't be meeting for a brew at the local pub."

She said it so casually that it caught him off guard and he laughed out loud, saying, "Well, *now* you're talkin' my language." He immediately wished he hadn't said it.

"How about today after work? Murphy's at 6 p.m.?"

He considered it for a moment.

"Suds on me," she nudged.

"You bet."

Okay, Ed had to admit he was intrigued. Carla was a strong woman, determined to promote her cause. But women like her could be problematic. She had that Cleopatra feel about her.

Ed realized what a rookie he was, but calling her back to say no would be *lame*.

He finished checking over the day's inventory report, put on his sunglasses, and then, just keeping himself distracted, inspected the new box truck in the parking lot.

When it came time to leave for his rendezvous with Carla, he felt resigned to it.

At least there will be beer.

At the lab Carla looked over the new data that had come in since yesterday. She had more than a hundred emails that had stacked up just since the night before. *Damn!* She realized she had turned her cell phone off last night and hadn't turned it back on. The phone now chimed with voicemails, no fewer than six. *What the hell . . .*

Then the phone rang in her hand. A familiar voice bellowed, "Where have you been?" Pedro Ramirez was practically shouting. "I've been trying to reach you for hours!"

Ramirez, her Costa Rican counterpart on the G.R.A.C.E. satellite team, was an intense man but a very fine scientist. It fleetingly occurred to Carla that maybe *intense* went with the territory of a climate scientist. She turned her attention to the conversation.

"Gosh, I'm sorry. I forgot to turn the blessed phone on. What's up?"

"Take a look at the Baltic Sea monitor."

Carla turned around to view that screen. An open sea filled the monitor.

"My God . . . ."

"*Exactamente*—and we're going to need Him."

"Is this live, Pedro? Because . . ."

"It's live. We are watching a massive positive feedback loop happening on top of the world." Carla knew the greater the dark surfaces on the Earth, the greater the amount of solar energy that would be absorbed by the planet. Without the reflective white surface areas of ice and snow, Earth's temperature would rise at an ever more frightening rate.

She stood paralyzed. Then she remembered the beer and Ed, and she resolved to somehow convince this man of the gravity of the hour. Somehow she had to find a way to speak to leaders without turning them off. What language did she need? What had been wrong with her approach so far? This was one of those times when she wished that her intuition about the situation were wrong.

Pedro was saying something about a freight train and humanity as she hung up and slowly let her body drop into a chair.

Murphy's was a university pub, busy and loud and offering a variety of great draft beers. Ed hadn't been there since Bonnie died. Weird, he thought, as the memory of many fun nights at this pub rushed back. Weird that he hadn't remembered those associations when Carla suggested the place. He felt a raw pain in his chest. He'd thought that was gone. *Shit! What the hell am I doing?*

Carla appeared through the double doors. She'd put on jeans and a halter top and let her hair go free. He felt befuddled observing her advance across the lobby toward him. He managed a tentative smile and held out his hand. She took it, and as she continued to hold his hand and look into his eyes, Ed swallowed hard and gestured toward the bar.

"Let's sit at a booth," she said. He followed, feeling angry for taking the bait.

They ordered. An awkward silence ensued. It was broken when the waitress brought salsa and chips. Ed dove in, and he felt Carla studying him. The waitress clumped tall mugs of icy beer onto the table. Ed held up his mug and reached across the table to clink it against hers.

"Let the games begin," Ed blurted, wishing for comic relief even as he fortified himself for an emotional conversation.

"This is not a game, Ed," she said. "Today I received visual images of the Baltic Sea, a sea that normally carries year-round ice pack. The region is ice free."

Ed regarded her. She was indeed beautiful, and sure of herself. He secretly wished he could be that sure about anything again.

"Well, that may be true, and it surely means things are changing." He noticed Carla's cheeks turn pink with emotion. "But change is part of the natural pattern." He watched as her eyes narrowed. There was a little line of froth on her upper lip.

Carla's green eyes glistened as she began. "This is the challenge of scientists, to communicate information about something with which none of us has experience. The last human community that experienced climate change like this lived in caves."

She munched on some chips, then asked, "Exactly what do you do at the food bank?"

Ed described the whole operation, what it was like to run a 23-million-dollar business.

"But to tell you the truth, I'm having trouble getting the food I usually stock." Ed was feeling the alcohol. His guard was down. He was beat from a stressful day.

"Why is that, Ed? Is there a shortage?"

"The Pacific tuna industry has been shut down." He felt like prey. She was studying him again, watching his body language.

"Excuse me, Ed. Why aren't you making the connection? Warming, acidic seas are finishing them off by destroying the phytoplankton at the base of their food chain," she said.

"You probably know more about that." He took a hefty bite from the burger that had been delivered during their conversation.

"Actually, yes," she said, eating her fries.

Ed held up both palms in a *told-you-so* gesture that made them both laugh.

"The warming seas promote algal blooms that rob plankton of oxygen. Those millions of little creatures form the basis of the tuna's natural food chain."

Ed noticed the pulsating hollow of her neck, the finely sprinkled freckles around her bare shoulders. He caught himself.

She continued, "Temperatures on the planet are regulated in big systems that most people don't completely grasp. The polar caps by virtue of the albedo factor reflect an enormous amount of solar energy."

"First time I knew the polar caps have a libido," he quipped.

She looked ready to pounce back. He gave her a teasing smile that appeared to briefly disarm her. Ed felt he'd gained ground.

She forged on with her explanation, trying to give as persuasive an argument as possible. Ed listened. Finally he responded. "What I hear you saying is that climate change could, or as you contend, *will* affect the economy."

He watched her squirm. Then she nodded in agreement. "That's a narrow perspective, but yes, it will affect the economy."

"Then why not say that?"

She looked at him for a few seconds, and then said, "It's true that few businesspeople take into account the ecosystem services that are the bedrock of the economy."

"There you go again, using scientific terms . . . 'ecosystem services.'"

He was playing with his napkin, folding it in myriad ways. He waited while she processed his statement. He could see her doing it.

Ed's attention snapped back to his original misgivings about meeting with her.

"Don't think I'm accepting your viewpoint, Carla. I'm just saying that this country has always believed that the power of individuals pursuing their right to happiness is the best way to create economic freedom for everyone. If you're talking about regulating that process, yes, you're going to get a strong push back."

Carla ordered coffee, which prompted Ed to say he needed to get home to his son.

"Oh? You have a son?"

"Daniel. Fourteen. He's a good kid."

He noticed her looking for a wedding band and withdrew his hand from the table, reaching for his wallet.

"This one is on me," Carla reacted. "I want to continue this discussion another time soon. Will you humor me?"

"Uh, I'm really busy at the food bank," he said, done with this nonsense.

"I'm busy, too, but maybe sometime soon we could find the time to continue this."

"Uh-huh. Well, I'm not sure we need to be so worried."

"Tuna, Ed. Think about it. It's here already."

She could be exasperatingly insistent. He was tired and wanted to break away.

"Goodbye, Dr. Connor." He was standing by the table, looking down at her round face lit in its halo of flame-red hair.

Later at home Ed couldn't sleep. How had he let a woman get under his skin? Gradually, as he combed over the evening at the pub, it dawned on him that he was attracted to her, that in spite of her opinions, he really liked her spirit . . . and more.

20

Ed and Daniel converged in the kitchen on a Saturday morning. Ed's unshaven face matched Daniel's unruly hair. They shuffled around in bare feet, getting their breakfast as if they were in parallel universes—close but with different operating instructions. Ed sat down with a bowl of cereal, a banana, and a gallon of milk. He proceeded to slice the banana over the cereal, then poured in milk until it lapped at the edges of the bowl.

Daniel cracked three eggs, shredded some cheese, and chopped a tomato while listening to his father's annoying habit of slurping his cereal. He added some herbs and then stood there with a spatula, ready to flip the omelet at the perfect moment.

"What are you doing today? Going to the museum?" his father asked.

"No, remember? The museum is closed, except at night."

"Oh, that's right. But I thought you said you might be working out there with the staff on animal care."

"Yeah, but it's not organized yet, I guess." Daniel wondered if it would ever happen. He flipped his omelet and turned off the stove.

"I've got a request," Ed said. "The food bank's garden coordinator is looking for help at the garden. I have to put in a few hours this morning. Could you go with me and help her out?"

Daniel had sat down across from his dad. He salted his omelet and poured a little Tabasco sauce on it.

"You make that just like your mother did," Ed observed.

Daniel ignored the compliment and said, "I was planning to do some online research this morning."

"In your pajamas, right?"

Daniel smiled. "Yeah, in my pajamas, Dad. I also want to watch the World Series this afternoon."

"That's right, I forgot about that," Ed said, standing up.

"Dad, I really don't want to roast in the blazing sun pulling weeds on my Saturday morning."

Ed explained that a court-ordered teen would be working there with Jenny and that she wanted to match him with a "normal" teen. Daniel looked up at his father and they burst out laughing.

"Well, as close to normal as she can get," Ed teased. "It won't be but a couple of hours by the time everyone gets there."

Daniel let out a sigh and shrugged.

"For you, Dad, only for you. But you have to promise me I'll be back for the Series. It starts at noon."

"Great, I might just watch with you."

As they cleaned up the dishes and parted ways to shower and dress, Ed said, "Hey, thanks, Son. I really appreciate this."

"You owe me one!" Daniel said, and he meant it.

The food bank sprawled over a square block in an industrial part of Tucson. In front of the warehouse, mesquite trees and desert willows provided welcome circles of shade for vehicles. Inside, the building remained cool, cavernous, and lit up only in areas where staff loaded and stacked boxes of food. Tall bay doors received a stream of trucks dropping off product from America's biggest food producers. Hundreds of volunteers, court-ordered youth offenders, and staff members packed emergency food boxes while other staff members used forklifts to stack them.

A few years before, the idea of food security had begun to take root as a permanent solution to intractable hunger and poverty. The food bank had hired a garden coordinator to establish a demonstration garden where people could learn to grow their own food in a desert climate and obtain heirloom seeds for hearty varieties to grow at home. The native seeds were the same as those grown by the Tohono O'odham people over thousands of years and field-tested to grow best in extreme heat and aridity. Beans, corn, squash, herbs, and specialty items like mesquite flour made by grinding the pods of the mesquite tree—all were available at the food bank for people who wanted to garden with native seeds. Periodically families brought in sacks of mesquite pods which were then ground by the food bank into sweet-tasting, multi-use flour.

On that Saturday morning Daniel followed the winding path from the parking lot, a route guarded by tall sunflower plants and enlivened by darting hummingbirds feeding at the throats of garden blossoms. He passed a bed of aromatic basil and sage and ambled to the ramada at the back of the thousand-square-foot garden, where Jenny sat at a table sorting seeds.

"Daniel! What a surprise!" She stood and reached to give him a hug.

"Let me look at you. Wow, you've grown into a man!"

Daniel's mother and Jenny had become friends as a result of the frequent gatherings of the food bank staff at Daniel's home. Jenny was someone Daniel had known from his earliest memories. But since his mother's funeral he hadn't seen her.

"This garden is great!" Daniel said as he sat down and automatically started sorting with her.

"You think? It takes a lot of people to keep it that way, especially with the extended growing season. Glad you'll be lending me a hand today. We have another volunteer who's working off hours as part of his parole agreement. I thought he might do better if there was another boy about his age to work with . . . at least to get him started. Are you okay with that?"

"Yes. But I don't know what I'm supposed to do. You know I'm not knowledgeable about gardening . . . only about the desert."

"Well, that's the best background you can have for it. I didn't expect you to be an expert; I wanted someone who would be learning along with Enrique."

Just then another boy came down the sandy path toward Jenny and Daniel. Of medium height, he wore black mid-calf basketball shorts, a chartreuse Nike shirt, and white high-tops. His black curly hair was cut back from his face, thick on top, hanging in ringlets to his shoulders. A bright gold chain hung from his neck. It shone in the sunlight.

Daniel looked down at his crumpled cargo pants and faded museum T-shirt and wished he had paid more attention to how he dressed.

"Excuse me," Enrique addressed Jenny. "I'm supposed to—" He glanced at Daniel, embarrassed to say why he was there.

"Are you Enrique Santos?" Jenny asked.

"Yes, *ma'am*, that's me."

"Great. I'm Jenny and this is Daniel. He's also volunteering this morning."

Enrique stepped toward Daniel, looked him in the eye, and stuck out his hand for a gangster grip and back slap. Daniel followed along with it all, and got a whiff of Enrique's heavy cologne.

For a moment everyone just stood silently, looking from one to the other. Finally Jenny stammered, "Let me show you two young men what I hope to get done this morning."

She took the boys to an area where she was growing a variety of chilies. The soil was choked with weeds, and Jenny had found aphids and nematodes on the plants. She pointed out the insects to Daniel and Enrique, explaining that she'd tried a few things but that the insects just kept eating away at the chiles.

"You can use a spray on them," Enrique offered.

"My dad uses ground onion mixed with detergent and water as a spray," Daniel pitched in.

"Well, I ordered the superheroes of the garden world to gobble up the aphids." She asked Daniel and Enrique to look closely at the clumps of aphids munching away. Then she gave each boy two boxes of praying mantis babies, so tiny they could barely be seen unless they moved.

"Oh, man, that is bad, dude," Enrique said, gazing into his box at the teeming mass of tiny mantises rubbing their arms together as if anticipating a feast.

"How many are in here?" Daniel asked, transfixed. There appeared to be hundreds in each box.

"Would you believe that each box has just one egg case? All those babes hatched from the one egg."

Jenny explained that they needed to weed first and make sure to pull up the roots of the grass and weeds. Then they should shake the baby mantises over the two long rows of chile plants. She showed them the tool shed.

"If you get hot or thirsty I've got a cooler of iced Gatorade and water. Also some protein bars. Thanks fellas, I'll check back on you in a little while."

Jenny left Daniel and Enrique to figure it out from there.

Enrique said, "Green or red chiles?" gesturing to the two rows.

"Red," Daniel said. They grabbed a hoe each, weeders, and plastic bags, and dove in. Each worked along his own row; both rows were about fifty feet long. They dug up slugs, snails, and pill bugs.

Daniel said, "Looks like every critter in the world likes chiles."

The sun beat down. Finally Enrique said he had to get out of the sun. He went to the food bank's ramada to get a drink and sit in the shade. Daniel joined him. As they sat together, Daniel gestured toward Enrique's high-tops and took a long drink from an icy water bottle.

Enrique studied his high-tops, which were covered with mud. "Yeah, wrong choice for gardening."

"But you look good," Daniel said.

There was a pause. Daniel asked, "Where do you go to school?"

"Mission Viejo," Enrique said, and gestured to Daniel to say *his* school.

"Tucson Prep."

Enrique raised his chin in recognition of the special school where students earned college credits and were offered internships in the community. His school had nothing like that. The only thing the two boys seemed to share was their age: thirteen.

They went back to weeding. About an hour later they were

drenched with sweat. One more trip to the ramada, a protein bar each, and some Gatorade, and they were ready to unleash the baby mantises on the aphid hordes. Jenny checked in on them.

"Wow, you guys are weeding machines. Best job anyone has done."

"We're ready for the aphid wars," Daniel said. He looked at Enrique. "Ready, dude?"

"Bring 'em on!" Enrique said.

Each took a box of mantises and flicked them all along the chili rows, stopping occasionally to watch the action taking place on such a miniature scale.

"They're like the Terminators of the insect world," Enrique said in wonderment.

Jenny looked on. She called them to the ramada when they were finished.

"Sit down and rest." Daniel and Enrique were soaked with sweat and visibly tired.

Ed came down the path.

"Sitting down on the job, huh?" He could see they had worked hard. He introduced himself to Enrique, who stood up, wiped his sweaty hand on his shorts, and shook Ed's hand.

"These kids did more work in two hours than a dozen volunteers could. Show him what you did, guys," Jenny said, gesturing to Daniel and Enrique.

The boys showed Ed the long rows, freshly weeded, and then the mantises on the aphids. Ed leaned close to the chilies and watched the action for a minute or two.

"That's amazing," he said. Then he remembered the time. "Hey, Daniel, we need to get going if we're going to catch the games."

They said goodbye. Daniel turned to Enrique and said, "Hey, man, it was fun," with a sarcastic grin that made Enrique laugh.

As Ed and Daniel hurried to their truck, Enrique watched with wistful eyes.

Daniel intuitively turned and gave Enrique a thumbs-up.

21

Sonya Morales had sent word to her contact in Mexico via her best friend Samantha, a small-business owner in Nogales. She had known "Sam" since childhood. Their parents had been neighbors, raising children together, weathering marital and life storms as confidants, and sending their kids into the world with everything they could muster.

Sonya and Sam had shared their developmental years all the way from babyhood to womanhood. Both girls had grown up among strong men in their fathers and brothers. Following the impulse of their generation, Sonya and Samantha had learned to look out for themselves, but always with the confidence that strong men would be there for them if they failed. For Sonya these men were still her father and brothers, and for Sam they were now the members of her husband's family dynasty in Nogales. Sam had opened a high-end tourist shop in Avenida Obregón, Nogales's main shopping street, where she sold art and cultural items from the interior of Mexico. Her husband considered the shop his wife's "hobby," but Sam was a serious businesswoman.

Sonya's life had taken an unexpected turn when she'd been accosted by a trio of boys on her walk home from high school one late afternoon. By the grace of God she'd managed to escape their attempted gang rape when a passerby heard her screaming for help in the alleyway. Ever since the drug cartels had infiltrated her hometown, rape had become a more common offense among drug pushers and even neighborhood gangs. That experience had set Sonya's life on a trajectory that was different from the one her mother had planned for her. Yet it made sense. With her father a judge and her brothers a legal team, Sonya had felt empowered to enter a profession where she might right some of the wrong. Sonya had enrolled in a criminal justice degree program at the University of Arizona, graduating with honors.

After Sonya's subsequent graduation from the Border Patrol Academy, Samantha and Sonya had begun to work together as friends, both striving to make things right for girls and women.

Sam's heart often took her to places where most girls never ventured. She and Sonya were each daredevils in their own way, intrigued with the underworld, occasionally reckless but usually careful and informed. Too many women and girls had been raped, beaten, and murdered for the two of them to turn a blind eye.

But now Sonya was dealing with danger on a scale that exceeded that of drug cartels. She was looking for links between the cartels and terrorists. Should she even allow Sam to help? And if she did call on her, would Sam balk at the increased danger? There was only one way to know.

When Sonya decided to call, it was their dinner hour. Sam and her husband Tomás dined late, after Sam's shop had closed.

"*¡Hola, amiga! ¿Cómo estás?*" Sonya greeted her friend.

"*¡Qué sorpresa!*" Sam said.

Tomás looked up at her from his meal with a quizzical look.

Sam whispered, "Sonya."

Her husband's face went blank. He knew that when Sonya called, it meant trouble for him. The last time Sam had helped Sonya it had taken his entire family's help to cover up her participation, which had involved relaying information during Sonya's investigation of a missing girl. Sonya had suspected that the girl's disappearance was due to human trafficking, a scourge that affected families with daughters in Nogales and even Tucson. Girls were pawns in the cartels' drug trade, and unfortunately thugs on both sides of the border were complicit in the dark world created by greed, sex crimes, and what could only be described as loss of the human soul.

"Tell her not to call here directly!" he said with consternation. The Mexican warlords could tap into the phone anytime they wanted. Sam waved for Tomás to be quiet. He rose and left the table in a huff.

The friends now spoke in code.

"I'm looking for a new . . . *outfit* to wear, something made in 'Hermosillo,' perhaps." A group working out of Hermosillo, Sam noted.

"What do you want it for?"

"*Algo muy importante*—a trip to Lake Havasu." So there must be some action happening in northern Arizona.

"For the Border Patrol?" Sam said. "I didn't know you serious types ever partied!"

"Very funny. Just because I wear pants all day."

"I'm thinking you should wear 'red' with some 'blue' to set it off." Red and blue, their code for border issues.

"Maybe."

"When do you need it, um, the *outfit*?" Sam would get information for her.

"Yesterday!"

"Ha! That's just like you, always impatient and impulsive."

"I have my reasons. Could be *earthshaking*, if I'm not, uh, *dressed* well."

Could "earthshaking" mean a bomb? Sam was fascinated. She figured the cartels or mafia were responsible for whatever Sonya was investigating. *But why Lake Havasu? So far north?* Then it struck her. The pump lift for the CAP system was not far from there on the lake near the Bill Williams River. *My God.*

"Well, it takes a few days for me to locate the right *weaver* to make the *outfit*, and then it will need to be made and delivered. Let's meet at La Roca when I've located a weaver."

Sonya asked, "Got the coupon?" They laughed. Getting free margaritas with a coupon at their favorite restaurant, La Roca, was their ritual excuse for meeting up.

"Oh, one last thing," Sam continued. "How much are you willing to pay for it? The outfit?"

"Whatever it takes," Sonya said.

22

Luna draped herself over a living room chair, wishing her mother would lighten up. Even on a holiday weekend, Isabel Lopez was giving her daughter tasks to do.

"Mom," Luna said, with that certain tone kids use when they believe there is no chance they'll get what they ask for but try anyway.

Luna's mother looked up briefly, then looked down again at her needlepoint. Their one tiny air conditioner clattered pitifully in the window near where they sat.

"Did you ever weave baskets, like Mrs. Romero?" Luna asked.

"No. My mother taught me to bead and I just stuck with that. Why?"

"She showed us a beautiful basket that she made, and told us a story about the design that she wove into it."

"Uh-huh?" her mother said, encouraging her to go on.

"Well, I'm still trying to figure out what it means."

Luna went to the desk where her parents always sat to pay bills and write letters. She found a pencil and a pad of paper, returned to her chair, and sketched what she had seen on the Tohono O'odham elder's basket. She held it out for her mother to see.

"Oh, yes. I know that design," her mother said.

Luna waited for the answer to her real question—what it *meant*—

but it was not forthcoming.

"Tell me how you spent the afternoon with her," her mother said instead. She continued sewing, occasionally glancing up at Luna.

Luna remembered that afternoon vividly.

She and Danila had sat at a long table on the screened-in porch at the Romeros' house, surrounded by piles of yucca leaves, bear grass, and Devil's Claw pods. Weeks of collecting, cutting their hands on bear grass, and roaming the desert on very hot days with Mrs. Romero had strained the girls' patience. Luna remembered Mrs. Romero's warning that to make a basket was a complex activity that took at least a year. She and Danila were just beginning to understand what that meant.

Mrs. Romero had said that making baskets was not for art only; baskets were to be used daily.

"Baskets in the past were part of everyday life, made to hold water and food and to store objects. They were also traded. We still sell them today."

Luna studied a wall adorned with beautiful baskets, intricately woven in soft earth tones. Some were made of white yucca and green bear grass in dramatic geometric patterns coiling out from the center like a galaxy of flung stars. Some were starburst patterns, and still others showed animals or people. Luna's heart beat with excitement as she planned the kind of basket she would make first.

"How do you decide which design or symbols to use on a basket?" Luna asked.

"It depends," Mrs. Romero said. "What is your purpose for making it? What is its function?"

Luna thought for a moment. "I'd like to make a gift for my parents."

"That's the finest basketry possible. It's a good goal, but for your first basket you might want to start with something simple," her teacher said with a warm smile of encouragement.

Luna held up her scratched arms. Danila chuckled, looking at her own.

"Yeah, simple might be good," Danila joked.

Luna observed that Mrs. Romero ignored their complaints.

"Now we are going to prepare the fibers for weaving. First they must be properly dried. I began the drying process after each of our collecting trips. It's been about seven days for this bear grass, and you can see that it's turning white; that means it's easier to handle." Mrs. Romero held it out for the girls to touch.

Using a finished basket to help with her explanations, Mrs. Romero described the "warp" and the "weft," showing them how stitches were made by the weft. She used a beautiful green and white basket made with white yucca as the weft and green bear grass as the warp. Luna saw hundreds, even thousands of very tight stitches. Her excitement cooled a little as she began to understand the magnitude of what she and Danila were undertaking—just making such stitches would require months of practice.

Luna noticed the elder's hands for the first time. They were strong hands with calluses on the thumbs and forefingers, and the outside of her right palm—the part of the hand that she used to hold the grass secure—was very thick. Luna looked down at her own hands, soft and youthful, with their gaily painted fingernails. *Do I want my hands to look like that?* she asked herself.

Suddenly Luna realized that the room had gone quiet. She looked up into the golden-brown eyes of Mrs. Romero, whose face wore a wry smile.

"What?" Luna asked, looking back and forth between Mrs. Romero and Danila.

"Rethinking your commitment?" Mrs. Romero asked in a strange jolly tone.

Luna felt her cheeks growing hot. She did not like that her determination was being questioned. Then she knew that she would never quit—she'd put Mrs. Romero's doubts to rest.

The elder put down the basket. "Let me tell you a story," she said and removed a huge basket from the wall. An intricate design of people and animals encircled the rim, while the center held a maze. A lone human figure stood at the entrance to the maze. Mrs. Romero moved to a more comfortable porch chair and signaled for Luna and

Danila to join her. Once everyone was settled, she held the basket in her lap and began the story.

After Se-eh-ha returned to his home in the Greasy Mountains, he decided to build a new home, a dwelling that would be like a labyrinth with winding passages. His purpose was to bewilder the enemy should they come to destroy him. "I'll be safe in my lodge in the center of my maze dwelling," he told himself.

One morning after he had finished his new home, Se-eh-ha rose very early. The day was calm and bright, but not the heart of Se-eh-ha. It was troubled. He sought to ease his feelings by reminding himself, "Am I not their Creator and Elder Brother?"

He climbed to the top of his new ki (house), shading his eyes from the bright sunlight. As was his custom, he looked toward the east. He saw a thick cloud of dust appear on the horizon. "Ha! I know the enemy is on its way to destroy me. We'll see who is more powerful!" Se-eh-ha hurriedly went back to his lodge, way down in the heart of the maze.

Before long the warriors arrived, shouting their war cry. They found the entrance of the maze wide open. Never had they seen such a strange-looking dwelling. It was like the mouth of a big monster, ready to swallow anyone who entered. One by one the warriors walked in. They quickly walked through the narrow, dark, winding halls. Soon the warriors were groping their way. It was so dark! Some fell, gasping for lack of air. The winding halls were soon cluttered with warriors, stumbling and piling on top of each other.

All the while Se-eh-ha sat smug and content in his lodge. He knew the enemy had all perished. Once again Se-eh-ha was the Conqueror.

It is told by the Old Ones the Se-eh-ha's ki (house) is located in the South Mountains near Phoenix, Arizona. In one of the gorges of these mountains were found an olla and a grinding stone which the Pimas believe are relics of the past and of the maze dwelling of Se-eh-ha.

Today the maze pattern is still woven into the maze baskets. It is like the pattern of life—with obstacles to dim the way. But happy is the man who rises to the top.

"So, Mom, what does it mean?" Luna now asked her mother, who had been listening quietly to her daughter's retelling of Mrs. Romero's story. Luna wanted to know the meaning not only of the maze design on Mrs. Romero's basket, but the meaning of that folktale.

"It's a story for your whole life, a great story," her mother said with a smile on her lips.

Luna waited for her mother to give an explanation. But she never did tell her, leaving it up to her daughter to figure it out. But at least she did say that it was a great story.

Frustrated and bored, Luna drew another maze on the pad of paper, trying to remember the course by which the one on the basket had led back to the entrance. It was confusing. While she drew, it came to her that many things go in circles: life to death to life again, seasons of the year, revolutions around the sun—even the circulation of her blood, which she had just learned about in her science class. Blood coursed out of one side of her heart, around her body, and back in through the other side.

Luna's gaze fell on her mother's hands, which were sewing stitches in the embroidery. They were not at all like Mrs. Romero's hands. Her mother's veins protruded blue and were painful-looking. Hers were hands of labor—hands that made bread, changed diapers, combed hair, swept floors, prepared meals, and tucked children in at night. Luna tried to imagine her when she'd been young, when her hands had probably been smooth and soft, like her own.

She left the room and returned with a few strands each of bear grass and yucca fibers, settled into a chair near her mother, and began to practice weaving. She and her mother stayed there without speaking until the sun dropped in a red blaze.

Luna was still thinking about the maze story later that night as she lay in her bed. Their home on the reservation was many miles from Tucson. The sky was black and stars twinkled through her window. A sense of timelessness came over her as the window fan pulled warm air out of the bedroom and the overhead fan sent waves of cool air down onto her skin.

She could hear coyotes yipping on the ridges.

This was her homeland, the place where she belonged.

23

As summer temperatures extended into October, the health of the people and the stability of the water supply preoccupied the minds of scientists, business leaders, and city and county agencies. Even the most stubborn climate deniers admitted that the situation was dire—no matter the causes. Action was required.

One morning Ed received a notice about shipments of imported fruit that were rotting on docks because cargo ships could not enter their ports. The recent rise in sea levels made it too dangerous. Ed had just finished reading a forecast of an expected rise in food costs due to lower production in the main food-growing areas of the US and in parts of the world that were experiencing either record rainfall and flooding, or the opposite, drought and record heat. Coffee prices soared as yields diminished. Food shipments lost at sea during mega-storms and cargo planes grounded in the record heat—each of these images bore down on his mind like a locomotive coming around a bend, horns blasting its arrival.

He realized what a damn fool he'd been. The thought deflated his chest and he slumped over the reports, deep in thought. Then he stood, took a deep breath, and walked out into the busy warehouse to find Frank.

"Get everyone together, Frank," he said. "We've got some serious planning to do."

In late October the temperature hovered above one hundred degrees. The expected fall cooling did not happen right away. People without adequate cooling moved into temporary shelters, including one that had been set up at the Tucson Convention Center, which had once hosted large concerts and dance performances. Churches took in whole neighborhoods when the grid flickered and threatened to shut down, and on particularly hot nights they sheltered the oldest and youngest members of the congregation, who were more vulnerable to heat extremes.

When once-stable sources of food waned, Ed and his staff gleaned ever more food from Tucson's groceries, restaurants, and burgeoning number of community gardens and backyard food producers.

The food bank's diesel-powered generator was utilized weekly as regional power outages became regular occurrences with the overloaded grid. In the previous month thirty-eight Tucsonans had died of hyperthermia, though the deaths were not reported as such. The victims were old people whom most assumed had reached the end of their natural lives anyway.

Then on a day that became unforgettable to Ed, the food bank was called upon to temporarily harbor the first overflow from the morgue. It was just a couple of bodies in containers, brought in at night, but it was impossible to keep the public from learning about the new morgue.

That was the point at which Ed finally admitted he was wrong. He felt a disturbing fear fill his chest, as well as confusion about his resistance to the idea that the world climate was changing. What had made him resist it so? Then he knew: he was scared of losing control. Everything he knew, had ever been taught, was based on the idea that human beings could control just about anything they put their minds to. But now he saw the hubris and even the insanity of such an assumption. Wow! In that moment he felt his compass spin out of control. It pulled him back into the memory of his father's sudden death, which had left him the breadwinner of his family.

Control, yes, it was all about control. This was the habit of mind that he'd developed as a lonely teenager working to support his mother and siblings, and he had carried it into adulthood without any awareness—or with no awareness until now.

One evening, in spite of her worries—or perhaps because of them—Carla decided to lure Ed over for dinner. She found her cell phone and prayed that the network was live.

"Hey, it's Carla," she said cheerfully when Ed answered.

"Hi," he said in a dispirited tone. She hesitated a moment, listening to his breathing. Then she took a breath of her own and dove into the unknown.

"A little bird told me that you have a weakness for Irish stew." It was really just a wild guess, but she knew he *was* Irish.

"How did you know *that*?" A pause. "Of course no one can make it like my mom did," he teased, knowing Carla couldn't pass up a challenge.

"Wanna bet? I'll put my mother up against yours any day."

"Oh, yeah?"

"I'm after that," Carla said in her best Irish brogue.

They agreed to get together the following Saturday night.

Carla smiled, thinking of his quirkiness, even of how she liked his unpredictability. She was a risk taker after all.

Inviting his son seemed natural too.

She didn't have to tell him that Irish stew was about the only thing she could make from scratch, having neglected her kitchen for the lab.

That Saturday Carla called upon the spirits of her grandmothers. These goddesses in her family lineage reached back in time to the Green Isle. She preferred to call them her "kitchen witches." She managed to find a butcher with lamb chops and paid a fortune for them. Thinking about the two men coming to her home felt good. On the day of the dinner she braised the chops in their own fat and roughly chopped carrots, onions, and potatoes. The witches guided Carla to add a few good shakes of Worcestershire sauce and a heaping tablespoon of pearl barley. They watched over Carla's shoulder as she arranged the meat in a heavy oven dish and supervised as she layered the potatoes on top of the vegetables and poured stock over them.

"Do I have enough salt?" she asked the gossamer forms of her kitchen crones. Sensing their reply, she added a few additional shakes.

Balancing on one sandaled foot, Carla held the heavy casserole in both hands, gingerly opened the oven door with her toes and shoved in the concoction.

I wonder if I should offer Ed's son a half pint with the stew, Carla wondered. She couldn't imagine Irish stew without Guinness to wash it down.

Then she asked her ghosts to keep the power on for the evening.

Ed hadn't been sure how to approach Daniel about the dinner invitation from Carla. Hell, he wasn't sure why he'd accepted it. He'd worried that Daniel might be upset, so he'd put off telling him until the actual day of the invitation, and now that it was here, he was feeling pressure and embarrassment at his ineptness in talking to his own son.

That Saturday morning they moved the washing machine to the back patio where Ed had re-plumbed a water line to harvest grey water from their shower and washing machine. Each time they used the washer, a different line would receive the rinse water and send it to trees and shrubs for deep watering. The weekend before, he had enjoyed mapping out the irrigation lines with Daniel, who'd planned how to reach each of their fruit trees and gardens.

"Son, we have an invitation to dinner tonight," Ed blurted out as he worked on the washer.

"From who?" Daniel sat on a stool, watching his father.

"Whom," his father corrected. "A scientist who's on the Emergency Task Force with me," he said. He sweated profusely, tightening down the washers on the water line. He looked up momentarily at Daniel.

"Oh," Daniel said, surprised. There was a brief silence then he asked, "And why am I going?"

"I thought you might enjoy meeting her, since you like science," he said, now looking sideways to see his son's reaction to the gender information.

"Her?" Daniel said. "A woman?"

"Yeah . . . a woman."

"And her husband and family?"

Ed stopped working and turned to look at Daniel. He cleared his throat. "No, just her. She's not married." Actually Ed didn't even know that for sure. Divorced? Kids? He really knew nothing about Carla. "Here, help me move the washer."

Father and son huffed and puffed as they moved the washer closer to the outside wall. Ed stopped and leaned an elbow on the washer. "It was just one of those things. She asked us over, and I couldn't think of a reason to say no!"

Daniel stared incredulously at him.

"But . . ." Ed hesitated. "She's kind of cute."

A look close to horror passed over Daniel's face. Ed felt like an oaf. He could see now that Daniel was definitely not prepared for this. *Hell's bells, neither am I.*

"So, why am *I* coming along?"

"Because Car . . . uh, Dr. Connor wants to meet you."

Ed could see that Daniel was even more annoyed now. He would be too, if he were Daniel. Then his son said something so surprising that it took him a few seconds to comprehend it.

"You know, Dad, I think it's great you've found someone you like."

Impulsively Ed said, "Oh, hey, man, I'm sorry . . . this is not a *date*."

Daniel just laughed. "Yes, Dad, this *is* a date. Don't you get it?"

"Carla and I are just working together on the Task Force. We're not dating or anything like that," Ed protested.

"Oh," Daniel looked up and grinned. "Let's see. You're just working together, but a single, apparently cute, woman has invited you, a widower, and your son to dinner. Whew! For a minute there I thought we might have another woman moving in!"

Ed stood tall, speechless, and ready to counter. Then he realized it *was* funny.

"Not on your life!" he said and pretended to bat his son over the head.

After they'd finished installing the grey-water system, Daniel excused himself to shower. As the trickle of cool water spattered on his hot skin, he thought about the sudden turn of events in his life. A woman was now in the picture . . . dropped like a bomb on the brokered peace he'd managed to create for himself since his mother died. He realized suddenly that his father, as clueless as he could be, might actually be moving on. It was shocking to Daniel. He felt a knot of resentment in his gut. But shouldn't he be glad? Living alone with his father was akin to dwelling with a statue—a static version of the flesh-and-blood original. Was it possible a woman had moved his father's broken heart?

Daniel wondered what she was like. He couldn't imagine anyone other than his mother. What if he didn't like her?

As the sun set behind the Tucson Mountains, Ed and Daniel arrived at Carla's home near the university. Father and son had been silent on the drive over, which had made Daniel nervous. They pulled up in front of her house, a modern adobe partially hidden behind a curved stucco wall decorated with Mexican tiles.

"Pretty nice," Daniel said, encouraged a little.

Ed was silent but nodded in agreement. They found a courtyard under an arched walkway. Daniel led the way under a green canopy of mesquite limbs casting cool shade. Flowering cacti in colorful lacquered pots peppered the veranda.

Daniel got a whiff of something cooking in the kitchen.

"Mmmm. Dad, do you smell that?!" Daniel said, turning to look at Ed. But his father was transfixed. Carla had come out to greet them.

She was dressed in a billowy blue blouse, gathered at her waist, and a pair of jean capris. *Wow, she's definitely not what I thought a scientist would look like*, Daniel thought. And then a follow-up reflection: *And she's interested in my dad?* His mouth gaped a little, but he caught himself and snapped it shut as he accepted her light hug and kiss on the cheek.

The cool, spacious living room held mission-style furniture, comfortable and with clean lines. Daniel was impressed, and he could see his dad was too.

"What's that heavenly aroma?" Ed asked, sniffing the air like a hound dog.

He's so not cool. Daniel wanted to hide.

"My family's contribution to mankind," Carla quipped. "Hey," she said, looking more thoroughly at Daniel. Her green eyes pierced him like a pin piercing an insect on a specimen board. "I know where I've seen you!"

"Wh . . . where?" Daniel's voice broke, and it was Ed's turn to laugh.

"You were the docent at the coati exhibit."

"Yep, that must have been Daniel," Ed said. "That's his favorite exhibit."

Carla grinned. "Come on, you two. Let's get you started with a drink and some goodies."

They followed Carla into the open tiled kitchen like obedient puppies. Carla opened the oven to check the stew. "Almost ready."

Then she turned to Ed. She stood about a foot shorter than him. Daniel laughed to himself as he watched his father's cheeks grow red and his eyes widen as if he were caught in crosshairs.

"Ed, I have a question for you," she said in her familiar Irish brogue. She stepped up close to him, grasping his forearm gently with one hand and gesturing with the other toward Daniel.

"Are we going to let this lad have his own pint?"

There was a pause. Ed was taken aback.

"Well, Dad?" Daniel asked, grinning broadly.

Carla echoed him. "Well, Dad, what do you think?"

Ed looked from Carla to his son and back. The moment was charged.

"Why not?" he finally gave in. "When in Ireland . . ."

"Thanks, Dad!" Daniel said, amazed and grateful. Carla was full of surprises. He began to think he might like this woman.

Carla poured frothing Guinness into large mugs and invited the men to platters of snacks she'd lined up on the tiled kitchen bar. They sat on tall barstools and watched as Carla prepared a roux. Ed and Daniel were enamored with her. They exchanged a few favorable nods when she wasn't looking. Why would his father hesitate? With each gulp of beer Daniel got happier and less cautious. This was the New World, and he was an explorer.

Through the sliding glass doors off the dining room, Daniel saw what appeared to be a rose garden near the patio. Carla's place was palatial compared to the Spartan-style living he and his father had accepted without Bonnie. With each passing month his mother's warmth and scent faded like smoke on a fleeting breeze. Just briefly, Daniel stood at the edge of that abyss again. He bet his father might be feeling the same way. But now Carla was here, in living color.

While Daniel chatted with Carla about the museum, he noticed that she watched his dad. As the evening progressed Daniel began to feel a sense of wonder, especially when she poured thick brown gravy over the top of the potatoes. He was starving, and the prospect of real food whet his appetite.

"Sure beats Hamburger Helper," Daniel said matter-of-factly. His father's face lit up.

"What do you mean, Danny boy?" he said, feigning surprise. "Why, we're gourmet cooks!"

"Could one of you get the salad out of the fridge?" Carla asked as she returned the stew to the oven. "Ten minutes and we'll be in heaven."

She did not see father and son practically collide over the salad. Daniel edged Ed out.

The Guinness had relaxed Ed too, and Daniel began to notice a little ease in him, a little more responsiveness to Carla. It was fun to watch. Daniel had never been in on a scene like this. He brought the salad and dressing to the dining table and Carla added a loaf of warm bread.

"God, Carla, this is wonderful," Ed said with his old enthusiasm. "I have to admit I'm starving! Daniel and I worked most of the day putting in a gray-water system."

The three chatted, mostly Carla and Ed. They laughed a lot, which felt good. Carla asked a lot of questions about the museum's animals. She really seemed interested in what Daniel had to say. She was smart—he could tell. For all he had dreaded this, it turned out to be a great night. Daniel's worry and loneliness vanished with the good food, the Guinness, and the glow of Carla Connor. She *was* pretty. Daniel had to agree with his dad.

Later Ed played moving images of Carla over and over in his mind, remembering also the look on Daniel's face as he beamed under her attention and how they'd both enjoyed her humor. Lying with hands behind his head, Ed grinned in the dark as he recalled the look of Daniel when he'd had a little buzz on. As far as he knew, the half pint at Carla's had been his son's first drink. Maybe that was a sign, like an initiation at the hearth of a woman they might come to love together.

Yet Ed's pragmatic side pulled back on his heart's desire to plunge headlong into Carla's embrace. His forehead creased as he came back to reality. He was having second thoughts about climate change. As bad as things were at the food bank, as severely as the drought had advanced, Ed just couldn't accept that the great American way of life wouldn't rally through these hard times. He saw the world as a glass half full; Carla saw it as half empty. Right?

Ed turned over, grabbing a pillow between his arms, and fell into a deep sleep, determined not to fall into any woman's trap.

24

Samantha facilitated contact with an informant in Hermosillo who proved useful to Sonya. It would be tricky business going through his networks without tripping the attention of a jackal in the cartels or mafia. Sonya could not be sure she hadn't done so already. But there were a few leads to Nogales. International trade, horse breeding, agribusiness, and border corruption converged in this international city where the twin cities of Nogales, Arizona and Nogales, Sonora Mexico were separated by a physical border that had been imposed by the Gadsden Purchase. The border crossing offered riches if one was willing to risk one's life. Many a dark figure had crossed in underground tunnels literally under the noses of Border Patrol officers.

Sonya had witnessed the dramatic change in crime first through her father's eyes, and now through her own experiences. Nothing was off the table when it came to the violence, greed, and twisted behavior she'd encountered in her career on the US-Mexico border.

"Okay. This is great work, Sonya," Bob Minor said. Sonya had taken the information she had to his office, believing her part in the investigation was complete.

"I'm a little worried about my informant in Hermosillo and my connection in Nogales," she said. "Please give the word that neither can be revealed, contacted, or in any way connected back to this information." Sonya knew the risks only too well.

"Of course," Bob assured her. "One more thing. We uncovered part of what might be a terrorist plot this morning. I avoided contacting you about it and asked others to report directly to me to keep you focused on your work, which you can see was fruitful."

Sonya's mouth tightened and she started to protest, but Bob cut her off.

"I know you don't like anyone to interfere in your territory, but this was simply too big, and your contact might be a critical link. I'm telling you now."

"What happened? What did you learn?" Sonya was sitting on the edge of her chair now, peering into Bob's eyes with both furor and curiosity.

"The big cat escaped," Bob said and waited for Sonya's next question. When she'd asked it he held up both hands in a "How should I know?" gesture.

"They were out searching for the jaguar when one of the men spotted something under the CAP canal bulwark. It turned out to be a bomb."

Bob could not look at Sonya now. "Go figure" was all he could muster while he tried to convey the insanity of the last few hours.

"Was it set to go off?" Sonya asked.

"Oh, yeah, Master Sargent," Bob affirmed in his Marine jargon. "Remote control. It was deactivated at Davis-Monthan Air Force Base. Our security team is scrutinizing the bomb as we speak."

Extreme stress contorted Bob's face, which appeared drawn and gray. Sonya worried that the stress might kill him. He had gained a lot of weight, and these days he ate and drank without any regard for his health. Like all of them he'd been compensating.

"I want you to choose one or two people you trust; doesn't matter what agency they're from . . . but I want you guys to be the team that investigates the leads along with me."

Sonya was shocked. "What about Homeland Security, the FBI— the agencies with the responsibility and expertise?"

"This has to be very local, Sonya," Bob continued. "Discreet, careful."

She sat immobile, trying to discern her feelings. Terror at being put in grave danger while having little authority; doubt that she was up to the task.

"I want to start with obvious links: the Border Patrol, the reservation, the businessman downtown who's been under surveillance for other reasons." Bob shuffled through a folder of documents. "I've already started a background check and review of his immigration papers," he said, handing her the folder.

Sonya took it in silence and thumbed through the papers. She knew the family being investigated. They did business with Sam. Impossible, yet she resolved to do the work—on her own.

Sonya felt Bob studying her face. "Look, Sonya. I did not want to drag you into this. It's dangerous, I know. But you are one of the best officers we have in the region, utterly trustworthy, and you've got the long history of the city and region in your head."

Too bad that can't be translated into a promotion and a raise, she thought as she handed back the file to Bob and turned toward the door and the dark underbelly of the night.

Sonya and Bob would need to organize an undercover sting operation after choosing a few experienced team members. News broadcasts would have to be squelched, which was never a perfect science. Bob said he was already on that. Sonya asked him to keep DEA agents out of the picture for now. They were notorious for bungling sensitive operations.

Then Sonya assembled the team. First there was a talented data-mining specialist from the Marine Corps Air Station Yuma who had been recommended by the Base Commander. Considered a genius in math and code, Addrian would liaison with Ft. Huachuca, the US Army Intelligence Center in southeast Arizona.

She also contacted Albert Pope, a recently retired tribal sheriff who'd served as Bob Minor's tribal liaison. A decorated World War

II veteran, Albert used good judgment and possessed more contacts and local knowledge than he was willing to admit. Sonya had worked with Albert in unraveling complex immigration cases.

Her third team member would be a talented undercover Arizona police officer, a man who'd frequently investigated drug-related crimes for the state. She had worked many times with Richard Green in successfully nabbing human traffickers in Mexico.

Green drove down from Phoenix to set up in the mayor's headquarters along with the Homeland Security and FBI agents who had assembled there, at the same time as the governor began to bring resources into Nogales. Statewide water-management personnel and local authorities were checking every dam and canal for other bombs, and the National Guard was being called to the same locations. Davis-Monthan Air Force Base, the Yuma Proving Ground, and the Marine Corps Air Station in Yuma would assist with reconnaissance. This was a national security crisis.

The cities and states supported by the water-management system in the Southwest represented a huge chunk of the American economy. Major agribusiness, clean power generation, and the wealth of the metropolises of Los Angeles, Las Vegas, and Phoenix, as well as that of smaller Tucson—they all depended on the Colorado River's unbroken flow of water. And Nogales was the largest international trade border for that region. If the cities and citizens of the American Southwest were suddenly put in peril—either from a grid failure, or sudden loss of CAP water or food—the entire nation would be thrown into a crisis. The major border crossings would be an open door swinging in both directions. It would be a terrorist's dream and could well enable an attack grander than that on the Twin Towers.

Sonya always marveled at the quirky and daring mind of the mayor. But she regretted for the first time the confidence he had in her. They both knew that federal agents, even state agents, could bungle a highly sensitive operation in a second. Corrupt Border Patrol agents, seduced to the wrong side by money or sexual favors, were common now. They were the weak links at the border, allowing individuals and shipments of drugs and people into the United States while lining their pockets.

No one knew the cartels and border issues better than Sonya and her family. Bob had convinced the governor to give her a little time to do the lead investigating, during which the mayor's office would orient the feds to the region. Bob would engage the backup by all the agencies and military if he could just have a few days. The governor could not control what the federal agents would or wouldn't do, but he approved Bob's moving ahead with a "look-see" to be performed by Sonya and her team. They might all go to jail later. But Sonya knew, as she understood that Bob knew, that if anyone could put a finger on a member of a group, it would be her. She likened herself to a police dog, picking up a scent where others missed it. Maybe it was in her genes, or maybe it was pure anger fueled by her indignation, shame, and trauma from that long-ago attempt to violate her body and soul.

25

Duma was airlifted to a wildlife rehabilitation center in Phoenix. Due to the venom coursing through his body he could not be sedated immediately. He drifted in delirium, striking out when he could. Agents and animal personnel secured him with restraints at great peril to themselves. The cat appeared to have a reserve of strength beyond credulity.

Duma's leg and paw had swelled to double their normal size. The day after his arrival at the wildlife center, Kim examined the paw. There was already some necrosis around the area where the snake had struck. She expertly excised it and repaired the wound. The cat's vital signs were strong. She had no doubt he would survive, but for what? She thought about this as she helped the jaguar revive another time. What kind of life would he have now? The Wildlife Center specialized in harboring orphaned and injured animals that could not be released into the wild. It was located near Phoenix, a city now on the verge of collapse from record heat and impending water shortages.

Kim removed her surgical garb and went to the office of the center's director, Ron Butler. They were longtime acquaintances in the animal-care world.

"What's the story about the Ghost Cat? Will it survive?" Ron asked, handing Kim a cup of coffee.

"Unfortunately for the cat, it will survive. It has nine lives, I think." Her feeble attempt at humor drifted off her tongue. Kim felt tired and weary from her constant concern about the heat and blackouts, and the knowledge that her job at the museum would soon come to an end.

There was silence between them while both drank coffee and thought.

"What's the chance that we might get this jaguar released into a wilderness area?" Ron asked Kim.

"Zero, by state and federal regs on both sides of the border," Kim said, looking out the window behind Ron at the red rocks, green scrubland, and blue sky. A lone white cumulus cloud drifted high above.

"However, I know some of the scientists at Pronatura. That's a leading nonprofit organization in Mexico for protecting wildlife. Maybe I can hold sway with them. They might pull some strings for this cat."

Ron was following Kim's thought process. She had clearly struggled to determine how best to move forward on this animal's situation. Had she lost objectivity?

"I'm not sure we can keep it here," he said. "It will need a large area, and special security and care. This is a killer cat that we aren't prepared to handle."

Kim knew that was true. With the museum closing, it could not be harbored there either.

"What about San Diego, the Wildlife Center there?" Ron asked.

"I was in touch with their director a couple of days ago, before the cat escaped. They said they would consult with their team. That may be a possibility."

Kim stood, thanked Ron, and left for her car. On the drive home she planned what would be needed to transport Duma across the Imperial Valley and the Laguna Mountains to San Diego. They would need a large climate-controlled truck. From Phoenix it would be nearly an eight-hour trip. None of it could happen until Duma completely recovered from the snakebite wound.

Kim reviewed the plans that she and Luis were making regarding which museum animals should be relocated and which would have to stay at the museum. She forecast a need for a skeleton crew to stay behind for animals that could not be relocated or released.

The monotony of the drive through low desert scrub between Phoenix and Tucson served as a hypnotic force. Kim's mind wandered. Images flashed of an ark releasing its furred and feathered passengers into a new world. She saw Duma, healed and strong, and she and Luis releasing him into the forested wilderness of his homeland.

Then she came to her senses and a thought intruded. Her profession's code of ethics instructed those in it to "do no harm." *Figuring that out in the present time was impossible*, she thought. *Was it ethical to capture, imprison, or kill animals just because they had accidently crossed into human communities?*

She felt the old angst writhe in her core. An irrational plan sprouted in her mind. All bets were off when the forces that impinged on living communities called for a new set of rules.

26

Engineers at Lake Powell adjusted the flow from the shrinking reservoir in concert with their counterparts at Lake Mead. Additional water from the upper system would no longer be released downstream. The reservoirs that held the lifeblood of the Rio Colorado were dangerously below capacity. This reality spelled catastrophe for the cities fed by the lower Colorado River system— but for none more than Tucson, which sweltered at the dripping end of the Central Arizona Project (CAP), a 336-mile system of aqueducts and pumping stations that carried water across the dry central valley and delivered it to Phoenix before bringing it south to Tucson.

Giant turbines pumped Arizona's share of water by first lifting it thousands of feet into a mountain range, from whose heights it was moved by gravity across the arid state to Phoenix and Tucson. The dreaded day would soon arrive when the turbines came to a stop as Lake Mead sank below the *dead pool* level. With a nearly depleted aquifer, Tucson was notably vulnerable to prolonged drought, and climate change intensified the impact of drought by creating high temperatures that caused water to evaporate at an even greater rate.

For two decades southern Arizona had been lying under a blanket of hot dry air, and there was no indication that the drought would end anytime soon. Experts predicted that a mega-drought could last as long as thirty-five to a hundred years. That was the pattern seen in the tree-ring research.

After the level of Lake Mead fell below the drought level of 1,075 feet, Arizona's share of Colorado River water was further reduced. This was the result of a 2007 agreement among the three states in the Lower Basin Group that gave the lion's share of water to California. The Southwest region entered a new era as climate change imposed the realization that a desert is inhospitable to large cities. US citizens accepted the truth before tycoons and government agencies were willing to admit it. Incredibly, Las Vegas rushed to build additional aqueducts to drain the Great Basin aquifer.

Carla worked around the clock at the Climate Center, barely keeping up with events around the globe. Strong climate shifts sped up exponentially, driven by reinforcing factors. The oceans continued to absorb huge amounts of solar energy trapped in the atmosphere by increasingly concentrated carbon dioxide and methane emissions. And while the world had moved to reduce emissions, the plan wasn't nearly as aggressive as it needed to be. World leaders didn't grasp the seriousness of the planet's human-induced fever. Earth's atmosphere heated disproportionately with the continued increase in carbon dioxide concentration. Scientists warned that there was no way to predict exactly what would happen to Earth's climate. Had they already passed several thresholds—indicators of the health of the biosphere? Forests, once the big carbon sinks, were collapsing around the world. The trees were closing the tiny holes in the undersides of their leaves to preserve their water. These trees were consequently unable to photosynthesize—no longer taking in carbon dioxide, and therefore ushering in their own demise.

News channels began to report an exodus of people from the Southwest as water became an uncertainty. In low-lying areas flooding caused related health problems. People moved to higher, drier ground. Carla saw it first in her own lab when Rajiv left, putting aside his career to return to his family in India. A terrible flood had claimed the life of Rajiv's uncle. Typhoid fever was rampant in his hometown.

Carla accepted his decision stoically, although it was a huge loss for her. They had worked together seamlessly. His departure would be just one of thousands of similar decisions as people began adjusting to new climate realities.

Few citizens were paying attention to the quiet exodus from Tucson—with the exception of the mayor and his city leadership staff. The local economy depended on growth. For the first time plans to build out remaining land in Tucson's southwest were seriously in doubt. Even basics like a stable water and power supply could not be guaranteed.

Determined to leave a new legacy, Lou Taylor assembled the best thinkers, planners, and designers in the region at a retreat. He chose the historic Arizona Inn in the heart of Tucson as the setting. Elegant, and exhibiting that particular genteel ease of Western culture, the inn achieved the blend of history and modernity that he hoped would shape his city's new ethic.

They were only twenty people in all, but among them were water, power, climate-science, culture, nonprofit, and finance gurus whom Lou knew personally, independent thinkers whose vision could extend outside the prevailing paradigm.

"I won't mince words," he began. "We are in a historic water crisis. Our city is growing, with the population expected to double by 2035. Climate scientists concur that we are in a mega-drought that could last for decades." He let that information percolate while he drank from a large glass of sweetened tea dripping with condensed water.

"There is no way out," he said, standing in front of the team that was assembled on the porch overlooking the tennis courts. "There is only a way in. I met with John Weston recently. Many of you may know him as the 'Water Guru' from California. He confirmed for me what I've been thinking . . . that we've been living in this desert since the late 1600s and still don't know how to live in a desert." Lou gestured toward Brent Lawrence, a young, well-known water harvester. "Some of you do, and frankly, I'll admit, I didn't even consider conservation as a primary solution. I guess I was a water buffalo, believing that engineering hardscapes like dams and canals—big-scale operations—were the only way to manage municipal systems for a city this large.

"Well, those days are over. Weston, and Brent here, have convinced me that we can overhaul this city's use of water and maybe, just maybe, get ourselves somewhere close to a system that renews itself each year." He paused, then said, "Folks, this is not another retreat that ends up with a published report and little action. We are here to save lives, to reinvent this city and the way we do—well, just about everything."

While Lou had personally invited each person at the table, not until that moment did they grasp the enormity of the present moment. It was perfectly quiet.

He looked down the long table at all the people from whom he expected solutions, whom he wanted to help him form a campaign that city officials, business sectors, and the public could get behind.

"Let's get started."

Lou sat down with hope that the weight of the world might be lifted a little from his shoulders. While breakfast was served, Sharon Briggs, a talented facilitator, outlined a process for the work that would take place over the next three days.

In South Tucson, Rudolfo Ramirez sat with South Tucson's mayor, Pepe Montoya, and his key staff. A team of water and energy specialists from South Tucson had just returned from Burlington, Vermont—a small city with a history of independent thinking—where they'd learned how that city had achieved energy independence. Their program combined renewable energy (solar, wind, and hydropower) with traditionally generated energy purchased from local producers with environmentally sound practices. They could keep going, off the grid entirely, in an emergency.

Listening to other Americans describing how they'd freed their city from corporate control of a common resource like energy had inspired Pepe Montoya's staff.

"Residents were induced with tax and rebate incentives, grants, and subsidies to place solar panels on their roofs or to install wind turbines on their properties," Montoya said. "That is the key. That's where we have to start—policy." He was gesturing to Congressman Ramirez. "That's where you come in, Rudolfo."

Energy independence would help many lower-income families stabilize their energy bills.

Discussion in the South Tucson offices that morning moved from determining all the potential sources of energy the city could utilize, to ways to implement the plan. Congressman Ramirez outlined sources of federal funding for low-income, under-represented communities like theirs. He and his staff would manage applications for that funding.

"In the meantime, we want to start right now. Energy efficiency has to be a big part of our overall plan. It makes no sense to have renewable energy in a leaky house or building. We can start employing people to help us tighten the envelope on every house. The other plan is to install rainwater-harvesting systems at the same time." He smiled. "We're going backward to go forward." He was referring to the cisterns that had been on every small farm in past centuries.

Rudolfo Ramirez interjected his desire to create an efficient system to recruit, train, and employ a Youth Corps. "There are so many hopeless poor kids in South Tucson who could use a job and a career path. It's that, or the gangs win out. This is a huge opportunity for families. We need an efficient system; no long lines and long waits. We've raised people's expectations, and we have to make this work. How do we do that?"

The plan that evolved would engage churches, neighborhood associations, public and private schools, and police precincts to disseminate information to families so youths could learn more about the program. Training would be contracted by the city of South Tucson and reorganized to support entry-level and then progressively more skilled training for youths who wished to pursue construction, engineering, or sustainability planning. This would take the combined efforts of thousands of individuals.

The mayor and congressman discussed the need for a well-advertised community meeting to bring residents together to help promote, lead people toward, and finally reach the large goal ahead of them. It would be held at an iconic location.

27

Dolores strolled hand in hand with Roberto to Saint Augustine Cathedral on a warm fall night. Families streamed through its heavy wooden doors. No one chatted outside as they once had. People picked up bottles of water as they entered the sanctuary. Inside a sea of droning floor fans moved the air around the huge interior.

Dolores noted that she had felt only slight relief at sundown. That little chill of desert nights had vanished. Sweat coursed down her temples. Roberto joined the volunteers handing out water while Dolores went forward to pray. She picked up a colorful paper fan from a pile in a large basket at the entrance of the sanctuary, dipped her fingers in holy water, crossed herself, and then found a pew near the front. The relief of a quiet mind enveloped her as she repeated the holy words. The glory of the Mexican baroque architecture and the vaulted rotunda framing a massive sculpture of Christ crowned in gold inspired quiet and reverence as the cathedral filled to capacity.

This night the people of Tucson had come together in the place of their beginning to consider an uncertain future. A period of unusually hot days and nights had settled over the city. Temperatures of 120° were common. In every household air conditioners, swamp coolers, and fans ran 24/7, loading the grid so that it frequently failed. At those times only people with gas- or solar-powered generators were able to keep cool. Families streamed to shelters and relief centers while emergency crews fanned out into neighborhoods, responding to calls for help. It was a frightening time, unprecedented in memory.

Even Dolores and Roberto questioned the viability of their town. Their dream of reconstructing a neighborhood felt unrealistic under the conditions. Dolores glimpsed Enrique in the crowd, the one student she'd thought had little chance of attending.

Roberto joined Dolores for the introduction of the speaker by Father Castillo. He reminded the audience that Congressman Ramirez was a native-born son of South Tucson.

"Tonight, my friends, we welcome a man who is one of us." The audience murmured in recognition of the man who'd grown up among them, a familiar figure in the cultural and political life of their community. As the congressman rose and ascended the steps to the pulpit, the crowd stood to clap, making a thunderous sound in the vaulted space. Dolores felt a thrill move through her. Roberto took Dolores's hand in his own.

Dressed in linen slacks and a white *guayabera*, his wavy brown hair glistening with gel, Rudolfo Ramirez stood before them humbly, gesturing for them all to be seated.

He held up a glass of water placed next to the podium. "*¡Éste es el nuevo tequila!* This is the new tequila!" he joked in Spanish. He grinned at the priest sitting next to his wife in the pew. Then he drank from the glass and set it down.

"Pardon my little joke. But it is true that water is the new gold." He paused, then asserted, "We *tucsonenses* know the true value of water. Our ancestors farmed by the Santa Cruz River, growing wheat, barley, and corn in their fields. They had their own system of water laws, so that no one went without water when they needed it.

Heads nodded and people murmured to each other. It was good to be reminded of that long-ago tradition.

"Even this church was built by *mexicanos,* brick by adobe brick." The grassroots construction of the original cathedral was another achievement to celebrate.

"Our relatives brought arts and culture to Tucson and, together with the original people, our ancestors imbued this place with beauty and vibrant commerce. We come from those founders."

He had the crowd in his hands now. Everyone felt renewed pride.

"In our present time it is easy to forget that legacy of leadership as we struggle with poverty, crime, and now climate change."

He stepped from the podium toward the crowd.

"The time has come for action. We must prepare for the coming changes. Rather than be frightened, I want you to think of these times as an opportunity.

"Tonight I wish to share how we can move forward as a community and as neighborhoods to secure our families and businesses for a warmer, drier time."

Ramirez captivated their hearts and minds. He spoke the truth without fear. The crowd listened in rapt attention.

"The more frequent blackouts are showing us our regional vulnerabilities. Power and water must be assured."

The cathedral was suddenly very quiet, every person following the congressman's words as if he were giving them life itself.

"What if a neighborhood made its own electric power?"

He paused to let them think about it.

"This is actually being done in other states in the country. It's called a 'solar commons,' and in it public space on the grid is opened to everyone. The money generated from leases is used to make it possible for everyone to join in.

"Investors can also buy a solar array for a neighborhood, or a business, that independently generates and stores solar energy. Some people call these 'solar gardens.' They are doing this in Colorado right now.

"When the grid goes down, the neighborhood continues to generate its own power. When the grid is up and running, the collective sells the solar energy to the power company."

"Now I know you're probably thinking, *Is this science fiction?*"

The crowd burst out laughing, their relief palpable.

A man in the front row spoke out, "What about water?"

The congressman repeated, "Yes, what about water? That is the question for this city and the whole Southwest. You can plan on renegotiation of the Colorado River Compact as part of an ongoing effort to make sure all the cities, tribal nations, and farms have water. But let's face it: water must be conserved much more than it is now."

The congressman paused briefly. The crowd was still. Water was the limiting factor. Everyone knew it.

"Let's go back to our deep roots again. What did the O'odham people do? They collected the monsoon rains to grow food. Basin farming. Today there is something called a dry well. It can be constructed by pitching a few neighborhood streets to direct runoff into a well below. There are examples in Tucson now."

Another pregnant pause. "Remember when streets were lined with fruit-bearing shade trees? Well, that kind of thing has got a new name: urban forest. The dry wells can water little forests of trees along streets. And with solar cooperatives we begin to see the possibility for neighborhoods to create resiliency against blackouts, drought, and heat, and to grow more food locally. This is what I mean by opportunity. These challenges can drive innovation."

The audience broke into applause. Ramirez walked down the aisle now as he addressed individuals.

"Do you know everyone on your block? This is a priority! We lost people in the last blackout because we were not organized." He addressed another row of citizens. "Do you know how to tell heatstroke from dehydration? Do you know where to go to cool down or find water?

"Our neighborhoods are not as strong as they used to be. Yet we have a long tradition of taking care of each other. We just need to revive our sense of community."

To Enrique it seemed that the congressman was speaking directly to him. More than the spirit of the community was under repair that night.

"Every home, every neighborhood must have reliable, affordable energy." The congressman strode down the aisle looking at people, face to face. "Imagine!"

He stopped in front of *Señora* Maria Alejandra Chavez, president of the St. Augustine's Women's Society. She smiled up at him from the delicate lace mantilla that surrounded her beautiful face.

"South Tucson can lead by organizing business, government, and community groups so that we are all working together. Let's be the ones, the leaders."

As the congressman walked past Dolores, she turned to see him point to Enrique.

"Teens like this young man can become tomorrow's leaders if we prepare a path for them." The congressman turned to address the larger audience. "No more dropouts, no more gangs: we will make sure students are involved in this transformation because it's *their* future that is under construction."

Enrique's face glowed in the soft lights. Dolores studied his face. Her student was spellbound.

Rudolfo stopped beside Pepe Montoya, patting his shoulder. The mayor looked up and grinned at him.

"We've got a plan," the congressman asserted. The crowd applauded as Ramirez sat down and the mayor of South Tucson walked to the podium.

Mayor Montoya instructed each family to pick up folders of information as they left the cathedral. Inside were forms to sign up for neighborhood training for heat emergencies; information on business participation and on how the solar cooperatives would be created, and a flyer inviting the youth to gather at the Sam Lena Library to learn more about getting involved in the energy activities.

He thanked the congressman and turned the night over to Father Castillo for the Benediction. Many people, Dolores included, fell to their knees in prayers of gratitude.

Everyone crowded into the fellowship hall afterward. Enrique pulled his mother along as he pushed toward the tables on which lay the folders that held their hopes and dreams. He could not wait to share all of this with his *abuelita* and Mrs. Carillo, both of whom had stayed behind so he and his mother could attend the historic gathering.

28

The day when it happened dawned warmer than usual. Air conditioners and fans hummed nonstop across the southwestern states. The average low and high temperatures in Phoenix and Tucson hovered well above normal, with no change in sight. A high-pressure system seemed permanently "parked" over the region. There were no clouds to bring relief. For the first time, Tucson joined Phoenix when the average morning low—one of the most important indicators of dangerous heat—stayed above ninety degrees. Hospitals began to fill with heat-prostrated patients.

The electrical grid had shown signs of wavering the week before when production had fallen below demand. Engineers and technicians had watched as load-shedding systems shut down parts of the grid to keep the imbalance from spreading across the whole network.

The city called upon citizens to turn up their thermostats and to avoid using appliances at peak hours. However, it was not long before the "nonpeak" hours became the peak hours. Instructions for maintaining body temperature by creating cooling effects with hand-held fans and wet bandanas, avoiding strenuous work, and staying inside, dominated radio and TV channels. Emergency and social-service crews checked in at trailer parks, poor neighborhoods, and the residences of the known elderly. Many people without air conditioning showed signs of hyperthermia; a few were rushed to hospitals. Some homebound elderly people expired before getting assistance.

Then in one stroke, at the hottest hour of the day, the grid failed. Like dominoes toppling as each knocks over the next in line, substations and transformers passed along the overage, shutting down nodes on the network. Over hundreds of miles—darkening and silencing communities as it failed—the massive electrical web collapsed. An eerie silence and an ocean of hot air enveloped desert cities, flowing into every home, office, and indoor space, and terrifying the public. Families, businesses, and workers waited. Usually the grid was back up within minutes or even seconds. But nothing happened. Only the oppressive heat persisted.

It would take time before engineers could determine the extent of the failure, as the massive overload caused one system after another to shut down and send its excess electricity on down the line. The interconnected patchwork of power linkages, utilities, and substations reacted throughout their connections, each shedding load, then overloading the next and causing *it* to shut down, and so on until the whole of the Southwest was without power. It would not be a simple task of reconnecting lines but would rather involve the complex reloading of segments, all the while keeping a balance between energy produced and energy used.

Cities and rural communities along the grid were without any power for days, some for weeks. Traffic came to a standstill, commerce plummeted, food rotted, communication failed, water stopped flowing, and regional security vanished. Chaos reigned on the streets, in households, and seats of power.

Western culture came to a spectacular halt.

For a time the generators at the natural history museum kept critical exhibit areas on reduced power. Kim and her staff monitored temperatures in the various indoor exhibits. A popular exhibit, the Cave, proved a lifesaver. Its rock-lined recesses provided cooler air—a welcome retreat from the intense heat. Staff moved more heat-sensitive animals in cages to its dark, cool areas. Kim noticed that her staff lingered there too. She was very concerned about hyperthermia. From her own experience she knew how it could creep up on a person, and once recognized it was often too late. Kim gave strict orders to her staff to drink plenty of water and to watch each other for signs of overheating: pale, dry skin and feelings of nausea and dizziness. She handed out packets of mineral salts for them to mix in their water during the day.

Backup generators continued to circulate water in the aquariums and otter and beaver pond exhibits. The museum could keep going in this manner as long as the blackout did not last longer than a week. Maintaining water quality and the right pH and mineral balance in marine aquatic exhibits would be problematic without proper circulation. For now, desert plants in the museum's botanical displays would receive no additional water. They were well adapted to extreme temperatures, and though they might shrivel they would still survive.

After they'd done all they could do, the skeleton crew returned home to their families with hope that the grid would soon be restored. Kim remained behind for a brief period, motoring around the grounds in a go-cart for a final check on the animals. Rounding the trail leading to the entrance, she turned to look out onto the Sonoran Desert beyond the museum's grounds. Seen in the intense sunlight and through the wavering hot air, the desert appeared to be on fire.

Early on the second day of the blackout, Ed and Daniel joined Frank at the food bank and found the warehouse still surprisingly cool inside. With its thick cement walls and thirty-foot ceiling it maintained its temperature longer than other buildings at the community complex. However, the fans no longer circulated air and Ed realized it would not be long before the place reeked from the odor of rotting vegetables. Nevertheless, for probably another day or two the warehouse might provide refuge from the inferno of hot air lying over the desert city. Unsure how soon the blackout would be resolved, Ed took an optimistic approach. They would just wait. If it were only a couple of days, they could probably save most of the shelf-ready food, and perhaps some of the food in the freezers would make it through.

Trucks from outside the darkened city continued to arrive with produce, but the bay doors on the receiving platforms could not be opened. Ed was not keen to expend his staff's energy on heavy-duty unloading and storing. He directed truckers to the Air Force base to seek other potential storage facilities. Angry and bewildered about where they could drop their truckloads of food, they idled in the parking lot, unsure of what to do.

Ed and Daniel pitched in to help staff move food from one cooler to another so that one was left empty. Ed told them this was thermodynamically more efficient. No one questioned it. He thought Daniel might, but the young man was concentrating on the task at hand. Ed figured the morgues would fill to capacity if the blackout continued.

He instructed everyone to minimize the opening of refrigerated storage units. Backup generators should keep them humming for a few days. Because the warehouse was cooler than the homes of some staff members, Ed allowed staff to move their families in and use the facilities in exchange for keeping minimal service going for anyone in need of food or water and able to get to the food bank.

Ed invoked the grid gods for mercy, and left with Daniel for home.

Carla's lab was equipped with backup power sources, but they delivered reduced power. Even in the cooled, circulating air sweat bristled on Carla's skin, dampening her hair. Circles of sweat stained her lab tech's shirts and blouses. Where vents pumped cooler air, beads of condensation dripped onto the floor.

Her main task that day, and on subsequent days and nights, was simple: read the climate models and follow weather reports to help emergency teams predict needed state and federal resources.

But Carla's attention was elsewhere. She wondered how Ed was handling the food bank and its stores of food, and imagined how Daniel must be helping. She wished she could be there with them. *How great it must be to deal with something as tangible as food.* Carla struggled with a barrage of data in bits and bytes. She was surprisingly unmotivated, perhaps emotionally exhausted.

Carla looked around the lab. Uncharacteristically she felt the excitement for her work wane while a need to go home waxed in her heart.

Suddenly she clapped her hands. "Listen up," she said, hearing her own voice as if someone else were speaking. Her students gathered around her. "How many of you have a place to go tonight—that has some cooling?"

A couple of students indicated they did.

"Go then. Don't come back until the blackout is over. Go take care of yourselves and your loved ones." To the remaining students, she said, "The rest of you are coming home with me. Get your stuff."

She grabbed a few things and programmed the lab robot so she could monitor data from home. In less than fifteen minutes she'd locked the lab and led three students down the emergency stairs and across the mall to her car.

To Carla, *this* seemed right, not pushing data or staring into a blue screen. Her internal compass pointed her toward home. She wished at the moment that she were going home to Ed and Daniel, and then realized that she'd ignored her own feelings for far too long.

"Hey, doc," came the voice of one of her students over her shoulder as they sped down a local street in Carla's Prius.

"Yes?" she said and looked into the rearview mirror at a young man's eager face.

"This is cool—I mean, thanks."

She just smiled back at him and realized that her students were feeling the same pull to be at home. Carla had already decided what she would prepare for her students from her garden and refrigerator.

For once she had food, leftover from shopping for Ed and Daniel.

The house would remain relatively cool due to its thick adobe walls. As soon as they'd pulled into the garage, Carla and one other student went out back to pick some fresh greens and tomatoes for a salad. They'd have a meal of cold cuts, cheese, and salad to stay cool. She instructed the others to make some snacks and relax. She was glad not to have come home alone to an empty house.

The blackout, having brought the usual frenetic activity in the metro city to a halt, reminded her again that her life was out of balance. She longed for human contact, for company. It was at that moment that she remembered her father's frequent admonition that family was everything—*the bedrock of civilization*, he had described it—and Carla realized anew that nothing would ever change that truth.

Enrique dabbed his grandmother's face with cold water, but her breathing grew shallow. He ran to fill the tub with water. But when he turned on the faucet, no water came out. In a panic now, he returned to his grandmother. Her breathing was more labored, her chest gurgled. He got a pillow from the sofa and gently wedged it behind her shoulders and back. That seemed to alleviate her struggle to breathe. Yet Enrique worried about her pallid face. He stroked her forehead. Dry . . . why wasn't she sweating? He was perspiring bucketsful in the stifling heat of the house. He gently shook his *abuelita*. She slowly opened her eyes, but they were strange-looking—dilated and unfocused.

He reached for his cell phone. The lines were dead. *No Signal*, the phone blinked at him. He looked at the door, then back at his grandmother. Then he bolted out the door for Mrs. Carillo's. He reached their house and found her, and before he could finish his sentence she ran past Enrique toward the Santos' home, yelling to her husband to follow.

The image of his *abuelita* that greeted them when they entered the house would remain emblazoned in his memory forever. She was slumped over, her hand stretched out toward the door. Mrs. Carillo gathered her into her arms and leaned her back into the chair. She stood. Enrique pushed her aside. He placed his fingers on her neck. He could detect no heartbeat. The labored breath and gurgle, the familiar signs of her continuance, were gone. His grandmother was utterly still. It took him a few seconds to comprehend what had happened.

He stood up, sweat pouring from his face and arms. As he looked down at her fragile body, a sob began to shake him. Mrs. Carillo put her hands on his shoulders. Enrique drew in a sharp breath to stop his tears. Rage replaced sorrow and slowly filled his body. Yes, he was enraged now, enraged about being poor, a Chicano in a gringo's world, abandoned by his father and betrayed by his brother, and recently jailed like a thug by police.

Mrs. Carillo could feel trouble brewing. She attempted to comfort him with words, but he didn't hear her, nor did he hear her husband, who stood by offering encouragement. Their consolations fell on deaf ears.

Enrique flashed back to the night at the church when Rudolfo Ramirez had promised a better world. It all seemed like a Hollywood hoax to him now in the presence of his grandmother, whose gentle spirit had just flickered out while the heat bore down on her.

Like a wounded bull in the ring, he wanted to hurt, to blindly destroy what had stabbed him over and over without provocation. His *abuelita's* shriveled and lifeless form only made his feelings of powerlessness more real. He could not change a thing in his life, yet he fumed with the desire to change everything.

Enrique turned from his grandmother's body and his neighbors, fists clinched and ready to strike. He lowered his head and charged out the door into the searing heat—to where, he did not know.

Susan Feathers

PART II

UNCHARTED WATERS

29

"What are *you* doing here?" Enrique yelled at his teacher when she came through the front door with a policeman behind her.

"*Mi'jo*, calm down," Mrs. Carrillo said with a worried look. She tried to put her arm around Enrique, but he did not want to be touched. He crouched like a threatened animal, turned away, and put his face in his hands.

"Just go away," he said. He was sitting at the dining room table, where Mrs. Carrillo had put a glass of water and a towel for the youth to use to wipe the sweat from his brow. The Carillos were one of the few families on the block with a generator. It powered a small window air conditioner and large fan—just enough to make the temperature bearable.

"We called Enrique's mother," she said in a whisper to Dolores and to Roberto, who was in his policeman's uniform. "Emergency personnel are at the house waiting for the funeral home to . . ." Her voice trailed off.

Dolores addressed her student. "Enrique, this is my husband Roberto."

Enrique did not move or answer.

"We just wanted to comfort you, to ask if there is anything we can do to help you and your mother," she said, sitting down at the table across from Enrique. Roberto had remained in the living room with Mrs. Carrillo.

"This is a very sad thing that has happened to you. I know it's hard."

Enrique listened, exhausted. He drank some water and wiped his face. He was clearly overheated.

"I don't want you to worry about school for now, okay?"

Enrique looked up at her and nodded.

"Will you stay here tonight—with Mrs. Carrillo, you and your mother, where it's cooler?"

"Where will they take my *abuelita*?" he asked, looking down at his hands and then toward Mrs. Carrillo in the next room. "Did they take her yet?" he asked his neighbor.

"No, not yet. The funeral home will come soon. I am watching, and I'll go down to make sure everything goes okay, *mi'jo*. Not to worry," she reassured him.

Roberto followed Denise Carrillo to the dining room table. He was worried that his uniform might frighten the young man.

Roberto said, "Enrique, I can help you with your parole officer. I know you need to check in with him, but I can let him know what's happening, that you may miss a few days at school." No one was sure at this point when the grid would go live again.

Enrique was surprised that Roberto knew about his parole, but he was glad and said, "Thank you."

Roberto moved to the table, sat down across from his wife, and pulled a pen and notepad from his shirt pocket. "What's his name?" he asked. Enrique told him the officer's name. Without phone service, Roberto would have to track him down at the precinct.

Just then Enrique's mother came through the door, her face streaming with tears and sweat. "Enrique!" She rushed to her son. Enrique stood to embrace her.

Dolores and Roberto retreated to the living room quietly.

"Thank you for notifying us, Mrs. Carrillo," Dolores said to Denise. "You know something like this could . . ."

Before Dolores could finish, Denise Carrillo took the young teacher's hands in hers.

"I understand. We are in this together."

157

"Will you let us know the date of the funeral?" Roberto leaned over his wife's shoulder to inquire. Denise took a card of Roberto's on which he'd written their phone number.

Denise looked up at them and whispered. "I am not sure what happens without power. The funeral may be soon; I just don't know.

After four sweltering days the grid went live again. In the interim Enrique's grandmother lay in a cooler at the food bank next to other victims of the heat wave.

The funeral was held at Santa Cruz Church in South Tucson—Enrique's home church. He usually attended with both his mother and grandmother, which made this day a somber one. As a boy at Confirmation, he'd sat on the right side of the aisle with the other boys, and the girls—dressed all in white—had sat to the left. Many of his childhood friends came to the funeral, surprising Enrique. In the turmoil of his year in detention, he had lost touch with them.

Enrique helped his mother to the pew and knelt to pray. He was dressed in clothes Mrs. Carrillo had found for him. The white shirt fit well, but the tie was long on him—as were the slacks, which bunched at his feet. However, Enrique's handsome face was all anyone noticed, especially his teacher Mrs. Olivarez. She and Roberto had attended the funeral at Mrs. Santos's invitation. With reduced power, the church and its occupants appeared to wave like sea anemones in an ocean current as their handheld fans moved to and fro, creating a little cool for each person. Water bottles given to each mourner were stashed next to holy books and hymnals.

It was surprisingly quiet. No cell phones, no music, no humming air conditioners, just the generator. No traffic, emergency sirens, or other stirrings of the modern community. In its own terrible way, the blackout had given pause to a culture of clamor.

Hundreds of candles burned with soft light, and the scent of roses—fresh cut from neighbors' gardens—filled the air. Enrique had lost his dear grandmother, whom he'd known from his very first memory and who had been his supporter throughout all the hard years, reminding him that he was good and had a rightful place in the world. He would never forget her . . . never.

Later, at the graveyard with his mother beside him, he tossed a white rose gently onto her coffin. *"Que Dios esté con usted,"* he said, his lip trembling. God be with you.

Everyone lingered at the Santos home after the funeral, sweating and drinking huge glasses of ice water or fresh lemonade, eating food that his neighbors and teacher had made. Each contributor had struggled, learning afresh how much everything depended on power. A few had used solar ovens that morning. Some had made tortillas on their grills.

Enrique realized that something important was happening to him. He couldn't exactly name it. To his great amazement, he was beginning to like Officer Olivarez. The officer had provided real help with Enrique's patrol officer, and now with his grandmother buried he felt a burden of responsibility lifted from him.

A few of Enrique's friends came to the funeral, and that felt new. Best of all, his new friend Luna came. She gave him a hug. When he looked at her he saw tears in her eyes, and that made his own tear up too. He was surprised to not feel embarrassed. Enrique was learning that it was okay to show emotion among his friends.

"Mrs. Olivarez invited anyone in our homeroom who wanted to go to the funeral. She and her husband brought us here," Luna told Enrique. They were gathered around the snacks. The other kids nodded, munching on chips and drinking sodas.

"You mean they drove all the way out to the rez?" he said, incredulous.

"No," Luna laughed. "It's too far. My parents drove me to their house."

Enrique looked across the room to where Mrs. Olivarez was standing with his mother and Mrs. Carrillo. She looked up and Enrique smiled. She smiled back. At that moment he understood his new feelings. He was part of something bigger than before—something like a family.

30

Months passed. In many ways Enrique's world was the same, but there were new possibilities too. The gangs were still around, hovering on the streets, waiting for an opportunity to mock him about his shorter hair, his books, and his work in the community garden near his school. He and his mom still had money problems, but the opportunity to learn a trade with the city was exciting. The city had more blackouts, but the neighborhood families figured out how to check on each other and make sure everyone had water, and they arranged for the older people to be moved to cooler houses or shelters right away. No one on his block had died in that period even though the blackouts and the heat had continued to bear down on the city. In Enrique's world it seemed people were more together than he ever remembered.

His brother was still in jail, but he would soon be released on parole. Enrique hoped he could get Diego into the training program too. Would his brother understand all the changes in him, or how he and his mother were part of the neighborhood watch program? Would he mock his little brother?

Enrique realized he was nervous about Diego coming home. He had worked hard to achieve a degree of peace and hopefulness, and he did not want to lose it.

One evening Enrique and his mother read the city's brochure on the new solar program, which had come in the mail that day.

A solar commons will be created. This is a public right-of-way with public spaces on the grid. The money it generates will be used to make it possible for low-income families to access cheap, clean energy. In South Tucson, construction and wiring of houses for low-cost or no-cost solar power requires volunteers and job trainees willing to join in outfitting each eligible family house. This is a community effort, with all hands on deck. Together we can make sure that Tucson families become energy independent and save money on utility bills, and we can create opportunities for community members—especially youth—to become gainfully employed.

The congressman and the mayor had come through on the solar commons. A solar farm was also under construction that would generate clean energy for South Tucson residents. They could now purchase or rent solar panels for additional power generation, especially for use in emergencies when the grid failed.

"*Mi'jo*," Mrs. Santos pleaded with her son, "We don't have the money to buy these things."

Enrique explained they would be able to qualify for low- or no-cost solar energy access. He knew that the concepts of solar commons, solar farms, solar panels, and substations were beyond his mother's comprehension at the moment, even though the brochure was written in Spanish. He would make a point to share what he learned from his training, which would begin next week.

The new system was difficult for everyone to understand in the beginning. Part of what the city would pay Enrique to do, after he finished his coursework, was to go house to house and answer people's questions, and help them fill out questionnaires. Later he would learn the science of the grid and actually learn about the wiring and installation of solar panels, all while earning "Solar Tech" credits that would go toward a certificate that would allow him to get a part-time job with his city.

At least that's what he'd heard from some of the other kids going to the training with him. Gerald said he wanted to study electrical engineering at the University of Arizona after he started working. Enrique had never dreamed of something like that for himself. Was that even possible?

"Mama, don't worry. There are ways for us to get solar energy. The mayor wants everybody to have a way to get it. I'll learn all about it next week," he said to his mother in a reassuring tone. He reached across the kitchen table to hold her wrinkled hands. *One day*, he thought, *she will not have to work cleaning hotel rooms*. He would earn enough for both of them.

"Are they really paying you to go to class?" she asked him, doubtful that there could be such a thing.

"Yes, each student will get a little money for transportation and food, and the class, computer, and materials will be free." Both of them were beaming as if the good fairy had just touched their lives with her magic wand and turned ordinary objects to gold.

"*Gracias a Dios*," she said softly.

Enrique left his mother to return to reading the materials that had come in the mail. He was glad to see that there would be some math in his training. He would be learning about grids, kilowatt hours, resistance, and materials science—whatever that meant—plus a lot about working in the business world.

If it had not been for Mrs. Carrillo, none of this would be happening, Enrique thought. She had called his teacher on that terrible afternoon when his *abuelita* had died. He also felt a twinge of guilt remembering how rude he had been to her. The memories felt surreal now. He was so full of hope today that how he'd felt back then seemed like part of another person's life.

What if I had gone with the Bloods? I was so close.

The memories and feelings were things that he pushed back. The dark, angry emotions and the burden of hopelessness were now despicable to him—a plague he had survived.

31

Luna handed her mother the gift. It was Valentine's Day.

Luna had proved a quick study, finishing her first basket in just eight months. Her heart beat a little faster in anticipation of her mother's reaction. Luna's father and uncle sat nearby watching. Mrs. Lopez ripped open the brightly colored tissue and drew in her breath.

"Ohhhh," she exclaimed and held it up for all to see. Woven in a spiral pattern, the luminous green of the bear grass against the white yucca fibers set off rows of near-perfect stitching. Luna's mother beamed with pride. "It's . . . amazing, Luna," she said, holding the basket out for the men to see.

"Excellent work, Luna," her father said, taking the basket from his wife to look at it closely.

Luna's heart swelled in gratitude for the praise. Her mother and father did not give it carelessly. To receive it meant that she truly had done good work on her first basket.

Luna explained how Mrs. Romero had taught her to be patient and had showed her how to collect everything before teaching her how to weave. It had been hard, even painful, she explained.

"There's probably even a little bit of my blood in this basket," she said, laughing.

Luna's uncle said he was glad she was learning one of the

Nation's oldest traditions. "I remember my mother and grandmother sitting in the shade of our ramada on a hot afternoon, weaving baskets while we kids rested."

Then something unexpected happened. Luna's mother retrieved the basket from her brother-in-law and stood before Luna, looking down. Her face was full of kindness, and a twinkle of good spirit moved like a spark across her brown eyes.

"My daughter, this gift means so much to me. You know that, right?"

Luna shook her head, a little nervous about what her mother was about to say.

"The first basket, in our tradition, always goes to the student's teacher . . . this basket must be given to Mrs. Romero." Then she smiled reassuringly at her daughter, whose face had gone blank.

"Let's drive it over to the Romeros' together," her father suggested.

Everyone in the family, including her uncle, worked to fill another basket with garden vegetables, saguaro syrup, and mesquite bread to give to the Romero family. In the Nation, giving represented an old tradition that nourished relationships as much as bodies.

That same day, now that she could make a basic basket, Luna made a commitment to continue learning from Mrs. Romero. Danila had dropped out. She just wasn't cut out for the frustration and long afternoons without her computer, cell phone, or TV. Mr. and Mrs. Romero kept their home natural—one of the few places where Luna experienced silence. At first she'd been bored, like Danila, but after a while she'd started looking forward to just hearing the sounds of nature, like the cactus wren calling from its nest in a saguaro, or the wind rustling through trees. She and the Romeros exchanged few words during those quiet moments, but much was "said."

Daniel mulled over his situation. He sat on an outcrop of boulders in the Tucson Mountains, having biked up Wasson's Peak Trail. Sitting among the saguaros and barrel cacti, the cactus wrens and Inca doves, he let the quiet of the desert soothe him. It was early on a Saturday morning. A slim, caramel-colored coyote trotted down the trail below him in search of a last morsel of food before finding respite in a shady spot. Soon the sun would breach the Rincon Mountains in the east and pour streams of hot sunrays down into the Tucson basin once again. He drank from his hydration pack, in which he'd mixed electrolytes with cool water. Daniel had become a careful biker since the higher temperatures had begun. In fact, he planned to bum a ride home with one of the docents later in the day. So much was changing. Life felt tenuous even to a teenager.

Daniel's mind roamed over the contours of his young life as his eyes roamed over the landscape before him. He felt a certain solidity forming in himself, a new sense of assuredness as he realized that he'd gained a healthy emotional separation from his father. Carla's presence had quickened the process, which was a good thing. It had been awful being alone with his father at home. He welcomed some normalcy. He also liked having two houses to choose from. Sometimes he was alone at one or the other, and that made him feel more independent too. He'd had a couple of get-togethers with friends from school at which a couple of beers had disappeared from the fridge along with most of the food.

The penetrating sun woke him from this reverie. He scrambled down the boulders to the trail below and steered his bike out onto the road toward the natural history museum.

Kim cooled herself at the museum's beaver pond under the shade of a large willow. She was talking to Rich Downey from the US Fish & Wildlife Service about the best remaining areas where beavers might survive and even reproduce.

"Bill Williams River is the best place," he was saying. "I talked to Rachel Burrows up there, and her people can help introduce this pair into an area where there are active populations of beavers below the Alamo Dam."

Rich watched the native fish swimming in the pond below.

"Of course, that river has been impacted just as much as the Colorado. In my view, they should drain Alamo Lake and return the river to its natural flow."

But that consideration wasn't the half of it. Release of long-captive animals was considered a "no-no" under normal circumstances because a captive animal might introduce a virus or bacterium that could devastate the healthy native populations. Normally that alone would have prevented Kim and Rich from considering such a risky scheme. But climate change had challenged the assumptions underlying the laws and regulations regarding animals. It had caused a fresh discussion about animal rights and conservation goals. The news was full of articles and interviews with zoo and aquarium directors who questioned whether animals should be kept on exhibit. Others promoted the role of zoos in protecting and conserving species. In every sector of the city, discussions brewed that challenged many assumptions and a way of life that most people had believed immutable—the American one.

Worsening climate events challenged every region.

Daniel meandered down to the riparian area. Kim turned to her youthful protégé and asked, "You up for a trip?"

"Probably," Daniel answered noncommittally.

Kim laughed.

Rich grinned. "Great, *amigo*. I could use the help."

The three crossed the trail to the otter exhibit.

"Now this is a problem," Rich said. "For all we know, there are no otter colonies that are truly making it in Arizona. With the demise of the Verde River and its ecology, there just isn't any place with the right conditions. I suppose we could call Rachel to see if she'd think of introducing them into the Bill Williams near Lake Havasu. They would have the whole reach down to the Imperial National Wildlife Refuge as habitat.

"This species," Rich said as he nodded toward the museum's otter pair twirling through their green pool, "is a Louisiana species introduced to the Verde River to try to boost the population of the mammal, but it might have overwhelmed the native species. We just aren't sure."

"Will these animals be able to survive?" Daniel asked.

"Good question," Kim said. She really had no idea. The museum's animals were maintained in conditions that were as natural as possible, but their food was supplied for them each day. Whether the otters could catch enough fish, frogs, and aquatic insects by themselves was unknown.

"Daniel, you're learning firsthand how all these systems are linked," Rich said. "People build a dam and channel a river bed, yet few understand the long-term consequences."

Daniel was beginning to understand. His year at the museum had been a real education—more meaningful than his years in school.

"It's a good time to relocate both the beavers and the otters," Rich was saying. "Mating season is in the winter months."

The three of them followed the path to the front patio, skirting the crowds of people who were carrying paper bags of closeout items from the gift shop to their cars. Dozens of museum members stood on the patio with somber faces or sat atop the flagstone walls near the parking lot to savor their last glimpse of the Sonoran Desert through the broad portal at the entrance.

After Rich had taken off in his Fish & Wildlife Service van, Kim and Daniel made a beeline to the museum's animal-care building. Kim gave Daniel instructions on the preparation of meals for the various animals still under their care.

As Daniel chopped vegetables and fruit and mixed in vitamins and oils, he imagined the release of the beavers and otters into the river. What would they experience after years and years of swimming from one side of a cement tank to the other, after eating food placed by humans in their dens, and after spending their lives under the watchful gaze of millions of visitors? What would *that* be like? He was reminded of his favorite movie, *The Shawshank Redemption*, in which a prisoner experiences utter confusion on returning to the "normal" world after decades of incarceration. Some prisoners even committed suicide after their release.

Would the beaver and otter pairs perish upon release into the wild? Would genetic memory show them how to forage on their own, defend themselves, and establish habitats?

As Daniel took meals to various exhibit animals, the thought began to form that his dream of becoming a biologist and working at a place like the museum was about to end, at least in the Southwest. It had the effect of draining his energy. He traipsed back to the prep kitchen, intending to go straight home. But instead he went out onto the trails and sought out the company of docents. He found Harold holding a kestrel on an oversized leather glove.

"The American kestrel is our country's smallest falcon," Harold was explaining to about a dozen members and visitors crowded in front of him. The slate-blue feathers against the bird's ruddy red breast and its sharp yellow beak made it a handsome bird to gaze upon. Daniel admired Harold's brilliant white shirt, pressed Khaki shorts, tanned body, and confident delivery. He made it look effortless, but Daniel knew otherwise. Harold's example reminded him that just showing up dependably, prepared and ready for the job, brought a certain quiet dignity to the museum's mission to educate the public even in the face of a rapidly deteriorating climate. It was good for Daniel at that particular moment. He waved to Harold, trotted to his bike, and left with a little more energy in his legs and with his spirit rising.

32

Sonya took chances. She knew it. That was the reason why she had no husband, no kids. She loved the law, and she was compelled to right the wrongs of just one beloved patch on the earth. But as she drove home, she knew that she was much more at risk perhaps than ever before, having pulled on the taut strands of the cartels' and mafia's webs of sinister activities. What creatures entangled in these webs, alerted by the vibrations of her investigation, lay in wait for her?

Arriving alone late at night, she let her eyes adjust after killing the headlights in front of the garage. Except for a nagging sense in her gut, all appeared in order. She turned in her seat to look down the street in both directions, then turned back to scan the vegetation in the front yard and look for any detectable movement inside the house. Her opponents used advanced technologies and could enter her security-protected home. That was something she'd learned from a previous intruder. So she'd bought a German shepherd, an intelligent, strong protector with a nice set of incisors. Jake gave her a sense of security she hadn't felt with any human-engineered device, including her .357 revolver.

The house was totally silent when it should have been full of barking and growling. She'd trained Jake to bark when any car pulled up to the house, when any person, including herself, approached the door. And Jake had learned it to the point of utter annoyance. So the fact that he was silent gave her a horrible feeling. He'd probably been killed, though she hoped that supposition was wrong. Sonya slowly backed out, watching to see whether any shadows moved in response. Where she failed to look, however, was above.

She was hyper-alert as her captors sped from her neighborhood. Sonya was bound and blindfolded, and her consciousness had split so that she was at once a terrified teenager and the courageous woman who strained to glean clues about the direction they were heading. The teenage Sonya shook with a fine motor tremor, feeling the urge to cry—no—to wail from the adrenaline pumping in her veins; the woman in her drew upon both mind and body to wage battle against her foe. Such was the state of Sonya's mind that these two parts of her were unaware of each other as she came to terms with her reality. There would be the usual outcome—intolerable to think about for even a split second. She heard more traffic, smelled cigarettes, and listened to the muffled voices of men. Was she in a van? If so, there would be someone with her in the back—where she reasoned she must be—watching her. She focused her attention, trying to detect whatever "thing" might be there. She heard breathing and smelled sweat.

Not long after, the vehicle pulled to a stop. They'd been traveling on a gravel road, so they were somewhere on the other side of town, Sonya surmised. She heard the "thing" move to open a door, then felt him grab her arm and heard him bark "Get out!" She stumbled forward and fell from the side door onto the ground. Instantly she sprang up and tried to escape, but two men grabbed her hard on either side. They dragged her into an unfamiliar place. The others followed. Were there four?

Suddenly the blindfold was yanked off, and she found herself faced by three men with distorted grins. Her mind felt disengaged from her body.

Sonya Morales had not reported for work, and Bob Minor was

frantic to find her. The FBI, Homeland Security, Border Patrol, and police teams were alerted. Bob called Sonya's team: Addrian Williams, Richard Green, and Albert Pope. Everyone rallied, terrified for the woman each admired for her courage and dedication.

Bob paced in his office, distraught and agitated. He knew that Sonya was savvy and might just be lying low to avoid providing intelligence to her enemies. Bob trusted her and thought that the situation would resolve itself. But in the corner of his consciousness, where his fears of the beasts and pestilences of the underworld lay, he pushed back the knowledge that Sonya might be their latest victim.

Alone, he mumbled to himself. *I know too much. If these malevolent ghouls got ahold of Sonya* . . . no, he couldn't let himself think about it. He was the one who'd called her into it. What in God's name had he been thinking?

His cell phone rang. He picked it up expectantly. "Minor here."

"Boss, we found her dog." It was his chief of police.

There was a pause. "Yes?" Bob urged, impatient but knowing.

"It's been strangled and mutilated . . . inside her house."

"Jesus," he said, a lump in his throat. "Any other signs or clues we can follow?"

"None. The house was locked tight. We could find no point of entry or exit, no evidence of the killer or killers. There was an eerie feeling in the house. The dog . . . I hope they strangled it first . . . ."

Bob was silent, thinking. His chief of police was thorough, and this only increased his anxiety.

"When is the last time anyone saw or talked to Sonya?" Bob asked.

"The security guard said she stayed late at the office. He left around midnight. Homeland Security has her computer and is tracing her cell phone records."

"What's next?"

"We've put out an all-unit alert to identify her or her car, and we have a team that is questioning neighbors, office mates, and family."

Bob had a hunch. "Chief, set up a meeting with the security guard, pronto. Bring him here."

He hung up. Whatever Sonya had been doing late at the office might give them a clue. Maybe the guard could throw light on her activities. Maybe he'd seen something, a vehicle or person.

Her dog, Jake, must have died a horrible death. Anyone who could do that to a dog could take Sonya apart without any remorse at all. Bob had read plenty of reports about what the mafia did to women. He fought to hold back his worst thoughts.

And then he left to meet up with Sonya's investigation team. He hoped that the three experts might pull a rabbit out of a hat.

33

Duma gained strength as his wound healed from the medicine and an enriched diet. But it was a cruel healing, for he became himself again inside a small enclosure where he did not belong. The scents of other creatures played in the cavities of his great nostrils. Sundry movements and strange or familiar vocalizations spurred his inclination to explore, while confinement prevented his normal activities. The visceral need for exertion by climbing, bounding, leaping, and stalking prey warred with his constraints and would eventually break him down from the inside out. He ate, slept, woke, and existed, but for what? How had he come here? For what reason? What place was this? Who were the two-leggeds? He resided in bafflement from sunup to sundown—each day an experience of agony.

One morning when he was stretching to alleviate the cramps in his legs, a man appeared before him. Duma did not lunge or make a sound. Something unusual about the man. He crouched to analyze. His nose sniffed for clues. No fear. Interesting.

The man sat down on the ground not far from the cage. Duma followed his every move. The man reached into a sack and pulled out a few man things and put them on the ground before him.

On first hearing the man speak, Duma rose but did not approach. Instead he pointed his ears forward. Then, letting roll a series of baritone grunts and breathy coughs, he approached the man, turned at the bars of the cage, and began strutting with his thick neck and head down. He displayed to the man his muscular back and forelegs, planting each round paw along the perimeter, marking the floor here and there with his water, establishing his prowess and territory, then returning to the center. The man did not move but made man talk as he watched the display. Duma grunted again—giving a warning, perhaps. He himself wasn't sure. He picked up no menace, but something else. What was it?

The man scooted closer to the cage. Duma approached and bared his fangs, but made no other sound. The jaguar and the man looked into each other's eyes. Connection. Confusion. Consternation. Yet it was a distraction, a novelty, and for that, for any temporary relief from his prison, Duma felt relief. Then he did something strange. He sat back on his haunches . . . in the presence of a two-legged, no less. Duma studied the man more carefully. Dark-skinned, shining black hair hanging long down his back. He smelled of earth. His eyes were dark pools—night sky in them. His movement was careful, strong like that of the small cats of Duma's homeland. Duma detected no malice, no wrong intention. The man was as clear in his intent as was Duma in his.

"The jaguar is a male, albino with barely visible markings under his white-gray coat, an absolutely magnificent cat who appears in pretty good condition for what he's been through." The man dropped the recorder into a shirt pocket and picked up his camera slowly and deliberately.

The jaguar followed every movement, but did not appear to mind the man's presence there. *Has it already become acclimated to life behind bars?* the man wondered. He hoped not.

For the next few minutes Duma tolerated the clicking and other strange sounds of the thing the man was holding up before his own face. Two-leggeds were indeed an indecipherable breed.

Finally the man rose, tall and square. Duma stood too. They regarded each other briefly. The man slowly turned from Duma, and just before he rounded the path that had led him to the enclosure, he glanced back at the caged jaguar.

Back at the news offices, Jarrod sat at his laptop downloading his photos and talking to his boss on speaker. "They've got this wild animal in a small enclosure hidden at the back of the exhibits, supposedly to recover from a snake bite and other wounds."

"Don't turn this into a sensation until you have all the facts," his boss warned. "How'd you find out about him anyway?"

"My daughter, would you believe?"

"Chrissy?"

"Yeah, her fourth-grade classmates have turned Duma's plight into a classroom project." Jarrod beamed as he looked at the photo of his feisty daughter on his desk.

"Duma? Sounds like Jungle Book." His boss chuckled.

"That's what the kids decided he should be named. They've never seen him, but only heard about his capture and escape down in Nogales. The classroom teacher is a member of the Sky Island Coalition, which studies and collaborates to conserve species from that area," Jarrod explained. "Jaguars are highly endangered and an albino jaguar is something really rare."

"Well, Jarrod, this might be a special-interest article, but let's get on to other matters of more importance. I want you to get down to city hall this afternoon to cover the press conference on the water situation. Spend your time on that first."

Jarrod agreed, but he would not drop the story on the jaguar. Chrissy's classmates were busy writing letters and launching a social-media campaign. He wouldn't let them down. These kids had tools and heart.

34

"San Diego will take the big cats," Luis announced. He slathered more cactus jelly on his toast, using it to pile the *huevos rancheros* onto his fork. Kim and Henry watched in awe as Luis shoveled the towering mass into his mouth with gusto. He was so concentrated on his breakfast that he didn't realize they were watching him.

The three were sitting on the patio of the museum's Ironwood Terrace Restaurant, which still served food to staff and docents. Its chef made the traditional Southwestern food with even more enthusiasm as plans to shut down the museum progressed. It was proving a common response among the staff to dig in more fiercely before it all ended.

Henry stirred his coffee in silence, looking into its brown swirl. "Well, good," Henry finally said. "Now, how do we transport them safely?"

Kim looked up from the yellow pad on which she was making notes. "We'll either have to hire professionals, which will cost us, or we rig up our own solution."

Luis pushed his empty plate aside and took a swig of juice. "I've got a crazy idea."

Henry and Kim looked up, surprised he had been following the conversation.

"Guess who's got big refrigerated trucks in town," Luis said.

"Walmart?" Kim guessed. Henry waited.

"The Community Food Bank," Luis said. "I've talked to Ed Flanagan, their operations manager. He's willing to work with us."

Kim's brain went into overdrive. "Fish & Wildlife can supply the cages. If Ed can help us secure them to the interior, and if we can load and transport them in an eight-hour period, it just might work."

"The tricky part," Henry interjected, "is getting a truck that large into proximity of the exhibit. Those twin mountain lions were just cubs when they came to us. Now they're full-grown cats who aren't going to like the move."

"That's the least of my worries, Henry," Kim said with a hint of derision in her voice. "How do we do this without seriously injuring them? They each weigh about two hundred pounds."

They were all silent for a few minutes, each thinking about different aspects of the problem. Kim said, "I know a guy who works with zoos and aquariums. He can lift the cages, animals inside, and place them in a vehicle and make it look easy. He's rather famous among zoos for his skill. He's expensive, but very careful. But he lives in St. Louis."

"Geez." Henry wasn't happy about paying for some guy's plane ticket. But he didn't know anyone else either. He looked at Luis and said, "Call Flanagan. Let's all go over to see his truck and ask him if he could help us get a crane for this guy."

He asked Kim to call her associate and find out if he was available soon and whether he had any other ideas for them. The mountain lion exhibit was set up to make the cats transportable by utility vans over short distances, not by vehicles that could travel over a desert, a mountain range, and into another state. And this was just the big cats. They still had deer, bighorn sheep, javelina, and wolves to go, along with dozens of other mammals whose fates had not yet been determined.

Luna's parents called her to the dining room table. That was rare. She worried that she'd done something wrong. Her parents were smiling, however, which put her more at ease.

"We got a call from the tribal chairwoman this morning," her father said calmly. "She explained that the mayor of South Tucson is looking for a young person to represent the Desert People on a Youth Council he is setting up. Mr. and Mrs. Romero nominated you."

Her mother's eyes sparkled as she studied Luna's reaction.

Luna was stunned. Her? "Wha . . . what's the Youth Council?"

"It's the mayor's way of involving young people in decisions we all make for the community. Our chairwoman explained that South Tucson is on a campaign to go solar, grow its own food, and help kids get off the streets, away from gangs, to get good jobs . . . ."

"Wow," Luna said, looking at her parents with wide eyes.

"Yeah," her father said. "Your mother and I believe you can do it, but it is a lot of responsibility. Do you think you could make time to do it well?"

"I don't know, Dad."

"You should be sure about it when you decide. Representing the Nation is an honor, but it requires a great deal of energy and commitment on your part."

Luna knew what he meant. Her parents were thoughtful that way. Whenever they accepted a task that would impact the community, they took it seriously, and they did it well.

"Don't make a decision now," her mother interjected. "The old ones say to wait three days before making a big decision. Talk to the Romeros if you wish. We can make an appointment with the chairwoman so you can learn what will be expected from the youth leaders."

"Thank you, Mom. I do need to think about it. I'm so busy with schoolwork, basket making, and other stuff, I'm not sure I can do it."

"You are going to be in town for school. We'll need to ask Aunt Sophie and Uncle Jerry if they can take you to meet with the council. Think about it. We could help you work it out."

Her mother was thinking ahead. Luna felt that her parents really wanted her to do it, but she wasn't sure. She was just beginning to learn more about tribal traditions from the Romeros. Could *she* represent the whole Nation?

An afterthought puzzled her. "Dad, why did they include the Tohono O'odham?"

"A couple thousand O'odham live in South Tucson, you know, like your aunt and uncle. After all, we *are* the Desert People," he said, chuckling. "We're the old ones on this land; maybe that's why. It's a good question. Maybe you could ask him."

"Who?"

"The mayor."

Luna would meet the mayor of South Tucson? That was pretty cool, she thought.

35

When Sonya awoke, dark memories flooded her consciousness, and they made her weep. Before she could even raise her head or stand, she recognized that the wholeness of the woman she'd been had broken down in this new stark reality. Every part of her ached from beating and violation, and her body, having been brutalized by demons in human form, lay exposed. She'd become an object to be used and discarded. She would rather have died than have awakened to this. Her condition was so dire that Sonya could barely think, and she tried simply to hang on to her memories of her family and the hope that her father and brothers, or Bob and her team, would find her. Whatever mental and emotional resources Sonya had possessed upon her capture had quickly vanished under conditions that even she could not have imagined.

Sonya's captors wanted to know how much the feds knew about the activities they were involved in and (Sonya inferred) about the terrorist attempt. Each time she came to consciousness she prayed for death to arrive and end the intense pain and emotional torture. How many girls and women had endured this, only to die undiscovered?

One night she was taken to a woman who helped her recover. Why had they let her live? She wasn't sure she cared to. Later she was moved again, and then a period of relative calm ensued. Sonya even had access to a decent bathroom. Another woman brought her some underwear and clothes, though these were only a few ratty second-hand rags.

After some time, Sonya began to hope. She started to think there was a chance that Bob and her SWAT team would find her. Richard Green and Albert Pope might find their way into the morass of undercover operations that the cartel operated.

Or maybe her family would pay a ransom.

Albert Pope's instinct proved a powerful weapon in a world gone digital. A network of neurons could not be hacked. Not to get him wrong: he valued data and especially the global positioning system (GPS) that did everything from the run the grid to keep track of a grandmother. But Pope understood that a good "hunch" was an invaluable part of the human toolbox for investigating a crime, especially in a blackout. In fact, the aptitude for sleuthing found renewed respect whenever the feds' machines went dead.

He figured that Sonya's whereabouts might be right under their noses. Perhaps she was in a place so familiar as to have become invisible to the security teams assembled to find her. Of course he did not share these views with everyone. Only Addrian Williams and Richard Green, his amazing team members, knew that he navigated by natural senses as much as digital maps. Addrian, able data-hound that she had proved to be, had positioned a drone near Sonya's house from the get-go. It was a little "hummingbird" that had rested in the Penstemon blooms and in the mesquite near Sonya's picture window. Addrian had kept constant vigil until her digital eye had gone blind, probably vaporized by another drone brought in by the mafia men who had followed Sonya to her home the night of her capture.

Pope had arrived amid the settling dust of the van that had swept Sonya away and had followed as far as he could before the trail ran cold. At least a couple of times the team thought they knew where she'd been taken, but the swat teams found no viable leads in either location.

Pope figured that Sonya, if she was still alive, would find a way at some point to contact a trusted site or friend.

36

Carla's research interests shifted to areas of science where she saw potential for large-scale solutions. She'd done what she could in her area of climate science. New reports showing carbon depletion in soils worldwide had caught her interest. Forests and grasslands had served as a carbon "sink" for millennia, with trees and plants taking carbon from the atmosphere during photosynthesis. But clearing of land for agriculture and city building had diminished that function. Humans had unknowingly interfered with the natural uptake of carbon from the atmosphere and its deposit into soil. If humankind could learn how to return carbon to the land, could warming be reduced—even reversed?

On the home front, at the Connor-Flanagan residences, the decision whether or not to use the oven became one of considerable importance. Adding heat to the house made no sense. With frequent blackouts and rising heat, Carla and Ed figured out what they could bake or broil that would be good as a cold leftover. They learned to warm up leftovers outdoors in covered glass dishes, and used the solar oven as a mainstay rather than as a novelty. Not long afterward the oven began to sit idle.

One night the family gathered at a table around a big platter of Mexican polenta pie that Carla had baked in the solar oven.

"I felt like women must have felt centuries ago baking in outdoor stone enclosures!" Carla said as she sliced the pie and dished it out to Ed and Daniel.

Her comment reminded Daniel of the ladies preparing fry bread and delicious tortillas at Mission San Xavier del Bac south of Tucson.

"The Tohono O'odham still cook outside," he reminded Carla.

"That's true, isn't it?" Carla affirmed.

"The food bank partners with O'odham elders," Ed said. "For some years we milled mesquite pods into flour. Apparently the pods contain something that regulates blood sugar." He ate his pie slowly these days, as life began its new pace in the Old Pueblo.

"No kidding?" Carla said, sitting up with renewed interest.

"Yes, and there are certain beans the O'odham have grown forever that do the same thing. I don't have all the details, but I know someone you can talk to if you want to learn more," Ed said, tearing a soft tortilla in two and slathering butter on it.

Daniel studied Carla and his father as they discussed these matters of food and culture. At school there was a buzz about obesity and fast food. He mulled this over with all the other changes in his life and environment realizing it was a sign of more changes to come.

Carla sought to learn more about Tucson's food security from experts who were recovering traditional farming practices. This gave her renewed hope, which was something she'd found she could not live without. Shocking her colleagues and administration, she secured a fellowship for a two-year sabbatical to visit scientists who were working on climate solutions. Once this began she realized that she'd never felt freer, and for the first time in years she couldn't wait to get out of bed in the morning. Carla believed that time was running out.

Through her studies and interviews with farmers, she learned about native seeds of the Americas and about traditional farming practices that held promise for renewing soil. Carla joined a local team of scientists working with Native Seeds/SEARCH, a seed bank based in Tucson that collected seeds from farmers throughout the

Americas. The seed bank established and maintained a searchable database for anyone looking for seeds that would grow well under varying environmental conditions. It amassed knowledge gained by native peoples over four thousand years of farming and by regional farmers under many conditions, and thus represented the region's best shot at successfully growing food fit to the region and climate conditions.

Carla was interested in knowing how native plants and trees might help restore the soil's ability to take up carbon dioxide and thereby resume its natural function as a carbon sink.

At a gathering of experts at the Mission Garden, an ethnologist named Sal Castillo spoke first. He gestured toward a bushy plant nearby.

"This plant is part of an accession of Tarahumara *Ojo de Cabra* beans," he explained, holding a handful of tiny blue-brown beans out for Carla and several other visiting scientists to examine.

"What does 'accession' mean?" Carla asked as she examined one of the beans.

"Accession, in this case, means that this variety of bean was grown by one farmer and protected from wind-borne genetic variation as it was grown out in other locations. The importance of heirloom seeds is the biodiversity of the genes they contain, uniquely adapted to specific conditions and locations. With all the disturbance in natural environments, the world has steadily been losing agri-biodiversity," Sal reflected. "Our group is growing these varieties here in Tucson to determine which ones are best adapted to our current conditions."

His enthusiasm was catching. Carla grasped the critical nature of the work at the Mission Garden and was determined to become part of it. Its location at the base of Sentinel Peak, on the edge of the dry Santa Cruz River bed, was no accident. This was Tucson's birthplace, a spot where thousands of years of continuous cultivation had fed the communities that had inhabited the valley.

The garden was near the site of Mission San Agustin de Tucson, established in 1757 as part of Father Francisco Kino's mission system. The location facilitated interpretation of Tucson's history in the context of agriculture. Prehistoric cultures, whose archeological remains lay under the old mission site, had grown corn, beans, and squash, all of which they had genetically engineered from the native seeds already present in the desert flora well before "civilization." In those ancient days, genetic engineering had taken the form of cross-pollination and the hand grafting of trees and food-producing shrubs.

A succession of cultures had followed these most ancient ones, each contributing something new. The Hohokam had invented the use of canals to channel water from the river into agricultural fields; the O'odham had later developed "basin farming" techniques that captured rain in shallow depressions, allowing it to soak deeply into their agricultural fields. Their settlement was called *S-cuk Son*, a designation preserved in the present-day name "Tucson."

By purposefully placing the Mission Garden in that place, the organizers had been making a statement. Embedded in the seeds and in the cultures that cultivated them was a certain kind of wisdom that now provided new direction, like a community compass, a direction that made sense at a time when the city's way of living was unsustainable and when food insecurity threatened the population.

Sal Castillo looked up from under his broad-brimmed hat into the large emerald eyes of a vibrant woman standing among the group of visiting scientists.

"Let me show you something amazing," he said effusively. He was directing his comments now to Carla in particular, sensing her sincere interest. They walked to a row of green shrubs loaded with tiny bright red tomatoes. He picked a few and turned to Carla.

"Taste these," he said, extending his hand to her.

Carla popped the tomatoes like candies into her mouth. The taste was sweet and the pulp watery. Her eyes lit up, and a trickle of juice dripped from one side of her mouth when she smiled.

"This is a perennial shrub of northwest Mexico," he said, handing the other scientists a few to taste.

Carla was dumbfounded. "Perennial? You mean these grow wild, year-round?"

185

"Yup," Sal said, laughing quietly. In his role at the garden Sal traveled the Americas in search of traditional varieties of native plants that were still being cultivated. Born in a small town in Sonora, Mexico, Sal had grown up around small farms and native gardens. His love of native plants and traditional cooking had grown into a career in ethnobotany, a discipline whose body of knowledge and research concerns had become more relevant over the course of his lifetime. He exuded the quiet peace of a person whose life and work blended seamlessly, and this was not wasted on Carla.

He has an unpretentious, lovely smile, Carla thought as she observed Sal that first day at the Garden. Deeply tanned, slender, sexy in a natural way, scientist and educator, he was charming to her as another attractive specimen of the human race. She was drawn to his exuberance about life, which was much like her own. Carla decided to devote herself to learning as much from him as possible.

Ed too was becoming disquieted by his work at the food bank. The problem wasn't the profession, just the circumstances. He knew that his work was relevant, but the continual crises with blackouts and the ever more frequent stashing of bodies in the food bank's cooler distressed him enormously. His passionate love for Carla pulled him toward something more exciting. She was growing, experimenting, and taking risks. This affected him. He recognized the inertia of his life. He'd been marching to the same tune for so long that he'd stopped even thinking about where it was taking him.

When his father had died so unexpectedly it was Ed who had started earning money for the family. Food was a big industry in the Chicago area where he was born. He'd readily found work at a large food distribution center and later at the largest food bank in the country. But it had not been his natural interest. He had once dreamed of studying architecture, but both that interest and his youth had been taken from him. Now, he wondered, might he return to that interest in some form? *It would be useful in this time and place*, he thought. *Could I help renovate housing to make it more compact and energy-efficient?* Ed loved the old adobe structures, which made sense in their region, and he enjoyed working wood. With new energy sources like solar, there were opportunities for incorporating new technology into existing home designs. The idea of blending old and new appealed to his sensibilities. Energy efficiency was overlooked by many, and he thought he could capitalize on this neglect by starting a business that would tighten the insulating "envelope" on the nearly 200,000 homes built in Tucson during the 50s. Ed saw it as a partnership among city, state, federal, and private partners like the one he dreamed he would own one day. Many low-income people lived in these older homes, people without resources for refitting their homes with proper insulation and new shade technology. If he could contract with government agencies he might draw enough business to last two lifetimes.

Ed decided to discuss it with Carla, but he had already made the decision to enroll in a construction course and learn the ropes.

Driving through the city's neighborhoods, he noticed things. For example, he'd see the orientation of houses on a street and understand how it could promote a certain way of life—or prevent it. These new insights made Ed feel that stones were being lifted from his eyes. He felt a sharp sense of purpose, one appropriate to the future that was unfolding before him.

That evening Ed and Carla were relaxing on the living room couch at her adobe home. They'd been spending more time together ever since the night they had first kissed and hungrily explored each other's bodies. One thing had led to another. It had happened on a night when Daniel was staying over at a friend's. Ed had never been one to show emotions, but that night his passions had surged and his usual self-control had vanished. A consummate sexual being, Carla excited every fiber in Ed's body. That night had marked the beginning of a new life for both of them—a New World of exploration and joy.

Tonight they were discussing the changes they'd each observed in people's behavior as they'd been out and about in Tucson. Like the temperature, people's tempers were blistering. Many people had lost their jobs, which made it doubly hard for them to respond to the new demands of climate change. Small pleasures were no more. It was almost impossible to get a good cup of coffee, a deprivation which on the surface seemed petty but which loomed large in people's minds. It was the same with a great shower, a good shave, a reliable hair dryer—just about every aspect of modern life. People were feeling the hardships of frequent blackouts or reduced power, and of the relentless heat.

Out of the blue Ed said, "I think we should consolidate. Move into one home."

Could I leave my beautiful home? Carla immediately wondered, assuming he would want to keep his house. *Do I want us to live together? Wouldn't it spoil the magic?*

"Adobe is much more efficient," Ed said. "I think we should live here at your place. What do you think?"

"What about Daniel?" Carla said, stalling.

"I don't know, but my hunch is that he either won't care or he'll be like me, ready for a change. Memories of Bonnie are all through the house." His voice trailed off.

Carla kissed his hands gently. She cradled her head against his firm chest, and looked up into his liquid amber eyes. Carla loved this man solidly. Yet there lingered an old but still fierce desire in her to be free. Having two houses let her maintain a safety zone into which she could retreat when her emotions irritated her. Relationships were tricky for Carla. Ed knew what it was to be married, to be in a committed relationship, but not only did Carla not share that experience; when she got right down to it, she didn't think that she even wanted that kind of permanent commitment.

Could Ed accept that?

37

It took months for the Solar Tech Program to get started, but Dolores and Denise had kept Enrique on track at school and at home. Now that he no longer needed to care for his grandmother after school, Dolores was able to find volunteer opportunities for her student, and Denise made sure Enrique came to her home after his activities. Mrs. Santos had finally gone back to work after power had been restored.

Meanwhile, Diego was released on parole. Having his brother back felt good to Enrique for the first few weeks, but then Diego changed. Enrique could tell the gangs were gaining ground with his brother. Diego was confused and shaken by his year in prison. He would not talk about it with Enrique or his mother. What had his brother experienced?

The changes began with Diego's resentment toward Enrique. He quipped about his brother being a teacher's pet, and called him a *bobo* for believing the promises of the city.

"Heh, Chicano, remember the Alamo," he'd say—over and over, like a broken record. During his brother's absence Enrique had grown up, and with the help of his mother, his neighbors, and Mr. and Mrs. Olivarez, he'd begun to feel the ground under his feet for the first time. He'd never had that before. Now he realized that his brother had not grown in the prison; Diego seemed like a little brother to him now.

"Get some new words, bro," he said to Diego. "Things have changed."

Diego grunted. He was lying on the couch while Enrique folded clothes on the dining room table. "Look at you!" he said to Enrique. "You're nothing but a *bajo*, little brother."

This infuriated Enrique. He whipped around to face Diego and said, "Oh, so your mother is a *bajo*, too? No!" He turned back to his stack of clothes, shaking with anger.

Diego was now fully awake. Drawing out each word in a mocking voice, he retorted, "*Hermanito*, don't get so mad." He rose, went to pee, and then left the house without another word.

Enrique wished his brother would just stay away, but he knew that he was too loyal to let his brother go. Somehow he had to help Diego find what he had found within himself. Hope.

Enrique sat with about twenty other kids in a classroom at Pima Community College. It was modern, with long curved desks that spanned the full width of the room. The instructor's lectern was set in an elevated console from which he or she could control a drop-down screen, video projection, and other electronic tools for teaching. To Enrique it was science fiction compared to his school in the barrio.

He only knew a few students; the rest had come from other schools or were older kids. "Hey, man," said Gerald, one of the boys from his school. Enrique grinned and stood to exchange a gangster grip with him.

"Who else is here from Mission Viejo?" Enrique asked. It looked as if all the students were boys. Just then a tall, slim girl flowed through the door on the far side of the classroom. She paused to scan the seats. She wore tight cropped jeans and had a cascade of thick brown hair held back by a pink baseball cap.

She chose a chair near Enrique but one row in front of him and proceeded to empty her backpack. He couldn't take his eyes off her.

She looked up and smiled when she saw he was staring at her.

"Hi," she said.

"Hi," he said back, and looked down at his textbook. She had flashed a beautiful smile.

Gerald, who was still standing by Enrique, slapped him on the back and leaned down to whisper, "Already lookin' up." He grinned at Enrique as he left to find a seat.

Just then two male instructors entered the room, one tall and the other very short. The tall one was older and dressed in a suit jacket with a white shirt open at the neckline, while the other one wore Dockers and a yellow T-shirt with "ECO TECH" in black lettering across the front.

"*Muy buenos días a todos*," the tall teacher addressed them. Welcome to all.

Everyone sat down and the room went silent. Enrique's heart beat faster. It was finally happening. After waiting for nearly a year, he wondered what he would be learning, and how it might all work out. Enrique still doubted it was true. It seemed impossible to believe anything good could happen in his barrio.

During the morning the instructors explained how the course would be taught, what they expected of the students, and the schedule. All the while Enrique could not help but look at that pink cap and thick wavy hair on the neck of the girl in front of him.

"This is a unique opportunity for each of you," Mr. Sparks was saying. "This class, if you successfully complete it, will earn you a Solar Tech I Certificate. That means you will be employable by the city of South Tucson and will be able to start working and earning income."

Everyone sat up straight and paid attention. Enrique was spellbound. This was what the congressman had promised. Enrique hoped he was smart enough to earn the certificate. He didn't know anything about energy.

Over the next two hours the students were introduced to all that the city planned to accomplish, and watched a presentation about the concept of the "commons" and what a solar commons would look like for South Tucson. The ideas were simple to Enrique, and equitable in nature, but the information about how it would be implemented through a "trust" was challenging. Enrique's head was spinning. He scanned the other students. Were *they* getting it?

"Let's take a twenty-minute break and then get started," the instructor said. "When you come back, pick up one of the binders with course assignments, and a textbook." He gestured to a table piled high with materials for the students. Then he gave them directions to the restrooms and invited them to enjoy the snacks and sodas set out for them in the back of the room.

Pink Hat stood up and moved toward the door with the others, glancing up at Enrique. He noticed a tiny brown mole near the girl's cherry-colored upper lip. Her skin was clear and very white.

"Pretty good, huh?" she said to him, smiling.

"Yeah . . . kinda unbelievable," Enrique said as they joined their classmates making their way into the wide halls.

They moved toward the restrooms, looking at the other students but staying together.

"See ya,'" she said as she disappeared into the women's restroom.

Enrique stood there engrossed in a jumble of thoughts.

"Interesting." It was Gerald, who stood just behind Enrique staring at the door of the ladies' restroom over his friend's shoulder. "Very interesting."

Gerald chewed a wad of spearmint gum, popping it periodically. He could be annoying.

Enrique was reading on his new laptop about the fundamentals of energy production when his mother shuffled into the kitchen to make coffee. She looked tired and old.

"*Mi'jo*, you look *muy importante* sitting at your laptop reading." She grinned. "Tell me about your first day," she said, starting to prepare dinner for her sons and a snack for herself for the night shift at the hotel.

"Ma, it was really great," Enrique said. "They told us we would be able to get a job when we finished the first course, a Solar Tech certification." His mother beamed as she chopped onions.

"That's wonderful, Ricky," she said with affection and a wisp of disbelief.

He moved to a barstool at the kitchen counter, bringing his laptop with him. He watched her wrinkled hands, now chopping green pepper, and her graying hair, disheveled from sleep.

"Ma, it won't be long before you'll not have to work so much," he said.

She looked up at him. "I know. But first pass the course!"

Her good nature gave him a boost of confidence just when he was feeling the weight of responsibility for his family again. She helped him remember that he was young, a student in public school. She would not stop working until he got what he needed. All of that she communicated with her body, her attitude. She just worked and prayed. He loved her so.

But that good feeling was shattered when Diego burst through the front door, leaving it ajar. He was drunk. Sweaty body odor followed him into the kitchen as he mockingly hugged his mother, who pushed him away from her.

"*¡Eres un lío!*" she said. You are a mess. "Go take a bath."

Enrique closed the front door and returned to his work on the laptop.

"*Extraordinario*," Diego gawked. "Lookie who has a new laptop." He reached for it, but Enrique grabbed his arm and held it in a vise grip, standing and glaring at his brother.

Diego stopped when he saw tears streaming down his mother's face. Enrique let go as his brother stormed from the kitchen into the bedroom.

Enrique got tissues for his mother and handed them to her without a word. She composed herself and went back to her cooking.

Enrique said, "Mom. Don't worry."

They were quiet for a while, Enrique doing homework and his

mother preparing dinner. Then she went to get dressed for work.

Enrique could hear his brother snoring in the bedroom. He reflected on the fact that Diego had once been a young boy with his whole life ahead of him. Then Enrique recalled what Dolores Olivarez had said on an afternoon that he had spent helping her at school.

It had taken months before he'd learned to trust his teacher. They had been making nametags for a "parent night" when Enrique had shared with her his worries about his brother, telling her how he believed that Diego was using hardcore drugs.

Mrs. Olivarez said, "Things will happen to all of us, some good, some bad, but we have choices about how to respond. It's easy to cry, be angry, use drugs, or blame others. The hard thing is choosing to stand for what we believe is right and live by it, no matter what. That makes living meaningful and joyful."

No matter how chaotic his world was, Mrs. Olivarez had a way to set it right.

38

The air quivered with heat, even in the shade of Aunt Consuela's house. It was not yet 7 a.m. and Dolores was sweating buckets, sitting in her car with the window down. It dawned on her that she could no longer safely make her pilgrimage up the mountain. It might even be life-threatening to do it now. It was spring and already the morning temperature was in the nineties. The winter months had barely cooled. It was perpetual summer. What was she thinking? She wasn't, she decided. Perhaps she could just explore the old neighborhood near the bottom, with its lush shade trees.

Dolores locked the car, poured water onto a bandana and tied it around her neck. It felt delicious. Donning a hat, she set out to explore places not seen since childhood. Her sweaty fingers found the beads of her rosary, but she couldn't bring herself to begin the prayer. Even praying expended too much of her precious reserves. So she settled on strolling with no particular purpose.

The old adobe homes paled behind the curtain of shimmering air. The ancient trees slumped over like slaves beaten by the intense sun, holding their leafy arms up for protection. Among some sturdy roses still thriving in the heat she found a miniature grotto with a plaster statue of St. Francis holding a lamb. Dolores stopped in front of it. She drank from her thermos and wiped her brow. That old world of saints seemed irrelevant to her for the first time. St. Francis's exhortation to care for animals and the earth rang hollow in a time when clearly people no longer understood what that meant.

Whenever she was tired or confused, Dolores became morose. It was her shadow side. She kept it to herself, preferring to work it out in prayer. She saw prayer as a weapon in the battle for her soul and for the restoration of her faith, and it had become a daily practice of late.

She left St. Francis in his grotto and turned a corner that would lead her back to her car. Before her a path wound down to where she and her siblings used to swim. She decided to walk down to the dry arroyo. To her surprise, a long wall, beautifully constructed from adobe bricks, spanned the level field beyond the wash. She suddenly realized someone was rebuilding the old Presidio.

Dolores had found the back entrance to the Mission Gardens, where Colonel Hugh O'Conor had ordered his Spanish troops to build a presidio to protect Spain's northernmost outpost. She marched toward the structure with renewed excitement and found the front entrance.

Inside, a man and woman were watering rows of stout trees on which green fruit was forming. Others were harvesting corn from tall stalks. Dolores walked closer to the baskets of corn and noticed rainbows of colored kernels on the cobs.

Nearby a man was inspecting some fruit trees. His face and neck glistened with perspiration.

"*Buenos días*," she said to him. He turned to look up at her.

"*Buenos días, Señora*," he said as he stood up and dusted soil from his knees.

"I was just walking the neighborhood and discovered the wall. Isn't this where the old presidio used to stand?

"Yes, the very place," he said.

"What a surprise! How long has it been here?"

"Several years," he said. "Take a look around if you like. I'm Sal," he said.

"Dolores Olivarez," she said. "Are those quince?" She pointed to some lime-green orbs. Before Sal could answer, she exclaimed,

"And persimmons, and limes?"

Sal laughed with her. "Yes, these are varieties the Spanish missionaries brought with them."

Dolores left the man to explore the garden herself. There were grape arbors and some kind of beautiful green pods that she also didn't recognize. She made her way toward the back, where several people were watering and planting. Dolores entered the Timeline Gardens.

She read signs along the paths that told the story of each heirloom variety grown there. Chapolote corn, Kitt Peak tepary beans, ancestral cushaw squash, and black seed devil's claw, all grown thousands years before her time. Irrigation ditches and basins brought precious river and rainwater to crops in Hohokam and O'odham gardens, and the plowed-row agriculture of the Jesuit and Franciscan fathers, who had brought both the European plow and animals to pull it, was all represented in the Timeline Garden for the public. The place was a living library of what grew well in this place as determined over centuries of farming. Dolores realized that here was a resource through which people could rediscover how to live in a desert. Its value was incalculable. Quietly, the Garden's staff and volunteers were creating footprints for people to follow. And it was so beautiful along the paths with the sturdily growing trees and green plants, and with the wildflowers and the swarms of buzzing bees pollinating them. These varieties thrived in heat and dry soils. This could be done all over the city, Dolores realized.

After her self-guided tour, Dolores joined Sal under a shady ramada near the entrance.

"This is a garden of mystery and miracle!" she exclaimed to him. "I felt that I'd walked back in time." Her mind was spinning with ideas for her students and community gardeners.

Dolores noticed that a family had entered the garden and had begun to harvest vegetables. "Oh, can people pick from the garden?"

"When people come for food, we do not refuse them," Sal explained. "But we do not advertise the garden in that way because we are really a laboratory, learning which varieties to grow and the best conditions for the growth of these heirlooms. We collect seeds for storage and some for sale."

Just then Carla arrived with notebook and camera in hand. Her fiery locks curled from underneath her straw hat. Noticing her blossoming crop of freckles and irrepressible spirit, Dolores immediately liked Carla. Sal introduced them.

"This place blows my mind," Dolores said to Carla.

"Let me show you something," Carla said and gestured for Dolores to follow her. They walked to another area of the garden, which Dolores realized extended down toward the banks of the old riverbed. Mentally she oriented herself in relation to her aunt's house. Yes, this was near the swimming hole where she and her brothers had played after heavy monsoon rains. As she followed Carla along the path, it occurred to her that she was retracing her own life's path, circling back with more knowledge than before and learning things anew—a mysterious accretion.

39

The big van from the Fish & Wildlife Service carried the otter and beaver pairs in relative comfort, and there was plenty of room for Rich, Kim, and Daniel in the front cab. Daniel moved between the cab and the back of the van so that he could keep an eye on the animals. They had spent a dramatic morning removing aquatic mammals from the only home they had ever known. Daniel stared into the beady eyes of an otter as he hand-fed it chunks of apple and a boiled egg. He knew the otters must be stressed, having been pulled from their watery habitats, put into steel cages, and brought into a world with the sounds of traffic and the opening and slamming of doors.

Daniel was engrossed in thought as he half listened to Kim and Rich's conversation. They were discussing the site and the process they would use before releasing the animals.

The teen felt a rock in the pit of his stomach at the idea of being witness to these animals' greatest trial. Would they be able to survive the dramatic move? Was he just a worrywart, and would the animals in fact be ecstatic when finally released from their confinement into a free environment, even if it was different? Did they have feelings at all? He'd brought along a notepad and spontaneously began to write down these thoughts:

What happens to animals in captivity? Has anyone studied that? Will native animals accept captive animals as being the same as them? Look up the history of zoos. Ask Harold about clipping the wings of birds for interpretation. Wasn't that cruel?

They traveled through the metropolis of Phoenix with its crisscrossing highways and passed everything from high-rises to sun-parched trailer parks. Gorgeous sculptures, dramatic architecture, and highways with giant murals portraying ancient Hohokam culture greeted travelers through the city. The spot being located in the Valley of the Sun, the low desert underneath the asphalt had once received the unimpeded flows of the Gila and Salt rivers. Now dams held them back to create reservoirs for the vast city.

"Just think, Daniel," Rich said, almost yelling from the front seat to where Daniel sat in the back of the cab. "The old Hohokam lived here almost two thousand years ago."

"As many as two *hundred* thousand Hohokam people," Kim added. "Unbelievable."

Daniel moved to the front again. "What happened to them?"

"No one knows for sure. Some archeologists think a mega-drought, like the one we're experiencing, eventually forced them to leave. Others think it might have been a disease or maybe war."

Kim pointed to a canal flowing near the highway. "These canals were built on the traces of the Hohokam's original network of canals."

Daniel jotted down more notes.

Rich, Kim, and Daniel were silent as they continued on through the sprawling city. Daniel noticed how much of the valley was cemented over. It was architecturally beautiful, but not much land showed through. More notes.

They headed northwest across west central Arizona and north toward Kingman. Just east of Kingman the perennial headwaters of the Bill Williams River flowed for thirty miles before reaching the Alamo Dam and the Alamo Lake reservoir. With its thick stands of cottonwood and willow and rich diversity of wildlife, the river still supported one of the last remaining riparian habitats in Arizona. This was to be the location for the release of the otters and beavers.

After checking in at the Game & Fish office in Kingman, Rich, Kim, and Daniel drove toward the headwaters of the Bill Williams River. Daniel watched the landscape change as they neared the water. Huge sycamores with massive limbs and platter-sized leaves shaded the banks of the river where cottonwoods, alders, and willows also grew in profusion, their roots deep in the water. Signs for deer crossing began to line the road.

"Daniel, you're going to see how Arizona used to look before we drew down the water table," Rich said as he pulled off the secondary road onto a smaller forest road. The bumpy surface rattled the cages, causing the otters to hiss and crouch in the corners. Kim moved to the back. The beavers were wrapped around each other, heads buried under their arms.

"Slow down, Rich!" Kim yelled.

Rich slowed and rolled down the windows so they could hear the flowing river and birdsong, and breathe in the fresh air that carried the scent of rich earth.

Daniel was enchanted. This was one of the green belts he'd heard about; he knew that a long time ago, green belts had been all over Arizona, crisscrossing the desert and providing habitat for many animals and birds. It was like a scene from a Disney movie. But it was real.

Kim returned to the front. "We're close to the location the rangers suggested," Rich said to her. She consulted a map they'd given her.

"There," Kim said, pointing. Up ahead was an earthen landing where the rangers had once launched canoes. They parked and got out to explore the area and stretch their legs.

Daniel knelt beside the river. He could see fish near the bank, and on a log on a sand bar sat a row of freshwater turtles sunning themselves. All these elements indicated a perfect habitat for the otter pair. Now he was excited for them.

Kim called to him for help with the release. They unloaded bags of vegetables and fruit that would be hidden around the area to provide familiar and easy food in case the otters stayed around the release site.

Rich removed the otter cage with Daniel's help, and they carried it to the base of the dirt landing near the water's edge. The three of them gathered around. Kim opened the cage and pulled out the first otter with a thick-gloved hand. It was the female, who weighed about fifteen pounds. Rich fixed a radio collar around her neck. Then he reached in to extract the struggling male, who weighed about twenty pounds. Holding the otters, the two walked to the end of the landing where it sloped toward the water and put the animals down.

Daniel crouched down to watch. He took photos with his cell phone. The two animals did not move for a few seconds, but the male suddenly plunged into the river and the female, biting at the collar, followed him. He dove effortlessly under the surface, and she dove behind him. Daniel could see them gliding along the sandy bottom, headed for the sand bar. As the otter pair surfaced, the turtles dove in unison on the other side of the branch, with the otters in pursuit.

"I'll be damned," Rich said.

"Well, we'll see how they do," Kim said, but she was grinning from ear to ear.

"Do you think they'll survive?" Daniel asked, watching them swim away.

"Only about a third of reintroduced mammals survive in the wild. But this pair seems pretty resilient."

"Let's get on with the beavers. We've got to find an area with beaver activity," Rich said, walking back toward the van. He and Daniel loaded the empty cage into the truck, and the three companions rolled slowly down the road, looking on Kim's map for the places marked for abandoned dams.

The beavers were more at risk than the otters when it came to reintroduction. They had not been active dam builders at the museum pond. An artificial underwater cave environment had sheltered them. No one knew if they could remember how to build structures that would last. But many beavers did. The massive dams built by reintroduced beavers had improved the aquifers under some Arizona rivers by slowing the water as it moved against them, allowing it to sink deeper into the ground and replenish the aquifers.

Daniel was learning how the activity of wildlife affected the land. He scribbled more notes as they bumped along a dirt road.

Finally Rich pulled over near a slow-moving stretch of the river. Below them the water pooled, and just below the lip of the water Daniel could make out the outlines of the logs and branches of a huge beaver dam that stretched from one bank to the other.

"Look there," Rich pointed to the gnawed stump of a cottonwood tree. "Beaver activity!"

The process of reintroducing the beaver pair would be trickier than for the otters, which were smaller. Daniel knew beavers could weigh as much as fifty pounds, and their teeth were deadly sharp. Rich and Daniel slid the cage containing the beaver pair down a ramp, and then dragged it to the edge of the water.

Beaver societies were complex, and it was unknown whether the museum's beaver pair would be accepted into the society of beavers near this dam. They might be fought off, injured, or forced to go build a new dam. The beavers were sisters, so they would need a male. Did they still have the instinct for mating? No one knew.

With Rich and Daniel's assistance, Kim put a radio collar on one of the beavers. Then they stepped back to let the animals find their way. Less adept on the land than the otters, the beaver pair waddled toward the river's edge and eased into the water. They swam in circles just off the end of the landing, their powerful tails like giant water paddles. One of the sisters looked toward the dam with curiosity. The pair swam near each other, touching noses, then dove and disappeared into the water near the dam.

Kim, Rich, and Daniel ran down the road to find a place below the dam to watch. Crouching under the limbs of a willow, they waited in silence. On the downriver side of the dam a half dozen beavers were rebuilding an area of the structure that looked as if it had recently fallen away. Suddenly the museum beaver with the collar approached the dam with a branch in her mouth. She swam to one of the native beavers and offered the branch to it.

"Did you just see what I saw?" Kim whispered. She was breathing heavily with excitement.

"Was that an olive branch?" Rich chuckled.

"There are olive trees here?" Daniel asked.

"No, silly. He means an olive branch as in a peace offering," Kim said.

"Oh," Daniel said, caught up in the excitement of what they'd observed. It was like a human village with strangers coming to town. That little female beaver knew how to respect the "town beavers." *I'm definitely going to write about this*, he thought.

"Uh-oh," Kim said, peering through the brush.

They watched as the other of the pair was chased away by a large beaver. For some reason her companion had been accepted. They anxiously watched the lone member of the pair swim off and down the river, out of sight.

"Damn, I should have collared both," Kim lamented.

They crawled back out from under the willow and hiked downstream for about twenty minutes, looking toward the river for a glimpse of the lone beaver, but they never saw it. Finally they turned back to clean up the release area. It was time for them to head back to Tucson.

"I wish we could stay for a few days," Daniel said over Rich and Kim's shoulders as the van rumbled along the shaded forest road toward the highway.

Kim thought about it. Like so many of his peers, Daniel had probably never been to a wilderness area. "Tell you what, we'll plan a camping trip up here. There's so much wildlife to observe."

Just then a doe leapt across the road up in front of them. As they passed where it had been, Daniel looked into the wooded land. He thought he saw its fawn huddled in the brush.

40

Enrique joined the group with Pink Hat, whom he learned was named Esmeralda—Emmie for short. Gerald and another boy, Floyd, sat beside her. Emmie looked at Enrique from underneath her hat. Her chocolate brown eyes sparkled at him. Did he catch a tiny wink? She looked back at the group instructions on the table.

"I vote Emmie reads the instructions," Gerald blurted. Enrique would never do that to anyone, especially her. But she was cool about it.

Emmie read well, in a confident voice, like a seasoned radio host. The boys around the table were pleasantly surprised. Off to a good start.

"Okay. We have to figure out how sunlight is converted to electricity and why silicon is used for transmitting solar energy," she said. The four students went over the online tools they could use, along with notes from the teacher's lecture that morning.

"It's all about those electrons that get kicked out and wander around looking for something to do," Gerald said. Everyone giggled.

Floyd thought about that and said, "But silicon combines with four other silicon atoms. There is no free electron to dance around, right?"

"Rrrright," the other three said in unison, each wondering about it.

"Go on, bro," Enrique encouraged Gerald.

"So they don't use just silicon in the panels. They have to have something else to get a free electron on each atom."

They turned to the handouts on the table and shuffled through them.

"Okay, here's the answer," Enrique offered. "They combine it with phosphorus, which needs five electrons in its outer shell. See, look at the diagrams of the two kinds of atoms." Enrique pushed the diagram to the middle of the table.

"When it combines with silicon, there's an extra electron left over. Maybe that makes the current," Enrique said.

Esmeralda thought about it for a moment. "But why do you need the sun, then?"

That stumped everyone.

After class, Enrique walked Esmeralda to the front entrance.

"Hey, how'd you learn to read and speak so well?" Enrique asked her.

"Thank you," she said and laughed.

"What's so funny?" he said, laughing with her.

"Just how things work out. I mean, my parents got me a speech coach to help me overcome a stammer. Most of my life I've struggled to just finish a sentence."

For the first time Emmie looked directly into Enrique's big brown eyes. He felt an electric jolt go through him.

"I think you're cured," he said with a straight face, making them both laugh.

A horn honked. It was Emmie's mother, idling in a Mercedes at the curb. Emmie turned to wave goodbye to Enrique, whose confidence was collapsing like a blown tire. Now he knew his new flame came from a wealthy family. His family had no car at all.

He walked to the bus stop deep in thought. *Wait. No wealthy people live in my barrio.* Oh, could Emmie's family be involved with the mafia or cartels? She wore nice clothes. He'd noticed the sparkle of diamond studs in her earlobes, but he'd assumed they were artificial gemstones like the ones he and Diego had bought for their mother. Could they be real?

41

Penny realized that during the time her daughter would be alive the climate situation might devolve into a global crisis, the likes of which she could only imagine. Books and media portrayed dystopian futures. She had avoided talking about her deep concerns until recent events had made them impossible to ignore.

Before the long-lasting blackout and its attendant hardships, Penny had mentally pushed back hard realities with careful planning and the belief that somehow the nightmare would moderate itself. She was not unlike other Tucsonans in her disbelief that the region could become uninhabitable. People were too smart to let that happen, right?

One night Penny and Luis meandered to their beloved porch to watch the night sky. The nighttime drop in temperature from 118° to 98° made the air feel cool. Light breezes blew across the desert that surrounded their home. A great horned owl hooted through the silence and a golden moon rose before them. Silhouettes of bats occasionally flitted near saguaro tops or swooped near the porch, snatching insects out of the air. Coyotes yipped in the distance.

Penny watched her husband gazing upward. She took his hand and said, "Luis, I'm scared. We've got to do something to make sure Pearl will have a future. But I feel powerless to do that—I mean, for the first time in my life, I don't know what to do."

Luis studied her lovely round face, lit up by moonlight.

"I've been thinking that we might need to move," he said.

Penny started at his frank reply, but she'd had the same thought.

"But where could we go? If it's not a drought, it's flooding or hurricanes or some other kind of environmental disaster. For the first time I feel like our lives may be threatened."

He went back to gazing at the heavens. She was sorry to put this burden on his already overstressed mind. Her personal confidence had waned—an unaccustomed feeling for Penny.

At work Luis faced the dissolution of the museum and his life's endeavor, at least as he had known it. He wasn't sure that what he and Kim had come up with to advise Henry would have any appeal for him either. He was out of ideas.

Everything about their lives depended on the environment. Penny had known this intellectually, but now she suspected that she hadn't comprehended it fully. As the climate changed, their lives would, too . . . irrevocably. Pearl's future looked precarious.

"Remember that night I had the long dream, the night you stayed by me?" Luis said.

"Yes." Penny stared through the dark at her husband.

"I've been trying to understand it all this time. There was a jaguar that came to me, and when it did, I saw a river change from blue to red. Then long lines of people moved silently past me toward the river.

"What kind of people?" Penny asked. "Modern or ancient?"

"They looked like us, contemporary. And . . ." Luis hesitated, trying to recall the details, "there was a medallion hanging from the jaguar's neck."

Penny listened quietly. She was trying to decipher images he described.

"There was a red rose in the middle, surrounded by dragonflies, blue dragonflies."

Penny whispered, "*Río Colorado.*" She suddenly understood the meaning: the dream showed the red silted waters of the river before it had been dammed and channeled into the blue canals. Was the

208

dream a foretelling of events to come? Who were the people? Her generation? Pearl's?

"Penny," Luis said with more intensity, "maybe this time our plans are not the thing we should worry about."

"What do you mean?" Penny was pragmatic. Dreams might be helpful, but they weren't something she was going to rely on for assuring her daughter's future.

"I guess I mean that I'm feeling like we should be paying more attention to signs around us, signs that are like the dream, a direction we're not seeing right now."

Could her husband be right? Was it time for a new way of thinking, planning? It was totally against her grain to rely on something she could not see, feel, or touch. But maybe it *was* time for a new approach.

"What could the jaguar mean?" she asked, reengaged.

"In my homeland the jaguar is seen as a symbol of strength and spiritual power, but it also can be a deadly foe and ruler of the underworld. It's a shape-shifter."

They remained holding hands on the porch in silence, letting the symbols in the dream dance around in their minds, attempting to make sense of them.

Later, in bed, they made love. It had been a long time. Penny realized how much she'd missed the touch of her husband, the feeling of his muscular body on her own. She surrendered to waves of yearning and release, letting no thought intrude. Was it her imagination that their lovemaking had a new element, a kind of desperate reaching for safety and comfort?

42

"What is that design?" Luna asked Mrs. Romero, who held a gorgeous green and white basket. Her teacher handed it to her so that she could examine it more closely. Luna was breathless at its exquisite beauty. The basket felt alive in her hands. Her mind was filled with simple wanting. She too would weave this split-stitch pattern with a squash blossom center.

"I would like to try this pattern for my next basket," Luna said with more confidence.

"Ah," Mrs. Romero responded. "It's good to learn new techniques, but I advise you to stay with the method of your first basket until you perfect it, and then move to another." She smiled reassuringly at Luna to make sure the youth did not become discouraged.

"All right, I'll do a similar stitch, but this time I'd like to make the basket deeper, like a fruit bowl." Mrs. Romero agreed that that was a good plan.

Members of the Tohono O'odham basket weavers' society had stockpiled a good many grasses, so this time Luna would not need to gather her materials first.

The young teen began selecting dried grasses while sitting with Mrs. Romero on their screened-in porch. The older woman was creating a diminutive bowl, making intricate loops with her strong hands. From time to time Luna stopped to watch her skill.

The sun was dropping in the western sky, spilling brilliant colors where it touched the earth. The reduction in temperature had allowed a faint breeze to start up on the desert, and it blew gently through the screen, cooling the teacher and her student. The pungent scent of creosote bush reached Luna, filling her consciousness and leaving a welcome peace of mind.

About an hour later George Romero arrived home, followed shortly afterward by Luna's parents, who had been invited to dinner. Luna left her few swirls of bear grass and yucca fibers on the chair and went inside to help with dinner. Isabel Lopez carried a heavy casserole dish of baked green chili peppers swimming in a cheese sauce. Luna took it from her and put it on the dining room table. Of all her mother's dishes, she loved this one best.

"Welcome, friends," George Romero said, greeting them with outstretched hands. He nodded respectfully first to Luna's father, and then to her mother.

They mingled briefly in the living room, but soon the men went out to the porch and the women went to the kitchen to finish preparations.

"Luna, would you mind chopping up this melon?" Mrs. Romero asked.

Luna took it and began to cut into its tough skin. "What kind of melon is this?" she asked.

Mrs. Lopez was sitting at the breakfast bar watching the easy exchange between her daughter and Mrs. Romero. She felt glad that her daughter had confidence in herself and that she showed respect for her elders. Something very special had developed between the two of them that was good for Luna.

Mrs. Romero asked Luna's mother if she recognized the melon. Luna brought it over and her mother smelled it, rotating it in her hand. Then suddenly she exclaimed, "Oh my goodness, Flora, this is like the ones my grandparents grew in the old time basins, isn't it?"

"Yes! Doesn't it bring back memories?" Mrs. Romero said, turning toward her.

"I have not seen these for decades. Where did you get it?"

Luna took it back to slice it for a salad.

"They are growing the oldest plants of our elders over by Tjuk Shon."

"You mean the sacred place?"

Luna looked up. "What sacred place?"

"You know it as A Mountain," Mrs. Romero said as she lifted braised ribs out of a bean stew and put them onto a platter.

"Luna, it is where the old ones settled when they first came here and where they grew their crops. It's by the Santa Cruz River," Mrs. Lopez explained as she took the platter from Flora's hands and walked it to the dining room table.

"Let's call the men in," Mrs. Romero said, addressing Luna.

That night Luna listened quietly to the stories her parents shared with the Romeros. There was so much to learn about her people. But she reminded herself, *I am learning a traditional art form from a master. That's one way to learn history.*

As the adults chatted, Luna was left to think about the mayor's recent invitation for her to represent her community on the Youth Council. Although it was an honor to be chosen, she did not feel particularly excited about it. Her way was different. She wanted to learn her people's history, traditions, and language—the latter very difficult now that none but a few elders still spoke it.

It was the basket making, Luna told herself, that had led her inward and deeper, as if roots were growing from the soles of her feet and reaching down into the earth. Walking the desert, harvesting the grasses, feeling the textures—these things made new roots grow. She was not inclined to move outward right now and to try to be a leader. She had work to do inside herself. With that thought she remembered asking Mrs. Romero about the design on the maize basket when she'd been getting started as a basket maker. Suddenly Luna knew what the design meant. It was the path of life. A profound feeling of gratitude swept through her. When she looked up, both her mother and Mrs. Romero were smiling at her.

That same night at home, Luna fell into a deep sleep. Soon images danced before her mind's eye. Children were gathered around a hearth in a small adobe home. A hole in the roof allowed the smoke to flow upward and out into the cold night. An old woman rocked in her chair. Her white hair fell down her body, and the children could see that she sat upon the hair as on a cushion. Her face looked like a dry riverbed eroded by rivulets of rain. That night she told the children an old Pima story about a broken piece of pottery called a "sherd":

One day a small piece of pottery complained, "Once I was a useful olla, but now I am only a little sherd."

"What is your trouble?" asked Sandstorm, who was passing by and heard the little potsherd's grumblings.

"Long ago an Indian maiden of Hohokam land molded me into an olla, and I was so proud to hold water for the braves, their women, and their children. But one day great trouble came to the Hohokam and they left their villages in haste. In her hurry, the Hohokam maiden dropped me and ran to catch up with her fleeing people. Now I am just a broken piece of pottery," cried the little sherd.

"Do not weep, little sherd, for I am going to help you," said Sandstorm. "I am going to cover you with a soft blanket of sand so you will not be trampled to a powder. Some day you will become useful again, just wait and see."

Sandstorm blew, and blew, and blew, rolling a fine layer of sand over the little sherd.

Many harvests passed and the little potsherd began to get tired of waiting.

"Is this the end of me?" moaned the little sherd. "I'm wasting my time under a cover of sand!"

Again Sandstorm heard the little sherd's grumblings and decided it was time to do something. So Sandstorm asked Rain for help.

"But you know I am blind, so how can I see the place where you covered the sherd?" asked Rain.

"I'll lead you to the place," said Sandstorm, "but first let me

213

*blow on my reed flute so the little sherd will know we are coming."
Sandstorm began to blow softly.*

*Then as Sandstorm and Rain came close to where the little sherd
was covered, Sandstorm gave a mighty blast, causing most of the
blanket of sand to roll aside.*

*"Now, Rain, it's your turn. Let me see what you can do,"
challenged Sandstorm.*

*Rain fell, patter, patter, patter, all night long. In the morning
Sandstorm led Rain back to his home, for their work had ended.*

*Soon a Pima maiden came by to get sand to mix with clay to
make an olla. She found the little sherd that had been uncovered by
Sandstorm and Rain the night before.*

*"A-yah! Oh! What a beautiful piece of Hohokam pottery," she
exclaimed, taking the little sherd in her hand to study the pretty
pattern. The maiden took the little sherd home and skillfully copied
the design on her new olla.*

*"I'm so happy," whispered the little sherd. "Now I am useful,
and I will be a link between the Hohokam of the past and Pimas of
the present."*

*Because a sandstorm usually precedes the rain, the Pimas tell
their children, "The rain is blind and always has to be led by the
sandstorm."*

When she awoke, Luna remembered her dream. Was it a sign?
Would she be the one who found the sherd and incorporated the old
designs into a new time in her peoples' history? Luna wasn't sure,
but she considered the dream important.

43

Ed Flanagan shocked his boss with the announcement that he was leaving the food bank at the end of the year. He was going to remodel houses, no less. Betty Golden had now seen it all.

"Look, Betty," Ed said calmly. "Stacking bodies in the same cooler with food is not my idea of an honorable profession. And besides, making homes more energy efficient seems about as critical as providing food."

Betty couldn't argue with him. In a way, she was jealous.

"What am I going to do without you, Ed? The food industry is collapsing around us. You're jumping ship in the middle of the storm." She knew that would infuriate him, but she didn't care. She felt hopeless in the face of his news.

Predictably, Ed jumped up with a reddening face, told her that the ship had already sunk, and stormed out of her office.

Betty sat at her desk quietly letting tears roll down her cheeks. He was right. The venerable old food bank was giving out under the increasing pressure to supply food to hordes of people lining up for food boxes. The lines had grown longer. More people were out of jobs as businesses cut back on staff. Depressed economic activity had resulted in fewer customers. People had lost income, jobs, and hope as each wave of blackouts had shut down business activity and even routine living. New housing plans lay on architects' desks.

Betty had recently said goodbye to two friends who had joined the steadily growing exodus from Tucson and the smoldering west.

It wasn't supposed to be this way, Betty thought with her head in her hands. She began to think about her own family: her daughter inundated by the rising sea near her home on the coast of the Carolinas, and her son in the middle of tornado country. The usual road signs on the map of life had fallen away from Betty, and for the first time she felt lost and paralyzed. At least Ed had found his meaning and seemed reenergized by it. He was the most practical, level-headed person she knew. What should *she* be thinking about?

Kim dropped Daniel off at home. Carla and Ed were cooking and invited her to stay for supper. She fell naturally into the mix of cooks, accepting a bunch of lettuce and a pepper to chop when Carla set them down in front of her. Ed barbecued chicken on the grill, disappearing into the outdoor heat and then returning drenched in sweat, the only consolation being that the meat cooked faster in hotter temps.

Daniel showered upstairs, grateful that Kim could answer the questions he knew Carla and his dad would ask about their trip and the release of the animals. He felt raw inside and needed space to process all he had observed and felt during the trip: the sight of the animals swimming into a free but unknown future, his first experience of a truly wild area, and the realization that such wildness had been the norm not many years ago. What was the feeling that gnawed in his gut? Was it anger?

He dressed, flopped onto his bed, and thumbed through his journal from the trip. Then on his tablet he scrolled through photos, choosing the best for his article. Daniel decided that he would write about the trip after dinner. The growling in his stomach sent him downstairs, where the table had been set and Carla was dishing clumps of potato salad into a serving bowl.

"Pull up a chair, partner," Ed said, looking over his shoulder as Daniel entered the kitchen. "We've been hearing all about the trip." He skewered some chicken breasts, blackened to perfection, and put them onto a large platter. Everyone converged at the kitchen table and started passing dishes around, Carla chattering about the Mission Garden.

Daniel was content to eat with gusto while the adults talked, managing to evade most questions and keeping to himself. He offered to clean up, sending the adults to lounge in the living room and leaving himself to quietly work while images, feelings, and ideas swirled in his mind. After he'd finished, Daniel joined the adults in the living room for about thirty minutes, then excused himself.

He sat at his laptop and began to write about the trip to the Bill Williams River. He titled his essay, "Where the Deer and the Antelope Used to Roam."

44

Samantha was distraught over the disappearance of Sonya and the gruesome death of her dog. All signs pointed to none other than mafia goons with no social conscience. *If they could do that to animals, what would they do to women, or worse, to children?* The faces of her three children, all in elementary school, flashed before her mind's eye. Sam's heart was torn between the primal drive to protect her children and her fierce determination to defeat the forces that conspired to ruin their futures. Her entire family had been on alert for months.

Across town on the Mexico side of Nogales, in an abandoned warehouse, Sonya struggled minute by minute to hold her mind together. Why she had not been murdered was a puzzle. They'd done everything else they could do to break her down. She thought they might be using her as bait. Did the use of drones change the game completely? Sonya recalled the night of her capture. They'd known her whereabouts every minute of the day. Advanced technologies, which any person could now obtain for private purposes, had rendered privacy and safety dead. The rules of engagement transformed continuously. This was malevolent innovation.

To keep sane she had made a study of the going and coming of people, or of as much of these as she was allowed to see. Her location had changed three times. She wasn't sure what town she was in or which side of the border she was on, and she had lost track of time.

From bits of conversation that she overheard, Sonya surmised that her captors were affiliated with a cartel based in Hermosillo. Yet the group worked with others. Sonya was pretty sure they'd been involved in the attempt to blow up the canal system. She'd caught fragments of conversation, and when not blindfolded she read everything she could. Once she persuaded one of her captors to talk a little. But she'd had to trade sexual favors to make it happen, a despicable activity that she'd done out of sheer desperation.

She was crazy now, she knew that, insane from hatred and disgust for her captors.

Then José, the guy she'd seduced, left his laptop unsupervised. Sonya risked everything. She Twittered Sam using a remote access code. For long days and nights she lived in utter fear. Surely Addrian Williams, the ace hacker, had picked it up. Hope raised its weary head again, just barely.

Would Sam or her SWAT team decipher it, or would the cartel trace it to her somehow? That was very likely, but she didn't know what else to do. She was a caged animal—pacing, watching, ready.

When Sam received the bizarre tweet, it created a dilemma for her. She dared not respond, even if she thought it was Sonya. What tipped her off was the hashtag, #mango2. That had been her and Sonya's code for meeting at a particular beauty shop where the owner was crazy about mango-scented shampoo and lotions. They'd started calling themselves the Mango Twins after Tomás had said they reeked of overripe mangos.

Mango2. It could only be Sonya, and some kind of code about her whereabouts or condition. Sam needed help deciphering it. But the goons were probably in her computer. Could she even trust the Nogales police? The mafia had infiltrated them too. What could she do, whom could she contact? Sam felt paralyzed and at the same time compelled to do something. But what? Throughout the day her thoughts were of nothing else, and her nights were marked by constant vigilance for the sake of her friend. She hoped that somehow her concern would translate into a solution.

Addrian Williams picked up the tweet from Sonya to Sam. It served as a flame to dry wood. Time was of the essence. A blaze of renewed commitment raced through all the investigation teams, but through none as much as through the small unit led by this master snoop.

Every cell in Albert Pope's body seemed to become energized for the job. He'd surmised from Officer Olivarez that the gift shop was some kind of point on a grid of mysterious activity. Lines led south to Hermosillo and north to Tucson. But Pope did not let that distract him from an essential fact: the tweet had gone to a friend, not to the authorities. Why? Was there a reason why Sonya hadn't contacted her own team? It could only mean that the people who held her knew about him, Addrian, and Richard and were following their every move. It even occurred to Pope that his activities could be useful to the thugs who held her. Could he capitalize on that to lead them astray?

Dolores had learned about Sonya's disappearance through Roberto. Police departments and crime centers were alerted to her capture and ordered to report any activity that might seem related, no matter how farfetched it might seem to them. No stone would be left unturned.

For weeks Dolores kept vigil at the altar of Santa Cruz Church, where she prayed to the Holy Mother to protect Sonya and bring the criminals to justice. Head bowed, she let her mind drift in the quiet of the small chapel. A dark shadow lay over the borderlands and her city. Like arteries, the highways of the drug trade stretched from Sinaloa into Canada, major highways carrying substances to all points, ruining lives and making money, lots of it. Could nothing be done to stop it? People who bought or sold the drugs were as complicit as those who dealt them. The steady flame of her faith was flickering low, but she still believed she could make a difference by preventing children from being recruited by the cartel's mules on South Tucson's streets. That was the key. As a woman of faith she believed that love would eventually triumph over evil, but God was sure taking His time. She'd witnessed so many youths lost to drugs and violence. Would she lose Sonya too? Perhaps she was already gone.

In the old chapel of South Tucson, Dolores lit candles for Sonya, Enrique, and her community. She remained for some time in prayer.

45

The doors to the hummingbird exhibit had been left open, but the interior exhibit, with its water elements and trees and shrubs, was being maintained. The netting over the aviary had been removed, but many of the species remained. For a time the natural history museum continued as the ark of the desert and Henry Waxman the Noah of his time and place. But he was not leading them to a Promised Land.

As the arduous days passed, Henry Waxman could not shake the feeling that he was letting down the founders of the museum. They had had an exceptional vision in the 1950s. It was an idea borrowed from the American Museum of Natural History. For more than half a century the idea of setting living exhibits in their natural settings had remained a viable and powerful way to engage the public. Over its history the desert museum had evolved in response to new opportunities and challenges, becoming one of the most respected zoos and botanical gardens in the world.

Henry considered all these things while on walks around the grounds at dawn or dusk, and in private hours spent thumbing through the archives of the museum's glory years. One morning while he was exploring still more old photographs, a flash of insight made him sit up with a start.

"It's not just about enduring. It's also about becoming stronger, better for it," he said out loud. Another thought echoed in his brain: desert creatures don't just survive, they thrive!

He shut the large album in his hands, rising like an old warrior from the battlefield, war-weary yet victorious. He pulled his desert hat down low on his head, tightened the drawstring under his fleshy chin, and strode from the library across the front patio and down the steps to find Luis Munoz.

Luis, Kim, and Henry sat across from each other at a table in the Ironwood Grill.

"I just completely lost sight of our legacy and mission," Henry confessed. He guzzled tea and wiped his brow under his sweat-ringed hat.

"Our role must continue to change as our relationship with wildlife changes—not just because it's difficult to exhibit animals in these conditions, but because our role is to change with the new reality yet continue to do what we do best.

"Think about it," Henry said, looking at Luis and Kim intently. "Remember our first exhibits, cages along a trail? We responded to new animal research and the public's call to create conditions that were as close to natural as possible, and we changed how we exhibited animals. We not only did that, but we became leaders in designing realistic habitat enclosures. We showed resilience. It made us better. Then as we learned how ecosystems really work and came to understand the role of predators, it enabled us to help reestablish gray wolves in their native habitats—another act of resilience on our part."

By now Luis and Kim could see where Henry was going. Both of them leaned in toward their director, intent on his every word.

Henry straightened himself and leaned back. "Nope, we are not closing altogether; we are restructuring and redefining our work by showcasing society's relationship with wildlife *in these times*."

Henry leaned in closer to his two most important colleagues. "It's up to you to help me figure out what that means exactly."

Emitting a loud rasping sound like overgrown house cats, the cougar siblings retreated to the back of the overnight enclosure in their exhibit area. Kim, Luis, four museum keepers, and two Game & Fish biologists with pellet guns teamed up to help load the big cats into two reinforced crates for their upcoming journey. Henry sweated profusely as he and Ed watched the transport expert carefully lift the heavy crate to the exhibit. Luis signaled him back into the narrow opening.

Kim had trained the cougars to go into the crate to reach their morning meal. Today she'd only put water inside. The larger male cat easily jumped up into the crate while two of the keepers nudged back the female with long poles. Kim and Luis closed the crate door. The male rasped loudly inside.

The crate was slowly raised off the ground and the driver began the painstaking trip, threading along the trails toward the front of the museum. Luis followed, yelling directions to the driver. Meanwhile the female cat emitted threatening growls at the keepers. Kim stayed behind to reassure her.

The removal of the mountain lions took three hours, and it marked the end of an era for the region. These animals had become iconic symbols of the museum fifty years before with the arrival of the first cat to be named "George L. Mountain Lion," an orphaned cub that was afterward raised at the museum. A column about human behavior, ostensibly ghost-written by George L. (and afterward by each of his successors) would eventually begin appearing in the *Tucson Daily Star*. In those earlier, litigation-free days, George L. had thrilled visitors as he strolled the grounds on a leash. What had seemed right and proper then had changed with the times.

That, Henry thought as he watched the lions disappear, *that was a different time. Perhaps we were wrong about some things, like keeping large animals in enclosures, but it fit for that time and level of understanding. Now new insights will again drive us to reconsider how we relate to wildlife.*

But Henry knew himself too well to think he would be the one to lead that new charge. He was too much of the previous age. His heart was not in what lay ahead. Henry hoped Luis might step up to take his place and that the Board of Directors could understand the changes ahead and embrace them.

For the first time in months Henry seriously thought about his wife back east, waiting for him. They kept in touch by phone, but until now Henry had resented her firm conviction that he was crazy to stay in Tucson. Now he wondered whether she was right. The whole concept of transforming a desert into some Eastern version of itself was now not only in question; it was clearly apparent that it was wrong. John Wesley Powell's prescient warning to government and business leaders, so long ago, had fallen on deaf ears. One hundred years later his wisdom seemed proven, at least to Henry. Man cannot live outside the ecosystem that provides him air, water, shelter, commerce, and inspiration. A brand new way, or maybe a return to an old way, now promised the region its best hope for building communities that would fit with the arid lands in which they existed. He knew that if any Southwestern city could do that, it would be Tucson.

46

Roberto sat with Enrique in the Santos' living room. They were discussing the fact that Enrique was no longer on probation.

"You've done very well," Roberto said. "How is the solar tech program? Do you like it?"

"Yeah. We're just starting. There are some cool people running it," Enrique said, cautiously considering how he might ask Roberto to help him learn more about Emmie's family.

There was a pregnant silence. "Any girls in the class?" Roberto teased.

"Yeah, one. Esmeralda Martinez," Enrique said and watched Roberto's face for any reactions. He thought he saw his brow wrinkle briefly. "I think she must come from a rich family. Her mother drives a Mercedes," he said, casting another line to Roberto.

There was a brief silence. Then Roberto asked, "Is she cute?"

"Yeah," Enrique said, "and smart."

"That's good, she can help the rest of you *burros*!" They laughed. Then silence again.

"I just need to know if Emmie's family is rich from drugs," Enrique said finally.

"I see," said Roberto. "You want me to check for you?"

"Yeah."

"Okay. I'll find out what I can."

"I just . . . I want to stay away from that," Enrique said and looked up at Roberto.

"That's good, Enrique," Roberto said, rising from the chair. "I'll let you know."

Roberto returned to the precinct. All the way there he was thinking about the conversation with Enrique. Here was a boy who was trying to stay clean, but every way he turned the menace of drugs confronted him. First his brother, and now a new girl he was attracted to. Enrique was a classic example. Without Dolores and Mrs. Carrillo, Enrique would just be another statistic. *Yet here he is now reaching out to me for help.*

Roberto found that remarkable. *And thank God.* He knew the Martinez family had ties to the cartels, but the DEA had not been able to definitively link them. It could just be a blood link and not drug activity. Juan Miguel Martinez, Emmie's father, was a respected business leader.

Roberto talked to his colleagues, who directed him to a database of cartel families. He began to search for any ties to Juan Miguel. By later that evening he thought he might have found something.

The next morning he brokered permission from his precinct captain to spend some time running down his leads.

Roberto drove downtown to the Martinez's large home-furnishings store. He wore plain clothes to appear as any customer would, and he looked around at the furniture and rugs. One of the family members greeted him.

"*Buenos días*, may I help you find something?" A tall slim woman with long silver-streaked dark hair smiled warmly at him.

"*Buenos días*, yes, thank you," Roberto said. He gestured toward a couch with gorgeous woven cushion-tops. "That is a truly stunning couch. Is the maker in Mexico? Spain?"

"Ahhh . . . I love this one too. We have a merchant in Hermosillo who makes these. The weave," she said, walking to the couch and lifting one of the cushions, "is handmade by artisans."

Roberto walked over near the elegant woman, getting a whiff of expensive perfume and noticing the gold-crafted jewelry around her neck and wrists. *She might be the family matriarch, not a salesperson.* He ran his fingers over the colorful weave. Yes, it was expertly sewn.

"*Exquisito*," Roberto said with appreciation. "I must bring my wife to see this one." And he truly meant that, but knew his poor police salary and her little teacher's salary combined could never afford the $8,000 price tag.

"What exactly are you looking for?" she asked.

"Actually we want to refurbish our daughter's bedroom," he lied, wanting to spend more time with the woman in case she was a family member.

"Oh, come with me. How old is she?" They were walking to another section of the large elegant store, an old warehouse Juan Miguel had gutted and made into a showcase.

"She is fourteen," Roberto again lied, and half wondered what it might be like to have a teenage daughter to pamper.

"Ah! I just did the same for my granddaughter, who is about that age."

They examined a couple of canopy beds and elaborate dressers.

"Is this another handmade piece?" Roberto asked.

"Yes, from Oaxaca. My Emmie chose a piece like that one for her bedroom," the woman said reflectively.

"Is Emmie your granddaughter?" Roberto asked casually.

"*Sí*. Tell me about your daughter," she asked, and Roberto launched into a fabrication that both shocked him and filled him with wonderment.

"Well, let's see what we might put together for such a precious girl," the woman said, and Roberto followed her around for another half hour, listening to ideas for furniture, drapes, and rugs. Finally he excused himself, saying that he would return with his wife.

In his brief time with Mrs. Martinez, Roberto had gained three leads: a Hermosillo furniture factory, an artist in Oaxaca, and a store in Nogales where Mrs. Martinez's necklace had been crafted.

Daniel and Enrique met up among chilies again, but in a different garden.

"Hey, my man," Enrique extended his arm to give the other a gangster hug, and Daniel returned it with a slap on Enrique's back.

"Bro, what are you doing here?" Daniel asked.

"What are *you* doing here, *mi amigo*?" Enrique said, genuinely glad to see him.

Daniel turned toward Carla. "Enrique, meet my new . . . mom." Daniel seemed as surprised as Carla.

Enrique greeted the small pretty woman who was still staring at Daniel. When she finally turned to him, her radiant smile made him smile back.

Dolores observed the two, wide-eyed. Enrique had a new friend.

Enrique laughed at this teacher. "Mrs. Olivarez, meet my gardening buddy, Daniel. Hey, I don't even know your last name!"

"Flanagan," Daniel said.

"Ah," Enrique nodded toward Carla. "Irish, right."

Carla listened and said, "Later I'll tell you how the Irish and the Spanish came together in the Old Pueblo, but for now we need to find Sal and get started before it's too hot to do anything."

Carla marched toward the ramada, the others following single file on the soft, sandy paths bordered by lush green plants of many varieties. Giant round sunflower heads, heavy with whirls of shiny black seeds, shaded the soil all along one side, and corn plants waved their tassels at the gardeners bustling over the grounds. Enrique spotted melons under some low broad leaves. He made a mental note to take one home if possible. Enrique filled his lungs with the scent of warm, moist earth.

Carla introduced the boys to Sal. Enrique felt a natural connection. In some ways Sal resembled his brother, Diego—the eyes shaded by long lashes, the sharp jawline and smooth brown skin. But it was Sal's smile that reminded him most of his brother. That smile had cheered Enrique as a little boy back when he had worshipped his big brother. The memory made the morning's joy momentarily fade, and sorrow caused a sharp pain in Enrique's chest.

Carla and Dolores harvested seeds together. Dolores had permission to put aside some for her community garden. Enrique and Daniel assisted Sal with a new segment of an irrigation system, the boys learning as they worked together.

Enrique felt whole; he felt connected. The old pit in his core, the pit of oblivion and separation, faded from his perception as he worked in the garden with his teacher and friends.

As Carla selected seeds with Dolores, she realized that the knowledge they were gaining together was essential for the future, and that there were thousands of families who would need to learn the same skills. As sweat beaded on every surface of her body, she guzzled Gatorade and watched for signs of hyperthermia. A new understanding was dawning in her. If the city and neighborhoods did not organize on a large scale it simply wouldn't be possible to live in Tucson and have any reasonable quality of life.

Carla stood up to stretch and gazed across the Mission Gardens. It was a worthy enterprise, a teaching place. But much more food would need to be grown and a distribution system organized. The poor desert soil would need huge inputs of organic materials to enable it to function as a carbon sink. How had previous generations done that? From across the garden in a nearby barrio, the gentle clucking of chickens in a backyard could be heard on the still air.

Carla straightened up and started to laugh.

"What?" Dolores asked. She looked up at her new friend and smiled too.

"Every time I think I don't know what to do, I find the answers all around me," Carla said and knelt down to continue aerating the soil around the plants on her row.

Dolores stopped, waiting for Carla to explain. When she realized Carla was finished she said, "Sometimes I think there are these big mothering spirits that hover around us, beating on our heads, trying to impart knowledge and encouragement."

Carla did not look up but said, "I know those girls."

47

The jaguar was fully healed and at his prime age. Ron Butler from the Wildlife Center called Kim to say he could no longer house the cat safely. It had been nine long months.

"If I get one more bag of letters or another social media campaign directed at us from school children and their teachers, I will have to hire security guards."

The center's director was joking, but he was feeling public pressure for keeping a large feline for so long at a facility built for small animals and birds.

In fact, the keepers and volunteers were terrified of Duma. A coiled menace, his presence pervaded the whole of the fifteen-acre site. The center's director recommended to Kim that she work with Arizona Game & Fish to relocate him to his native habitat. The animal had paid its dues to *Homo sapiens*, he had said to her.

Later, Kim met with Luis to talk over their options.

"What about the San Diego Zoo Safari Park?" Luis asked.

Kim winced. The transportation of the mountain lions had been an ordeal she did not relish repeating. Besides, California was now dealing with worse environmental problems than Arizona. And the Phoenix Zoo was rethinking its mission in the midst of blackouts and water shortages, and was unwilling to take another jaguar.

She and Luis were having a late afternoon beer at the museum café. A basket of chips and generous bowl of spicy salsa sat between them. Luis munched and dipped while Kim thought about what could be the best outcome for the animal.

Should she share her compulsion to violate the law? In her mind's eye she traversed the desert lands that surrounded the high peaks of the Sky Islands and followed the jagged spine from the spot where the jaguar must have wandered across the border. Release the cat into the forests there?

She sighed deeply and said, "It's just so damn unfair. This animal did nothing but wander into the human mess of the border. I think we owe it a fair turnaround, but I would have to do something illegal—an act forbidden on both sides of the border."

Luis looked at her. "Reintroduce it?"

"Yes," Kim said flatly. She studied her friend and colleague. His eyelids flickered as he thought about it.

"I've thought a lot about this, Luis," she continued.

"It's hard to untangle something like this," Luis said thoughtfully. "I mean, our professional ethics are based on keeping animals in captivity from the time when they are orphaned or from their birth on site. The endangered species legislation concerns the impact reintroduction might have on native communities. But," he went on after pausing to chomp on another salsa-laden chip, "the jaguar came from the wild and has not been exposed to the public. If we target the area where it's most likely from, then reintroducing it might have a negligible impact on jaguar populations in the vicinity."

Kim listened carefully, processing the matter as Luis thought it through.

"I've been around and around in my own head about this," she said. "We represent the museum and abide by the principles established here. This is outside our normal responsibility. It's more the purview of state and federal agencies. However, now they are looking to us for advice and help."

Jaguars were rare in Arizona. Sightings were decades apart. Great conservation efforts by nonprofits like the Sky Island Coalition and by jaguar conservation teams aimed at protecting the native habitat and the dwindling remaining populations. Yet even in the present day, mining and other land-use interests threatened the remaining jaguar habitat. It was the usual conundrum.

Luis stood, and Kim intuitively knew he was headed for Henry's office. She followed him, and they found Henry packing photos and memorabilia. He glanced up at the two. Henry's eyes looked wistful to Kim. Maybe this was a bad time to talk to him.

"Ah, the harbingers of fate," Henry said with a wry grin. To him a visit from the two of them meant some new challenge.

Luis and Kim found seats in front of Henry's desk. He kept packing boxes by his chair. After a few minutes he turned and said formally, "Well, what is the nature of this visit?"

It was touching to Kim. Dismantling the museum had taken its toll on all of them. Without a plan for how it might continue in the dawn of a new age, the future seemed uncertain at best.

"It's about the Ghost Cat, Henry, the jaguar captured in Nogales," Luis said.

"I've been asked to help release it into the wild," Kim blurted out. *There, done, she'd said it and was glad.*

Surprisingly, Henry didn't react. A few minutes passed. He continued packing.

"I did not hear that, you hear?" Henry turned to look at both of them to make sure they got his meaning.

Luis glanced at Kim. This was their nod to proceed.

48

The day dawned bright and hot. Carla woke from a fitful sleep. She threw off the sheet and let the air cool her body. Each day now, an arduous journey, required thoughtful preparation. She showered in a small drizzle, mindful of how many minutes were currently allowed, and remembering when she'd stood below a heavy spray of hot water for as long as she wanted.

As she toweled off, Carla remembered Daniel's introduction at the garden. She was deeply touched. But there was something about it that bothered her. Carla had no intention of ever marrying Ed. They'd never talked about it, but of course it was logical that Daniel might expect it. He'd grown up in a traditional home—one father, one mother, married with children. She didn't know why, but that just didn't work for her. She'd been on the prowl all her adult life.

But now Daniel had intervened in her natural way of living, had rolled a big heavy boulder onto her life's path: the prospect of being a mother. This was problematic because she loved Daniel. He'd lost his mother and was now bonding with her. Not that she could take his mother's place, she thought as she poured coffee. Suddenly it occurred to her that drinking hot coffee on a hot morning was ridiculous. She sipped it anyway, becoming more agitated.

Normally Carla would take a long hard bike ride to dissipate such negative feelings. She prided herself on having a steady-as-you-go personality that her students and friends relied upon. But she felt that strength fraying in the personal restrictions caused by the extreme weather. Her pool was empty, a chalky hole in the ground left over from another life, and she no longer biked long distances, instead seeking indoor protection from the relentless sun and heat.

Carla's thoughts turned to her impulsive decision to leave climate science in favor of something more practical. What could the community grow in a mega-drought, what could they grow together should Tucson remain habitable? Could they plant thousands of trees along the old Santa Cruz River that would pull carbon into the soil and draw up the water table?

Or maybe it was time to leave. She found the thought disturbing when it intruded.

She put on a hat and sunglasses and went outside to walk. Her sun-hardy plants showed new signs of stress, and her once beautiful gardens were brown and withered. New water restrictions forbade even nighttime watering. She planned to start over using the ideas and native seeds that she'd learned about at the Mission Garden. But there had not been time for that yet.

Back inside, she sat on the couch with her cell phone and scrolled through her Twitter feed. The news was filled with rancor between community leaders, world terrorism, national violence, and more weather-related disasters. She was about to throw her cell across the couch when a text popped up from Daniel.

"ppm (parts per million) CO_2?"

"450," she wrote back. "WAYN?" Where are you now?

"Library."

"143"—I love you, Carla wrote.

"1432"—I love you, too.

Carla smiled. That was a first. She wiggled deeper into the soft cushions. She enjoyed her new relationship with Daniel. But he had called her his *new mom* when he introduced her. She was shocked because he had never called her that before. She wasn't sure how she felt about it.

Carla was more irritable now than ever before, and this was

caused by the changes in their lives. The climate robbed them of choices, diminished precious freedoms, and made everything harder to do.

Even me, Carla admitted. *I've been studying climate change for years, advocating action, but it never truly penetrated my understanding until now.*

She called Ed. "Want to come over for a he-man breakfast?"

And there it was—her natural impulse to call him, to gather her loved ones to her. In the crucible of the present moment she chose to be with Ed, and she thought that perhaps she could temper her passions enough to manage a committed relationship. Maybe that would be all right. She'd get used to being a mom, or she and Daniel could work out another perfectly agreeable word to describe her new relationship to him.

49

Sam's shop was modest in size but represented Mexico's best artisans, with colorful woven shawls and blankets, Mata Ortiz pottery with bold geometrical patterns, Tarahumara figurines, simple wooden carvings, and jewelry-filled glass cabinets.

Roberto held a gold chain in his fingers, studying its quality and design. Samantha explained that the jeweler lived in Nogales. Roberto bought Dolores a pair of earrings, and Sam took them to wrap them. While she was in the back of the shop, Roberto took the time to really look around. He'd noticed a parked car with a man inside who had followed his progress into the store. And he'd picked up on a certain tension in the air, as if the shopkeeper had been checking him out too.

When she returned with the gift wrapped in beautiful paper, he said, "A friend of mine referred me to your shop."

Samantha looked up quickly and then down again. Roberto noticed how her body tensed, and he detected a forced a smile when she said, "And who might that be?"

"Angelina Martinez."

Sam looked up. Roberto knew he had struck a vein. Terror filled her eyes.

"Do you know her?" he asked. "She is Juan Miguel Martinez's mother. They own—"

"Yes, I know of them," Sam said, looking down again. Then she said, "They are my competitors."

Just then a man entered the shop. It was the man from the parked car.

"May I help you?" Samantha asked him.

"Yes, I am looking for a gift," he said, walking behind Roberto.

The man approached the counter. He wore an expensive cologne that Roberto recognized. This was no ordinary thug, he thought.

Roberto thanked the storekeeper and left. He walked a short distance down one side of the street, then crossed and worked his way back under the awning of a store across from the shop. He noticed that a closure sign had gone up in the window and that the shades were drawn.

When Albert Pope first learned about the activities at the Nogales gift shop, he had a hunch and honed in on that location.

"Officer Olivarez?" Albert asked in his resonant bass voice.

"Yes. Who is this?" Roberto asked suspiciously. He'd never heard this deep voice and it was his home phone, not his precinct cell.

"Albert Pope, part of the Nogales investigation team for the disappearance of Sonya Morales. Are you familiar with the case?"

"Who isn't?" Roberto said, still wary. "How'd you get my home phone?"

"I'm sorry to use this number, but we're trying to keep our activity 'below the radar,' if you know what I mean." Pope chuckled softly at his use of the old World War II term, which was a galaxy away from today's advanced technologies.

"So that's why you're using a public telephone number?" Now Roberto laughed.

"Yeah. Anything that defies the expected," Pope said. "Could I drop by your house sometime today? I'm following up on a recent visit you made to Nogales."

So, thought Roberto, I was observed. Damn, that means the

mafia knows too. Immediately Roberto felt his chest tighten with the understanding that his activity could imperil Dolores. If the good guys had observed him, then he knew the others had too.

Pope waited in silence on the other end of the line. He understood what the young officer must be thinking, feeling. This was tricky business—each decision to continue creating a burden of risk.

"Not here. Meet me at the precinct on Stone and Cushing. One hour from now."

Pope notified Addrian and decided to take Richard Green with him. Officer Olivarez could probably give them a host of information. Yet the fact that he was only willing to meet him at the precinct told Pope that the officer was guarded.

Time passed slowly. Sonya became delusional. Her memory played tricks on her. This must be what prisoners of war experience, she thought, and she remembered what Senator John McCain had done to survive after his capture in Vietnam. Sonya, a precocious teen, had found the thumb-worn copy of McCain's memoir in her father's library. She had read it cover to cover without sleeping. McCain's description of the psychotic torturer, The Bug, seemed all too familiar. Her confinement, torture, and unrelenting fear were similar to what McCain described. She was a prisoner of the drug war. She'd forgotten his story, and now, remembering it, she felt hope welling in her like newly oxygenated blood. Human beings can endure the unendurable. Her will to live flamed, a tiny light in an underground mine, illuminating the encasing walls and persisting.

Sonya began a mental practice of recounting her life: when she'd been born, where she'd lived, the names of her family members, their birthdays and addresses, the names of their husbands, wives, and children. She paced off the room, the windows, using her body, mentally running mathematical formulas. She "built" a new house brick by brick, laying the foundation and plumbing, and then planted a garden. Then she mentally drew the blueprints of a real house for her to live in after she was rescued. The pieces of her shattered mind came together like shards of broken window glass in an explosion run in reverse, reforming a window through which she could see clearly. Her mental fog vanished. She began to plot an escape.

Duma studied the two-leggeds until he knew the habits of each one. The big cat sensed those who feared him most. He could smell it as he could with prey just before he took them down. He paced the perimeter of the indoor-outdoor enclosure, tracing his path over and over again, marking it with fresh spray, and tolerating the parade of two-leggeds that came and went like buzzing flies.

The cat's attention focused on escape, and he watched carefully the opening and closing of the enclosure on the days when a two-legged entered the cage. His red-rimmed glassy eyes followed each one carefully, calculating the options. Another stood by, watching with the fire stick that Duma had learned to fear.

But the jaguar's natural strength and power had diminished in captivity. His body no longer cried for meat and blood as it had before. His once-powerful muscles had atrophied in confinement. The old power, coiled and ready to spring, had dissipated. He panted in the heat, chasing an occasional mouse that he found foraging for seeds near the outer perimeter. It was Duma's entertainment to bat the warm bundle of meat, spear it with a long claw, and crush it between his strong jaws. There was little honor in it. On occasion the Ghost Cat lost his mind, charging at the chain-link walls, growling and huffing for long periods of time. He took pleasure in watching the two-leggeds dive from sight.

Retreating to a shaded corner of his cage, he collapsed in a heap of flesh and bone. He lay watching, watching for a chance to flee.

Kim studied the big cat inside the airlock that kept her safe and that prevented Duma from escaping when she opened the door of the enclosure. He was in terrible shape. Kim had shown the rehab personnel ways they could hide food or secure slabs of meat to a wooden frame shaped like the cat's natural prey. These techniques encouraged captive animals to hunt, to attack, to rip and tear their prey. However, Duma had come to them as a free-ranging predator with wild instincts when he had wandered over the border into human communities. The rehab center had done its best, but the poor cat was suffering.

"He's lost weight. I'm estimating that he weighs around 250 pounds now," Kim said to the men standing outside the airlock.

"We'll sedate him one last time . . . hopefully." Kim said this last phrase with some shame. How many times and in how many places had she participated in this animal's sad journey?

One of the men was a pilot who specialized in airlifting heavy objects. He'd never transported a large animal, but he had been in touch with a team that had airlifted a two-ton rhino and carried it successfully to a new location about the same distance away as the place to which they were taking Duma—the San Raphael Valley in the Huachuca Mountains. It was at the headwaters of the Santa Cruz River in the Sky Island habitat. It was an area of rich biodiversity that included perfect habitat for jaguars. It would be about an hour to an hour and a half from Phoenix to the Huachucas via an aircraft build for speed.

No one knew whether the cat would survive the ordeal. The relocation and release would take two teams, one at the wildlife center to prepare the cat for the trip, and the airlift team below the border for the reintroduction. Luis would manage the team at the release site. It was, after all, similar to Duma's homeland. Luis knew officials at the Mexican National Office of Wildlife whose charge was to protect biodiversity. They would do an expert job on a very difficult task. Luis contacted biologists at Pronatura, Mexico's largest conservation nonprofit organization, and asked them to join the release team.

The cost of the reintroduction was estimated at $10,000. But no one was counting. A wealthy donor at the museum had picked up the whole tab. Henry had leaned on him to help with relocating the mountain lions, and the Ghost Cat was another endangered mammal that the donor relished helping. On the matter of the illegality, everyone turned a blind eye. The story of Duma had reached legendary status in the region. While there were many who wished him destroyed, just as many wanted to see him restored to his homeland. No one could be said to be right or wrong in the matter. The convolutions of man and beast had exceeded comprehension in the crucible of climate change.

50

Emmie did not wear her pink hat to class that morning. She had let her long dark hair down, and it lay on her shoulders in glossy waves. As she walked toward him, Enrique felt unsteady. She was quite beautiful, and he drank in her image, the way she held her head erect, how her body moved, and the broad smile that lit her face. He was a goner, he thought. Hopeless.

"Hi, Ricky," she said, using his familial name. How did she know that?

"Hi," he said. After an awkward moment he turned to walk her toward the classroom. The hallway at the college was long, and with only summer classes in session it was almost vacant.

"Got your homework done?" she asked.

"Yep. You?"

"Not completely. My uncles came over last night, and they are loud. I couldn't concentrate."

"How many uncles do you have?" Enrique asked as they walked into the amphitheater of the classroom.

"Five," she said casually as they put down their backpacks and began to unpack the contents.

Gerald and Floyd arrived. Soon the classroom filled and the instructor asked everyone to sit down. He announced that they would take a short field trip the next day and told them to dress in casual, cool clothing. They would be visiting the location of the solar field that would begin generating solar power for the town later that month.

During class Enrique could not get the image of five uncles at Emmie's house out of his mind. *Were they and Emmie's father involved in the cartels?* Wait, he stopped himself. He was just assuming things, and that was unfair to Emmie.

The class material had become more challenging for all of them. After all, they were just teenagers! But on the other hand, the city had offered them a chance to move onto engineering career tracks— maybe go to college too. On scholarship. But it occurred suddenly to Enrique that it made no sense for Emmie to be there. Right? Why would she pursue this when her family could buy her a ticket into any university, any career in the world? His mind wandered when he should have been attending to his homework. *Why was she on this track with low-income kids?* He had not thought about it before.

In their subgroup work, Enrique and his three friends worked as a honed team, each with a special strength that made it fun to face a new challenge. Enrique found that he liked being part of a team. This surprised him. He'd been a loner most of his school life, that is until Mrs. Olivarez's homeroom. His teacher had discovered a gift in Enrique for mathematics and had encouraged him to develop it.

So now he was the one who led the mathematical portions of the team's work. Emmie led the team itself, aided by the natural deference of boys to a gorgeous girl. Gerald was good with community connections, like mobilizing people to join the solar energy commons. Floyd questioned everything. He always wanted more time to decide. That quality, Enrique decided, was invaluable, if also annoying. It was Emmie and Gerald who typed up the team's final reports. They were averaging an A-, something Enrique found miraculous.

But there was an evolving conflict. Gerald was falling for Emmie. Enrique realized it on a day when Gerald casually mentioned he'd spent the afternoon at Emmie's typing up a report for the team. It struck Enrique like a bolt of lightning.

"You were at her house?" he said, dumbstruck.

"Yeah. You should see it. A palace, man," Gerald said, oblivious to Enrique's reaction.

After class the two boys walked to the bus. Gerald acted like nothing was going on, talking more than Enrique could stand. Didn't he ever get tired of talking nonstop? Gerald's chatter only served to fuel the storm gathering inside Enrique's chest. But he was too proud to show his jealousy and hurt. After all, he and Emmie hadn't been on a date. They had just done their classwork together.

"What's her family like?" Enrique inquired, breaking through his inner turmoil.

"Have no idea. Only a maid and I guess a butler were there."

At his precinct Roberto began to piece together the picture of the Martinez family, and as he did so he became less sure that they were directly tied to the cartels. While there were distant relatives in Mexico who could be in the drug business, Roberto's department's research found no hot leads on the local family members. The furniture business was legitimate; the family members were on just about every nonprofit or foundation board in town. There was a veritable tribe of them involved in South Tucson's business and social services community. It was Emmie's parents who had given the mayor $250,000 to start up the solar tech program for youth. Roberto couldn't wait to tell Enrique. The young man had hit the jackpot with Emmie.

But Roberto had pulled on a thread at that shop in Nogales—tied to something dark. After Sheriff Pope interrogated him, he realized he was in way over his head.

51

Daniel's first published essay appeared in the *Arizona Daily Star*. He wrote about the trip to the Bill Williams River and the reintroduction of the otters and beavers. Due to his status as a junior docent at the museum, and in light of its pending closure, the public was hungry for such tales. The perspective of a teenager particularly hit home with readers. Online comments flooded the paper and caught the eye of the editor. After discussing it with his staff, Daniel was invited to contribute another essay a month later.

Readers liked Daniel's style of writing. It was natural. He reported and then reflected. There was no guile, no proselytizing, just the story, pure and strong. Daniel was making discoveries and his training at the natural history museum bolstered his confidence for writing about the desert.

The editor's invitation thrilled Daniel. It seemed effortless, the way he'd moved into writing about his experiences. He hadn't thought about anything beyond his wanting to write for an occupation. It was Carla who had suggested that he submit his work to the local paper.

"This is great writing, Daniel," she'd said after reading his first story. "You have a natural talent." She gave him some pointers about scientific nomenclature and about providing references and resources for readers. Between Carla, Luis, and Kim, Daniel even had an outstanding editorial team at his beckoning. He began to think a little more seriously about his opportunity for bringing important stories to his community, such as the story of the reintroduction of captive animals to natural habitats, and he also wanted to communicate his discovery and consternation that Arizona had once had so much biodiversity. Could they bring it back?

Other changes were happening. Ed cut back to part time at the food bank. Betty and Ed groomed Frank in preparation for his stepping up to the Operations Manager position. He would do a fine job, and Ed began to mentally separate himself from his life-long preoccupation with food banking. As he did so he became physically and mentally charged with new energy.

The community college program required actual construction and design work. He was by far the oldest student in the class, but he relished the physical demands and even tolerated the heat well out of sheer excitement over doing something he'd dreamed about as a boy. The scent of freshly hewn lumber and the mental challenges of deciphering space, preparing materials, meeting code regulations, and refitting homes so that they were in harmony with the ecology of the land kept him occupied day and night. He dreamed of redesigning some of the interior aspects of his own home. Carla encouraged him to think about including areas in his remodeling schemes for basin gardening, rainwater harvesting, ramadas, and outdoor showers. The two of them discussed how they might work together to help homeowners and landlords rethink how to conserve water and provide space for growing food and native vegetation on their properties.

At night the Flanagan house was a lively roundtable of shop talk among a budding builder, an avid native gardener, and a young writer. Both Ed and Carla had become more fit with their outdoor activities and more engaged in solving real-life problems. Their work took on new meaning, rekindling their imaginations and drive after their previous careers had grown stale.

It was about this time that Carla noticed another change in her body and mind. She could not put a finger on it. She woke each day with it: a mental disorientation and weird, super-sensitive skin. At first she thought she had an allergy to something in the garden. Finally she made an appointment with her doctor.

"Well, it's quite simple, Carla," Dr. Kingsley said with a smile. "You're pregnant."

Carla stared at him, wide-eyed, not believing what she'd just heard. "But . . . but we've always used condoms."

"As you know, that's not foolproof," her doctor said, removing his gloves at the sink.

"But I'm forty years old!"

By now she was fully realizing the reality that there was a baby growing inside of her. "Oh, God," she muttered, one hand on her abdomen.

"Who's the father?" her doctor asked.

"None of your business," she said frankly.

"Do you love him?" Her doctor had moved to the door. Before she could answer, he said, "Get dressed and come to my office."

After he'd closed the door, Carla sat for a while composing her thoughts, or rather sorting through a tumult of realizations, all coming at once.

Everything will change. I don't want to be a mother! I've never even thought about having kids. And I don't believe in having children in this unpredictable world.

"Oh, God," she said out loud again.

In the doctor's office, Carla cried hot tears. Over the years of her relationship with Dr. Kingsley, she had shared concerns about pregnancy, and he'd advised her to be careful on more than one occasion, even suggesting a tubal ligation, which she had rejected.

"You are early in the pregnancy, Carla. You have options."

She looked up at him, suddenly realizing his meaning.

"I could never. But I am not ready for this, never wanted this to happen. This," she paused to consider her thoughts, "is going to take time for me to process."

"Okay. Good," Dr. Kingsley said, reaching for his prescription pad. He did not really fathom the impact of his news upon the young woman sitting in front of him. The universe was spinning in her as her mind, body, and soul came into full awareness of the child coming through her into a new family, and an uncertain future.

Carla left with her prescription and an appointment with an obstetrician. She was still in a state of shock when she arrived at Ed's house. It was early afternoon, and she was exhausted from the emotional torrent and heat. Upstairs, she flopped on their bed—the bed, she thought, where this baby may have been conceived. She lay on her back studying the rotating fan, letting her thoughts roam wide and unfettered. Into her semiconscious mind came the grandmothers, her "kitchen witches," transformed into a mothering horde. They hovered around the bed and caused images of a tiny red-haired girl to play in front of Carla. She saw Ed holding the baby and Daniel playing with her.

Suddenly she came to her senses.

"What if Ed doesn't want a child?" she thought and sat up, sweat beading on her forehead, her body damp with perspiration in this upstairs room that overheated in the hot afternoons. This was the environment in which she and Ed had such phenomenal sex, wild animals in a steam room. Jumping in a cool shower afterward, and making love again. It must have been during one of those sprees that the condom had leaked, she surmised. They had been irresponsible, she thought, looking back. Both of them starved for affection.

Well, now we've made a baby and we've got to step up to the challenge. Yes, I love Ed. Yes, Carla answered the doctor.

She made her way to the shower, and as the water flowed over her she touched her abdomen again and whispered softly to the tiny life inside her. With that she found herself smiling. She toweled off and began to plan how she'd let Ed in on the good news.

And Daniel . . . she hadn't thought about his reaction. He might think it was totally weird, parents at his father's and her age. But she thought not. Daniel loved kids. Didn't he? Then another thought: marriage?

52

The class followed an engineer into a building near the solar farm. An expansive window framed row upon row of solar arrays turning slowly with the sun's path across the sky. They were calibrated to absorb the greatest concentration of solar energy over the hours of daylight.

"We have engineered the farm so that no towers cast shadows on any of the panels."

Sun Team Central, the name Enrique's group had given themselves, sat together, spellbound by the futuristic look of the solar arrays.

"What you are looking at is a farm: linked solar collectors that convert solar energy into electricity and send it on to the grid. Families in South Tucson that join the South Tucson Solar Commons get credit for the amount of solar generated here on this farm."

He paused to let that sink in. Floyd raised his hand. "You mean, the solar energy does not go directly to our houses?"

"That's right—it gets dumped into the whole system or the grid, but the people who buy into it help pay for this operation, and they get credited on their electric bill each month. Once we get this going fully, South Tucson residents may have a net zero electrical bill, but right from the beginning they'll see their electric bills go down."

"So," Enrique said slowly, thinking out loud, "what you are

telling us is that we are becoming energy producers, not consumers, right?"

The instructor smiled and pointed to Enrique. "Great! He's got it right. That is the hardest thing for us to get across to the public, and it will be your job to make that happen as you go out to houses in your neighborhoods. We become producers of solar energy, and we get credit for it. You'll be getting money, but it just shows up in a net decrease in the energy bill each month for every family."

He repeated, "In the beginning most people will see just a minimal decrease in their bill. But as more people buy into it, the more energy we produce, the more everyone will benefit."

This had a great appeal to Enrique. "Look, it's a real do-it-together thing," he whispered to his team. "That's what the Sun Team Central marketing message has to be about."

The current assignment challenged each class team to develop an outreach plan to help educate their families, neighborhoods, churches, and other groups about the new solar energy campaign. They could use any means possible—informational websites, social-marketing sites, social media, door-to-door canvassing, public meetings, music, art, or whatever other means their creativity could generate.

The rest of the morning was a walking tour around the facility, a box-lunch session with their instructors and the facility manager, and then the trip back to the college. Sun Team Central was on fire with ideas, and excited to finally see the big vision of how the city was setting up the system for South Tucson families and businesses to get in on the solar revolution.

That night at home, Enrique tried to explain it all to his mother and Mrs. Carrillo. While he was showing them the diagrams from the day's field trip, Mr. and Mrs. Olivarez rapped on the door.

They were warmly greeted by Mrs. Santos and Enrique.

"What's going on here?" Dolores asked Enrique, seeing the dining room table covered with diagrams and charts. Enrique and

Roberto joined her at the table.

"How about some lemonade and a piece of Denise's *tres leches* cake?" She gestured toward Mrs. Carrillo, who rose to help slice the cake she had made for the Santos family.

"*Tres leches?*" Roberto said. "I haven't had that for ages. My mother used to make it."

He followed Mrs. Santos and Mrs. Castillo into the kitchen, leaving Dolores alone with Enrique.

"Can you show me how this will work?" Dolores asked, pointing to a diagram.

"This is Barrio Sonombre, and here is a nearby vacant lot, where a solar array will be built to make energy for twenty families," Enrique said, pointing to the street map. "And here are the transmission lines that connect them to Tucson Electric Power and the grid.

"During normal times the families will be getting their power from the grid, but because the solar garden, here, is producing solar energy and dumping it into the power company's grid, the families will get a lower energy bill." Enrique looked up at his teacher with sparkling eyes.

"Uh-huh," followed Dolores. "So, what happens if the grid goes down?"

"Well, that's the beauty of the solar garden: it can disconnect from the grid and send solar energy to the individual homes, so there isn't any disruption to their power."

"Wow!" Dolores was amazed at how simple it was. "Why haven't we done this before?"

"I asked that too. Our instructors explained that solar technology has become cheaper with more and more people buying into it, and the battery technology keeps getting better."

Dolores turned to her student and said, "Enrique, I am so proud of you. You know that, right?"

Enrique blushed and looked down. It was clear to her that he was mastering something for the first time in his life. She observed a new confidence in her former student. Dolores couldn't help but compare this assured young man to the sullen boy who had been so withdrawn and wary in her homeroom on the first day of school. The fake attitude he'd used to cover up his fear was gone now, leaving a healthy youth who glowed with renewed hope of a future of which he was a part.

"Have you heard from Diego?" Dolores asked. He never mentioned his brother, but she knew that he'd been rearrested and was back in jail.

Enrique's face darkened and he turned away briefly.

Dolores wished that she hadn't asked. But then he said, "Did you know his name means 'teacher?'"

Dolores understood what Enrique was telling her. Her student had survived detention and parole, the loss of his beloved grandmother, and the experience of watching his brother ruin his life. All these things that could have turned him toward a path of self-destruction had only made him stronger.

Dolores made a mental note to write the congressman and the mayor about this transformation in Enrique. South Tucson had at least saved one youth's life with their Solar Tech program. And what a life it was that appeared to be unfolding! Her chest filled with joy.

Just then the women came in bringing glasses of lemonade, and Roberto followed them carrying some plates with slices of cake on them. Dolores helped Enrique clear away his charts so they could settle around the dining room table. Enrique planted himself on the couch with his laptop.

"Ricky," his mother called to him. "Don't be rude. Your teacher came all this way. Come join us."

"Ma, I have homework to do," he said.

Dolores put her hand gently on Mrs. Santos's hand. "Let him. He is going to save the world." She smiled and the women went back to their conversation and dessert. Roberto returned to the kitchen for another slice.

After offering compliments to the cook, Roberto joined Enrique in the living room. He leaned across the coffee table and whispered,

"I checked out everything I could think of. Looks like Emmie's family is A-OK. And Ricky, they are leaders in this community."

Enrique's look wasn't what Roberto had expected. He just listened, then looked back down at his computer.

"That's good," he said.

Roberto waited a little, hoping there may be more from him, but when the boy just went back to reading, he asked, "Is there a problem?"

"She seems to be more interested in Gerald, a guy in our group."

"Are you sure?" Roberto asked.

Enrique stopped reading and looked up. "Not really, but I think so. She invited him to her house to do homework."

"Oh, I see," Roberto said. There was silence between them.

"You're not going to let that stop you, are you?" Roberto asked, grinning.

Enrique looked down. Then he looked up. "No."

"That's my man! Don't let *el ladrón* take your girl!" Roberto said too loudly.

"Shhh," Enrique gestured, grinning.

Roberto leaned in and whispered, "And I found out her parents are the ones who gave a bunch of money to start the Solar Tech program. You hit the jackpot, Ricky!"

That last bit of information made Enrique stop and sit up. That was information he did not want. It took him by surprise and he had to think about it. His scholarship came from her family's money. He wasn't sure how he felt about it.

Roberto watched the flickering thoughts reflected in Enrique's brown eyes. He realized that that bit of knowledge might be unwelcome to him with his young man's point of view. He felt a pang in his chest and wished he could withdraw the comment. But it was done, and now Enrique had to deal with it.

"Sorry, bro. I probably shouldn't have told you that."

Enrique was silent, thinking about it, letting it sink in. "No," he said, looking into Roberto's kind face. "Thank you for it. I could not understand why Emmie was in the program, you know, being rich.

It's for poor kids like me."

"Hey, it's not just for poor students, it's for *motivated* teens who want to make something of their lives. Don't forget that." Roberto used his counselor tone.

Enrique smiled at him. Roberto was like a big brother.

"Yeah, but we're all poor just the same!" he said.

"You are richer than you think, my man," Roberto said as he rose.

Enrique looked up at Roberto, whom he'd come to respect—a policeman, no less. Enrique felt something. Maybe this feeling was like having a father.

"Hey, isn't there a dance at Sam Lena Community Center on Saturday night?" Roberto asked.

"I guess. Why?"

"Maybe Esmeralda would like to go." A barely visible grin hovered at the edges of Roberto's lips.

Enrique was silent for a few seconds. "Yeah, maybe." He grinned too and Roberto burst into laughter.

"I might even know a cheap ride for you two," he said. They high-fived and Roberto left Enrique to himself.

A hush filled the living room. Moonlight streamed through the front windows, shining softly over the threshold of the front door, which had been left open to create a cool breeze. The teen went to the door and stood in the gentle light. Stars blinked at the edges of the lunar aura. The fragrance of Mrs. Carrillo's roses wafted by, reminding him of all the good things that had miraculously come into his life. He half listened to the adults chatting in the dining room. He looked into the moon's bright face and breathed deeply.

53

The Romeros listened carefully to Luna's description of her dream, glancing at each other, exchanging thoughts without words. They could see the young teenager struggling with the possibility of representing her Nation when she was just beginning to understand its deeper traditions. It required a certain maturity and discernment that Luna felt she did not yet possess. They assured her that whatever she decided to do, they supported her. The elders perceived a delicate moment in the adolescent's development, one that must never be intruded upon by adults' wishes.

George Romero sat across from her. He'd just come inside, and sweat still glistened along his temples. The elder wiped his deeply tanned face with a handkerchief. His silvery white hair was pressed down where his hat had been. In accordance with custom, he avoided looking Luna directly in the eyes. Instead he looked down at the rug.

"It's a good thing to follow the path to learn about tribal customs. Not many young people care about them anymore. Flora and I got this knowledge from our parents and we've tried to pass it on to your generation. You are someone who wants to know. That is a good thing, and we are grateful to you."

He picked up a cold glass of water that Flora had put on a table near him and drank it reverently. When he'd set it down again, he continued: "You have the gifts of a leader. Flora is a good teacher.

She made sure you took no shortcuts, that you did things the right way to make your basket. It was not about making a basket, you see. It was about a way of doing something thoughtfully and skillfully."

Luna listened intently to Mr. Romero, occasionally looking at Mrs. Romero, who nodded at her husband's explanation.

"Your dream came from the ancestors. That is an old story that was told when I was a boy and before my time too. It comes from the time when the Hohokam left their ancestral home and came here to this valley. It was a time of great trouble, and people were confused, much like this time now. The dream is a gift to you, Luna. It is a call to lead."

Mrs. Romero looked at her student and said, "It is true. Those dreams are sacred, and when they come they are meant to be understood and acted upon. This dream that you had, Luna, is a great honor."

George added, "You see, they waited to see who would finish the basket. Your friend gave up, and no other youth expressed any interest in learning more after the saguaro harvest. But you did. Something in you reached out to Flora."

Luna felt dizzy. She had not expected this. She felt embarrassed, overwhelmed, and even wished it had not been said.

"You need time to think," George said, understanding her emotions. "Leadership has two sides, like a knife. One cuts deep if not handled right. Leading is a burden as much as a gift."

He said this gently, his Stetson grasped in his hand now. He stood up and excused himself, disappearing into the blazing afternoon.

Flora took Luna into her kitchen. "Sit down. You need to eat. It's good for grounding."

She prepared a burrito for her student as they discussed Luna's next basket project. For now, the subject of whether Luna would be the representative from the Nation on the mayor's Youth Council had been put to rest. It was up to Luna to decide. And she knew that whatever she decided would be all right with the Romeros.

Dolores worked the soil in her garden under the soft light of the moon. It was the only time she had for gardening at home, and at least the air cooled a little after sunset. Her mother sat on a porch swing, humming a tune while gazing at the night sky.

Roberto had been gone for a few days and she missed him. He had not told her what he was doing except that it was routine stuff. She was glad not to have to add one more worry to her list.

Dolores noticed movement out of the corner of her eye. It was a large hawk moth flitting around the garden. It found the long white blossom of a Datura plant and lit on the stamen to imbibe nectar. The hawk moth was the size of Dolores's outstretched fingers. She watched the dance between the flower and its pollinator in the moon's golden glow. Bats flitted over the streets feeding on insects attracted to the street and house lights.

Venus sparkled above and the tiny red orb of Mars was visible in the southern sky. Dolores felt the stresses of the day ebbing away in the soft night air and smelled the fresh scents of pungent herbs and perfume from the night bloomers that dotted their garden and those of neighbors. As a result of the renewed interest in growing food at home, her neighborhood now provided habitat for many desert species. The return of life encouraged Dolores that they were on the right track.

An occasional car went by the adobe home in the old barrio. Their neighborhood watch program had ushered in a new feeling of security in numbers. It was a tentative beginning, like the new roots of a young tree, but it had already established more confidence in the families who were so recently terrified to be out at night. With the ongoing threat of blackouts and further loss of normality, even possible loss of life, the decision to trust—to do something as simple as sitting on one's front porch—required courage.

From the enveloping black velvet night, someone called out to her mother from the house across the street.

"*Buenas noches, Señora Olivarez*," the voice sang. Then another from down the street rang out, "*Buenas noches, Señor Gomez*," and so on, rippling like water when a gentle breeze crosses the surface.

As Dolores methodically worked her way along row by row, turning over the soil and listening, the sounds of people's voices as they echoed each other's greetings sank into her soul. Her neighbors seemed to be making solemn oaths to go on being there for each other, to hold fast in the storm.

54

Carla brought a steaming platter of *carne asada* to her men. She set it down in the middle of the kitchen table with a flourish.

"Hmm, that smells downright wicked! If I didn't know you better, I would think you were casting a spell over us hungry *hombres*," Ed kidded. He was truly ravenous, and was so glad that they were not going vegetarian tonight. He'd been climbing, hammering, and sawing all day long, and his body cried out for protein.

"What is it?" Daniel said with his hands on his fork and knife, poised to stab one of the fillets onto his plate.

"*Asada*, bro," she said. "I marinated it overnight. Lots of jalapeño peppers, cilantro, limes, beer, and the kitchen sink." The men were already eating it.

She passed around grilled potato wedges and a salad. They were all having cold beers.

She waited until they'd satisfied their hunger and started to slow down. Then she made her announcement. After thinking about how to do it, she decided to include Daniel. It was a family affair and it would be a family taking care of the baby.

She clinked her glass for attention. Ed and Daniel looked up at her, surprised. "I have an announcement." She paused for emphasis. "We are going to need to rearrange the furniture."

Silence. "And why would that be?" Ed asked, a quizzical

expression on his face.

"That's what women do, Dad," Daniel said.

Ed sat with a curious smile on his face. Carla could tell he was running through all the reasons why she might have said such a thing.

"There will be one more of us soon," she said.

Another long silence. Both men were running through all the possibilities until finally Ed's face registered the meaning. He went completely pale and sat back in his chair, staring at Carla.

Daniel said, "You mean as in *a new family addition*?" He was grinning with excitement. He'd gotten it, and Carla could tell by his expression that Daniel loved the whole idea of a baby on the way.

"I'm too old!" Ed said with his hands on his chest. "Hell, *you're* too old!" he gestured at her, going through what Carla had gone through in the doctor's office.

Carla let things percolate. "I've got dessert." She proceeded to remove the platter and replace it with a beautiful lemon pie with waves and peaks of toasted meringue, Ed's favorite.

She could tell that Ed was immobilized. She cut him a slice and put it in front of him. Then she reached around his shoulders and delivered a kiss on his cheek.

"We're going to have a baby, sweetie," she said, hoping to melt through his shell.

Then she cut Daniel a slice, and as she handed it to him she said, "And you, dear boy, will have a little sister."

"Sister?" father and son said in unison.

"Saw it in a dream . . . the most precious little red-haired girl."

Ed stood up and motioned for her to come to him. He wrapped her in his arms, pulled back a little to look her in her green eyes, and said, "I got a tiger by the tail when I fell in love with you!"

Daniel grinned through a mouthful of lemon pie.

Carla had succeeded in winning over Ed and Daniel. She sat on Ed's lap as he teased her with a forkful of pie. When she tried to eat it, he withdrew it, saying, "Got to watch the calories, dear," and ate it himself.

"I'll just sneak a piece later," she warned.

After a few moments of silence, Ed said, "Seriously, is this really happening?"

"Yes." she said soberly. Then her face lit up. "This baby is going to spice up our lives. I just know it."

Ed began to chuckle. She got up from his lap and looked down on him.

"What's so funny, Dad?"

"You've gone from a hot climate scientist to a knocked-up gardener in just one year!"

Her face reddened, but even Carla couldn't deny the humor in it. She started laughing and then fell into Ed's arms, where her laughter turned to tears.

Ed held her close but with as much caution as he would use to handle fine china. Carla drew back after a while to look at Ed's tanned face. She felt intense love for him.

"We'll make this work, sweetheart," she said to him. He smiled, running his fingers through her waves of red hair. He kissed her gently.

"I think we are winning the contest for number of life-changing events in a year."

She rested her head against Ed's chest and thought about that. What he'd said was true. New careers, new family, new child.

It all seemed perfect somehow, albeit earth-shaking. *I was a single woman on a crusade to change the world*, Carla thought. *But instead, the world changed me.*

55

The Nogales police put a watch on the neighborhood of Sam's store after Roberto talked to the precinct captain. He was to report any further leads he might uncover.

"An investigator called me," Roberto told his captain. "An interesting man who asked a lot of specific questions. I taped it. We met here."

"Who was he?" the captain asked.

"Albert Pope."

"I know that guy. He was a tribal sheriff. God, he's one of the best investigators I ever worked with. Trustworthy. Quietly goes about solving cases, which he almost always does. And not by fancy means. The guy just has an instinct about people."

Roberto listened and felt better. He'd been concerned that his boss would think he'd overstepped his authority by letting Pope interview him without the captain's knowledge.

And there was one item that he hadn't completely run down. A certain "weaver" in Hermosillo. Roberto knew that whoever the weaver was, he or she was somehow affiliated with the cartels. Intel had traced emails from the shop to this informant and to Sinaloa, a place from which cartel activity emanated. But how did that relate to the capture of Officer Morales? She'd been investigating a bomb threat to CAP. What was the connection?

Roberto said, "I think I might just look into one more connection before I drop this investigation. Is that all right with you?"

His captain was not exactly thrilled about it. "You'll be in the big league if you go looking into those dark holes."

"I'll be careful."

"Let me think about it before you move on anything. Don't pull on any more strings until then."

The captain looked directly at Roberto to make sure the young officer would comply.

"I don't want to lose you, and you don't want to bring down your family—do you?"

Roberto looked up at that.

"I am not exaggerating, Roberto. These characters we're dealing with are the worst of the worst. They do not even count as human beings."

Bob Minor stood before a team of hotshots from the DEA, the Border Patrol, Homeland Security, and the CIA. For the mayor of an often maligned border town—more residential than consequential— Bob wielded power like a pro. For one thing, his imposing size got their attention. An ex-professional football star and former Marine, he still had that attitude of leadership and impenetrable will.

"How long has it been since she disappeared? And you supposed 'pros' tell me you can't find her?" They'd run down lead after lead. But someone wasn't coming clean; something nefarious was going on. Bob could smell it.

"Look, Bob," the DEA guy responded, "I think we have to move on."

Bob stared at him, causing the man to look down. The mayor decided to play his cards.

Bob said, "I happen to know that you are making deals with the cartels." He'd said it to bait them. He suspected it but was not sure.

The room was deadly silent. The CIA agent said that that was ridiculous. The US government would never bargain with a cartel.

"Oh, really," Bob said. "Well, let's see what was leaked to the *Wall Street Journal* recently." He threw a document across the desk.

Bob held out a thick forefinger, pointing to each of the members sitting around his desk. "Find her. I don't need to know what you are doing, but I know you are using her as a pawn. Now *get out!*"

Albert Pope sat in a frayed beach chair on a dry wash where the sand was packed. Under the shade of a mature willow he swigged cold beer and peered from under his large panama hat. He'd whittled down a long slender willow branch, and now he leaned over and used this to draw on his desert canvas.

Putting Sonya in the center, he began to draw lines out to all the people and groups she'd been associated with, including her captors. Resembling a web, the network of crisscrossing lines allowed Pope to find patterns, see vulnerabilities. He hoped something he hadn't thought of would pop out from the picture before him.

When the first drawing yielded nothing new, he moved his chair several feet away and did another mapping activity, this time putting the mafia and cartels in the center. This one showed activity between Sinaloa, Hermosillo, Sam's shop, and Tucson. Three of the locations were commercial, representing the sale of arts and crafts from Mexico in US shops. Nothing unusual. Sinaloa was the main source of drugs and the home of the most vicious organization. Surveillance from the Hermosillo weaver, the gift shop in Nogales, and the Martinez's store in South Tucson hadn't turned up anything until just before the last, long blackout that had sent half the Southwestern states into another crisis. The Hermosillo artist's popularity had increased several times just hours before the blackout.

Sonya had contacted the artisan, looking for clues to a possible connection between him and the attempt to blow up CAP infrastructure. Had she pulled on the wrong string and tipped off the terrorists planning to take down the Western grid? During that week no security had existed on the border. It was anyone's guess how greatly crime activity had increased with the grid down, but it was a certainty that advances had been made during the blackout. Surveillance cameras, computers, drones, security networks, even locks on jail cells, had all been rendered useless.

Pope stood up to stretch and survey his work from a better vantage point. A rustling noise caused him look up in time to observe a scraggy coyote trotting across the wash about 25 yards away. It never looked back at Pope, but trotted on, finally blending into the creosote and willows.

Only someone familiar with his nation could understand the impression this made on Pope. Coyotes were tricksters in his people's mythology. A shape shifter, Wily Coyote could never be trusted and usually showed up as something he wasn't. A contrary teacher, in disguise.

Returning to the suite of offices that housed the clandestine team of three, Pope shared his hunch with Addrian and Richard. They returned to ground zero. Everyone associated with any part of the investigation to find Sonya now came under the eyes of Pope and his partners. Going beyond the typical security review of US, state, and local security agencies, Sonya's team conducted deep dives into the professional and personal lives of everyone, including themselves. Bob Minor, mayor extraordinaire, secured permissions for them.

It took only ten hours to identify a member of the Border Patrol whose activities were tied to all points related to Sonya. They had a snitch. Following leads without tipping him off, the investigation teams located a warehouse on the east side of Nogales, Mexico—right under their noses, as Pope had intuited.

Independent of the US intelligence community, Bob was working with the Morales family because he suspected the feds were dealing Sonya as bait. That goaded him to the point where he worried about his own anger causing him to do something stupid. He felt responsible, that was it, and he hated the way the United States had lost its guiding principles. It had become like a third-world country. On top of that, Sonya's mother had been in and out of the hospital with near-fatal heart problems from worry over her daughter.

A text message buzzed. It was an unrecognized number. He hesitated.

"What the hell?" He opened the text.

This is confirmation of your order. Your package will arrive next day.

"Huh?" He hadn't ordered anything. Maybe his wife had, but why would he be notified? And what was she ordering now? Damn, he loved that woman, but she had a shopping gene.

Wait. This could be something else. He sent a message back: *Thanks, dude.*

Then he traced the message using a watchdog app. Almost as soon as he'd keyed in the mobile phone number, his phone went blank.

"What?" Bob turned off the power and booted it back up. It came back on, but the message was gone and so was his watchdog program.

He stomped out of his office and down the hall to his tech guru, and related what had just happened. Carl took the device and played around with it.

"Can you remember the mobile number you called?"

Bob took the phone back and tried several combinations, but each connected him either with a message that said, "Sorry, this number has been disconnected" or with an angry person at the other end.

"What could have done that to my phone and erased that program in such a flash? It was instantaneous."

Carl thought about it. "Whoever sent that message did not want a trace-back and had the skill to block your attempt to discover them. It has all the hallmarks of an advanced security system. It could be a cartel."

Bob just stood there looking at Carl.

Or it could be us. It might have been our own security system letting me know to expect something tomorrow. Could it be movement on Sonya? Is a deal going down?

Bob left the office and drove across town to the old section where the Morales family lived. Bob and his wife had shared many lovely dinners with Sonya and her family behind these white stucco walls. He knocked using the heavy brass knocker on the massive oak door of the territorial-style home and admired the landscaping that contrasted so interestingly with the rest of the dusty border town.

Regina Morales greeted him, dressed, as usual, in traditional Tehuana style, with a long skirt and blousy top.

"Oh, Mayor Minor, what a surprise!" Then her face clouded as she realized he may have bad news about her daughter. "What is it?" She grabbed his elbow and ushered him in.

"Not bad news, Regina. Maybe something, I don't know. Can we gather whatever family members are here to talk?"

"Of course. Alex and David are working, but Raphael and *Papá* are here." Regina referred to the patriarch, Pablo Morales, as Papá. Ricardo, the oldest son, lived in Mexico. This was Sonya's family, the people he'd come to know. Each in his or her own way was working to find the sister, daughter, beloved. The strain on the whole family was enormous.

They walked down a wide hallway decorated with large paintings, including one of Sonya with her mother. Bob loved to tease Sonya about it because in the portrait she wore an ornate dress, definitely not her current style. Looking at the painting, he felt a renewed sadness.

"*Papá*, look who's here!" Regina said with an upbeat tone as she and Bob entered the library. Judge Morales sat at a spacious desk, working as usual—more than usual, according to family reports. The judge had not slept through the night for a year. Sonya was precious to him, and the thought of his daughter in the hands of ghouls had hardened him over time.

"Judge." Bob stepped forward and extended his hand.

"Sit down," Morales said. "I hope you have good news." He examined Bob's face for any hint of the reason for his visit. "Do you?"

Regina had moved next to her husband and kissed him on his

balding head. "The mayor has maybe some new information. He wants Raphael here too."

"Well, get him," he directed. She left.

"Quick, tell me before she returns."

"The bad news is that the feds want to stop the investigation." He watched the fury form behind Pablo's glasses. "But wait, before you react. The way it went down, I think they are just putting me off. I believe they are actually close and want to clear the room of anyone that might trip them up."

Raphael barged into the room. "What have you heard?" he said before greeting the mayor.

"Sit down, sit down and calm down," his father directed.

Regina and Raphael pulled up chairs next to Bob so that they all sat facing the judge.

"He was just telling me that something might be ready to happen."

"*Dios guía mi vida*," Regina muttered and crossed herself.

"Today I received a strange text message." He repeated it for the family.

"Did you trace it?" Raphael asked.

Bob shook his head. "When I tried to search back to the caller, it wiped the message and program in an instant. My tech expert at the office said it was like I'd knocked on the door of an advanced security system."

"*Papá*, what could it mean?" Regina was in tears. Raphael moved to his mother's side and held her hand.

"I thought you should know. I have no idea if it means anything, if I did get contacted by someone with information about Sonya or if it's just a fluke." Bob spoke directly to the judge.

They sat together, all of them pondering the message and wondering how to react to it.

Regina broke the silence: "*Papá*, could it mean Sonya might be alive and maybe even, *Dios mio*, might be released soon?" Her pleading look said it all. Desperation.

"I can't stay," Bob said and stood up. "I have to get back to the office, but I'll keep you informed. If you are contacted by the feds, for now, don't share what you know. I have my reasons."

Pablo walked Bob out. On the driveway he said, "If they are getting her out, it means she is being traded for something. These can go very badly. I will hope, but I won't hope too much."

"You believe in God, right?" Bob said.

"Yes. We're Catholics, *amigo*," he said, slapping Bob on the back.

"I am praying for her," Bob said, and tears welled in his eyes.

56

Kim invited Daniel to accompany her to Phoenix to witness and write about the great white jaguar's release. They discussed the complex legal and political issues related to what she and Luis were doing. But she felt there were enough wrongdoers on all sides that the controversy would wash out eventually in court. Kim was taking a risk by allowing Daniel to expose the activity in the newspaper. It would probably end her career, but at this point, with the museum closing and climate change altering her notion of the future, she accepted it.

"Why can't animals just be released?" Daniel asked as Kim drove. They'd packed her van and had been on the road toward Interstate 10 by 5:30 a.m.

"Well, the answer to that would take days of explanation. But here are some pointers. First, reintroduction is usually done to help a native population of the same animal that is about to go extinct or that is genetically inbred. To have a healthy population of any animal, it takes lots of gene diversity so that each animal is given the best chance of having enough survival genes for that time and place. Think of it like a hand of cards. The more variety in the deck, the more in your hand, the more likely it is that you end up with a winning hand."

Daniel was scribbling notes fast.

"You should get a tape recorder, you know?" Kim said.

"That's a good idea," Daniel said, still making notes.

Kim paused to let him catch up. They were winding up Gates Pass among rolling hillsides. Green sentinels in a saguaro forest flickered in the illumination of the van's headlights—witnesses to her crime, she thought—and pointed in other directions as if telling her to go back.

"So," she continued once they were on the highway, "reintroduction is a science unto itself. Research about the native populations near the release site must be conducted, and the impact of the new animal or animals must be considered. Some concerns are whether the native population will be exposed to viruses or pathogens the captive animal has picked up. Another consideration is the disturbances in the relationships among the native species that reintroduction might cause. Introducing breeding males, for example, creates new competition pressures that weren't present before the reintroduction."

"So what about the captive animal? What do you have to consider for them?"

"Great question. See if you can answer it just using logic."

Daniel thought for a minute or two.

"It might not know what to do after being in a cage or enclosure most of its life. It might not know how to get food for itself."

"Good, what else? If you had all the time in the world?"

Daniel thought about the otters and beavers and how he'd wished to stay at the reintroduction site, follow them, learn whether they later came back to the cages and to the food they'd left. "I think watching to see what happens would be important."

"Yep. You'd make a great scientist. Sure you'd rather write? Or maybe do both?"

"I don't know. I'm leaving it open," he said.

"So, yes, we call it monitoring: keeping track of the reintroduced species, watching for changes in the native community. That's a very time-consuming process, but it gets you valuable information."

They drove on a little, Daniel thinking. "But we aren't doing any of that. We just dropped off the otters and beavers."

"Oh, Rich and his staff are following them through the radio collars, and the population on the river has been well studied. So all that documentation was in place."

"What about the jaguar?"

"The Ghost Cat is another matter entirely, and very problematic."

She related the whole tale of Duma's capture in Nogales, the escape, and the recapture. Then his removal to the Phoenix animal shelter. Daniel had known bits and pieces of the story, but now he was hearing the full saga.

"Luis is an expert on jaguars. They are native to his homeland."

"But an albino. How often does that happen?"

"It's rare, rare, rare," she said, changing lanes. "*Panthera onca* is the scientific name. Some jaguars are not truly albino, but have genes that alter their skin color. But our cat is a true albino, an animal born with a congenital abnormality that robs it of any color or pigment in its skin, hair, nails, or eyes."

Daniel was scribbling. "How did it get to Nogales?"

"Luis believes it wandered across the US-Mexico border in the Sky Island habitats where there is plenty of prey. Predators like the cat go where the prey are and don't care about much else. It probably was attracted to nearby ranches at the base of the mountains."

They were passing Casa Grande—more than halfway to Phoenix. The sun peeked over the mountains. "Only about another hour to go," Kim said. Daniel hunkered down to get all his questions answered.

"So what's going to happen today?" He reached into the back and opened the cooler lid. "What do you want to drink?"

"Soda, please," Kim answered. "Well, here's the skinny of it: we will sedate the cat, put it in a special sling, and a helicopter will airlift it to a location south of the border, about due south from Tucson. That's where Luis is right now with his team."

As Kim explained this plan, Daniel realized how much of a chance she was taking. *Would the animal survive the trip? Would they disturb the natural order of the ecosystem into which they were reintroducing it? Would the jaguar attack humans in the locale? Would it perish from other predators?*

She drank her soda in a few gulps and handed the bottle to Daniel.

"And if I sound like I know what I'm doing, don't believe it. I've never done anything like this, and I'm scared to death."

Kim and Daniel were both silent, looking ahead.

"Yep, that's the truth, Daniel. I'm scared to death." Her voice trailed away amid the hum of the tires on the road. The highway stretched to the horizon with only the usual line of semis at the early hour.

In Duma's dream he followed a forested path worn by himself, the deer he tracked, and fellow creatures of the Sky Islands. Sensory memories lingered. Earth smells, tangy scents left by other audacious males over which he recalled the pleasure of pouring his own powerful waters. The cacophony of forest sounds that were brought on the wind and to which he turned his ears, the cries of the black-feathered horde that led him to injured prey, wind rushing through giant trees before a storm, the steady drop of cones thudding to the soft forest floor. The musky scent of damp earth, the pleasure of a swim on a hot day, and the acrid scent of blood from the fish he caught and ate at leisure on a sandy bank. In his dream he felt his fangs rip at the thick flesh and how it quivered with life.

When he awoke, Duma sensed a change in the two-leggeds. He could hear that there were more of them around. He rose to better assess the situation. As he walked slowly toward the outdoor enclosure, he caught sight of a pack of them. They stared at him. Duma smelled their fear. It emboldened him. He growled and crouched. The pack of two-leggeds left. He drank water and returned to sleep and to his dreaming.

Kim and Daniel pulled into the rehab center's parking lot. The sun was fully up. Before they got out of the van, Kim turned to Daniel.

"Now listen carefully. You will not go near the jaguar at any time. This is one of those situations where it's possible it could escape. So you are going to be in a nearby building where you can see the action until I tell you otherwise."

Daniel was taken aback. She'd never talked to him in that parental tone or restricted his movement in any way. It made him mad, but she was emphatic, her eyes a little wild-looking.

"Okay," he whispered.

Kim introduced Daniel to the rehab center's director and showed him where he could sit and observe the action. As she started to leave, she said, "Just forgive me for now. I'm a little hyper."

"Yeah," Daniel said. But she had already left. He moved to the front of the observation room and sat in a spot where he had a good view of the enclosure. No jaguar in sight.

In the veterinary center Kim calculated the dose she thought the animal would need for the trip. Beyond a certain point it was just guessing. Based on her previous experience and knowledge of the cat's reactions, she was probably the person best equipped to figure it out. She loaded the dart gun.

From the far parking area outside the center came the sound of the pilot beginning his startup preflight procedures. Her heartbeat quickened. She joined the rehab team and helped them secure the jaguar in the sling. She reviewed the procedure with the team, configuring the sling and the harnesses on the ground where the pilot could maneuver safely.

Daniel sketched and watched with increasing anxiety. When the cat emerged from the interior of the enclosure, Daniel stood. The jaguar was magnificent, even in its present state. But he watched in horror when it suddenly lunged at the fence, scattering everyone. Now Daniel understood Kim's fear. She looked back at him and gave a weak smile. He nodded.

The next half hour was tense. After they'd laid out the sling in its final configuration, they radioed the pilot. Daniel could hear the blades cutting the air. How was this all going to happen? What if they dropped the animal, or worse, what if the sedative didn't work?

275

He broke into a nervous sweat, wiping his brow with one arm.

Kim and a keeper entered the enclosure. The cat emerged. Kim released a tranquilizer dart into Duma's hind leg from a safe distance. The cat went down but struggled to get up. It dragged itself a short distance and then fell limp. The team flowed into the enclosure and four men lifted the cat, carried it outside, and lay it on the sling. Kim guided the team, explaining how each of the cat's ankles would be harnessed with synthetic cable, with the sling and padding underneath the body. The Ghost Cat would be airlifted upside down like a baby in a bunting.

Daniel took photos through the glass, wishing he were right there. Suddenly the helicopter was above the keepers and Kim and was dropping a hook. The pilot hovered the aircraft and brought it right over the top of the animal. They secured the creature and gave the pilot a thumbs-up. All at once the cat was airborne above them. The copter tipped toward the southern border of Arizona, its blades slicing the air with greater velocity, and flew off with its load dangling below it.

Kim motioned for Daniel to come join her. Outside the team was jumping around, doing high fives, and loudly expressing their pride in a job well done and their relief that their worst fears hadn't been realized. Kim talked to Luis by cell phone and gave him the exact time when the helicopter had left.

"It all went like clockwork; now the hard part. Luis, I am praying it goes well on your end. You might have a live cat by the time it arrives. *Please* be careful."

She hung up and smiled at Daniel. "Well, how's that for a story?"

"Probably the best I'll ever have," he said. When he looked at his watch it was nearly 11 a.m. *How had four hours passed?*

"Let's go for breakfast," Kim said.

As they drove to the restaurant, Daniel noticed Kim's hands trembled on the steering wheel. He gained a new appreciation for her that day, and for the dramatic things that were being done to save animals. This he would write about so that others could know too.

57

The SWAT teams moved in on the warehouse in silence, surrounding it, climbing stealthily up its walls, pouring into all its openings—all in silence and synchronized by the base nearby. Approaching but not yet in earshot, a Huey gunship was making its way from Nogales. On command it would swoop over the building, hover long enough to pull up its cargo, and power out at full throttle.

There was a moment of total quiet before mayhem was loosed. On command the teams advanced into the hallways and began to take down anyone who appeared before them, working their way back to the room where Sonya listened in hope and fear. Her captor José panicked and crouched in a closet near her, but with the door slightly ajar. He settled himself, then peeked out of the closet and aimed a gun right at Sonya's head.

Sonya started praying as she heard the teams advance. Enough ammunition was flying to start a war. The door opened without a sound. Immediately Sonya caught the eyes of the first Seal and she looked at the closet without moving her head. The soldier let go a round of bullets that obliterated the door and the man inside, but not before José pulled the trigger. The bullets grazed Sonya's skull. She felt searing pain as if her head were on fire. More men came and held down her scalp and carried her outside to a basket that lifted her along with a Seal. Hands reached for them as they were whisked away from the horror that had been Sonya's life.

As the Huey headed for a Tucson hospital, the pilot noticed a Jet Ranger carrying a payload and heading toward the border. He called it in to home base, thinking it might be a drug run. The Border Patrol and Homeland Security authorized its interception. A gunship raced toward the projected path of the plane with its suspicious cargo.

For half a day no one heard anything about the rescue. The cartel was not advertising it and no one dared report it. The Nogales, Mexico, police cleared the building of bodies and collected evidence. The intelligence teams from Nogales arrived. Bob was notified.

Gradually Samantha and Tomás heard through their family's network. Sam was stunned that her friend had been captive only a few miles from her store. What had she been through? Tomás prevented his wife from going to Tucson or leaving their home. Everyone lay low. Tomás knew that the cartel would be watching.

Throughout the region a new understanding dawned with Sonya's rescue. The predatory cartels were looking for weaknesses to exploit. With the extreme drought, blackouts, and looming water crisis, the region faced more than climate change: the cartels, mafia, and terrorists would continue to exploit every vulnerability. And there were many.

Regina and Pablo rushed to Tucson with Sonya's brothers. The woman who lay before them was unrecognizable. Regina wept with Pablo. Yet Sonya's mother knew that her daughter's physical wounds were not the biggest challenge she would face. Regina was more worried about her daughter's mind and soul.

Sonya's head was bandaged where surgeons had repaired her skull. Damage had occurred to the tissue below it, the surgeon explained.

"Most of Sonya's injury was outside the brain, but the swelling and bleeding where her wounds occurred will affect motor and sensory areas. Otherwise, for what she's been through, your daughter is in pretty good shape. We just have to wait now."

But Regina was focused on something else. Would Sonya's natural optimism remain? Would her personality change? The emotional scars worried Sonya's mother the most.

"*Papá*, I'm finished with this drug business. We've got to move away from it, we've got to find a safe place and take Sonya with us."

Pablo said nothing. Sonya's brothers were silent. Regina knew they were gathering strength. These men of hers would never leave now. She knew that and felt her body fold under the weight of it. They would not stop until the cancer that invaded the whole region was eradicated. Even when that battle may have robbed them of their sister and daughter. What's more, Regina knew that if her daughter survived and retained her former self, she too would recommit herself to her quest to end the violence that plagued the border.

58

Luis and his Mexican colleagues from the Office of Wildlife and Pronatura awaited the arrival of the jaguar. The reintroduction site had been carefully researched by scientists and conservation officials, and by Luis, who knew the Sky Islands as home. These unique mountain habitats, like an archipelago of islands in a sea of desert and grasslands, stretched south from Tucson deep into northern Mexico. The pungent scent of pines stirred old memories of his childhood, when he had roamed the highlands and its rivers. The Santa Cruz River emanated from those peaks, flowing north from Mexico across the Arizona border.

Luis was deep in thought about that river connection and his own path into El Norte, which had been not unlike the jaguar's path. Now the cat would be returned to its native habitat. Should he also return home? It didn't seem like the place for him now. While the jaguar would find refuge in these mountains, Luis was beginning to see that his refuge was of a different nature. Was that what the jaguar in his dreams had foretold?

Suddenly he was shaken from his reverie by the roar of the approaching Ranger.

Everyone looked up as the aircraft came to hover overhead with the jaguar still secure in the swinging cradle underneath.

Luis quickly reviewed the procedures with the team. If the cat remained sedated they would remove the halter and ankle wraps, administer an antidote, and let him go free. If the cat was alert, they would cage him—a dangerous situation for the jaguar from the point of view of possible injury, and for the crew should the cat get free to strike.

But as they strained to observe the state of the animal above them, an unexpected Border Patrol helicopter rushed into view from the west.

Luis closed his eyes and reopened them to make sure it was real. He watched aghast as the gunship caught up with the Ranger, hovering at a safe distance. A voice bellowed over loudspeakers.

"If you drop that load, we are authorized to fire."

"Get on the radio and get that fucker out of here!" Luis yelled to his counterparts, gone mad with surprise and consternation.

Luis ran over to the Office of Wildlife truck. He got there in time to hear the three-way conversation among the Border Patrol, Pronatura, and the poor guy flying the Ranger (who was not bilingual). The Border Patrol pilot was translating between the Mexican officials and the American helicopter pilot.

"¿El tigre? ¡Ahora lo he visto todo! Now I've seen it all!" shouted the Border Patrol agent. "And you expect me to believe this?"

The American pilot screamed back, "Hey, we have an animal on the end of this harness, and I have a limited amount of fuel. We've got to put this jaguar down on the ground *now*."

There was a brief silence as the Border Patrol helicopter moved away and began its descent, sending the land crew scrambling behind vehicles to avoid the blast of leaves, grass, and dead limbs scattered by the aircraft's downdraft.

Luis studied Duma for any sign that the animal was awakening, but it appeared to be still. He turned to address the Border Patrol with a look of desperation on his face. He ran toward the copter, ignoring the rotating blades.

When the gunship had landed, patrol officers poured out and scrambled into the clearing with guns drawn. It looked more like a sting operation at that point. Luis waved at his team members, motioning for them to crouch behind vehicles to avert a horrible accident. His heart was pounding as he tried to sort it out, but it was all occurring too fast.

With his arms up like a criminal, Luis sprinted over to one of the Border Patrol officers.

"We've got to get this animal to the ground," he yelled and pointed at the payload under the Ranger. But the officers grabbed and fleeced him instead, gesturing for him to walk toward the Office of Wildlife vehicles. Luis's face went pale and his eyes widened like saucers.

"No, you've got it wrong!" But one of them grabbed Luis before he could finish and pushed him back toward the vehicles. He staggered in front of them, totally confused.

His team crouched, their guns pointing at the Border Patrol. At that moment Luis thought he might die. He could not breathe or even speak well enough to explain.

"Idiots! Can't you see this is a government agency?" yelled the Office of Wildlife officer.

"Drop your guns if you want to engage in a conversation!" a Border Patrol officer retorted.

Seeing Luis held in front of them, the Office of Wildlife officials dropped their guns and walked around in front of their vehicles with their arms raised.

Luis found his voice. "This is official business. We are relocating a jaguar to its homeland. Look above you, for God's sake!"

The Office of Wildlife representatives explained what was happening and showed their credentials. The Border Patrol took the team's guns in spite of Luis's protests. Finally they authorized the Ranger to drop its load, warning the pilot not to leave the area or risk pursuit under fire.

As Duma was lowered and the Border Patrol was able to see that the payload was indeed a large jaguar, they handed the guns back to the Wildlife representatives.

Luis gestured to the pilot to begin lowering Duma. As soon as the crew got their hands on the harness, Luis unlocked the tether so they could lower the cat gently to the ground. The Border Patrol officers walked closer to study the jaguar's white hide and pale rosettes. It was a rare sight for sure.

Luis began checking Duma's eyes and chest. The cat breathed deeply, showing signs of awakening. A biologist quickly embedded a tracking microchip in Duma's earlobe.

Then Luis instructed the crew to untie each of the ankle hoists, sending the Border Patrol scrambling to their copter. Once inside they gave the Ranger permission to leave the area, satisfied that this was a legitimate operation. The Ranger left immediately, ushering in welcome silence. Luis could think clearly again. He carefully examined the jaguar one last time.

Everyone went to their vehicles except Luis. He injected Duma with an antidote to the sedative. The animal slowly came to consciousness. As it struggled to stand, Luis trotted across to the vehicles where his colleagues waited.

Luis stared into the jaguar's handsome face. He traced the patterned markings and broad nose, the thick, red tongue hanging from its powerful jaw. He followed the deepening breath of the jaguar, visible on its rounded chest, detecting how the animal was gaining strength. The jaguar looked directly at Luis. A wave of perception spread over him, prickling his flesh. He knew that he was witness to something new.

What? What's that smell? Duma felt his limbs under him. He lifted his head, breathing in the scents, reading the language. *Wood and stream, yes! That was it!*

Duma stood shakily, then staggered a few yards toward the great old trees. Was he dreaming again? No.

Suddenly he became aware of the trucks idling on the road. His first response was to bound away, but his still-drugged body did not respond. He lingered a few moments, and then, noting that the trucks did not approach him, cautiously stepped toward the green pavilions that he knew. As he neared the edge of the forest he paused to look back at the two-leggeds watching him from their vehicles. Memories of their strange world rushed back to him. He steadied himself, drawing energy from the land—his homeland, his lifeblood.

And then the Ghost Cat vanished from sight.

EPILOGUE

The dark, clear sky formed a massive dome overhead in which the moon goddess held court, sparkling stars adorning her golden head. Below, the drums began their deep rhythm, the heartbeat of the earth, organic and elemental, focusing the crowd's attention, and settling chaotic minds. A broad line of skeletal ghouls and creatures, half beasts and half angelic beings, marched past throngs of celebrants lining the street. In their boney gargoyle hands, people held images of departed loved ones that appeared and disappeared like fireflies in the passing flames of torches along the parade route.

It was one of Tucson's greatest traditions, the All Souls' Procession, when people celebrated the Mexican holiday el Día de los Muertos, the day for honoring the departed. A giant platinum urn rolled on wheels, receiving into its vessel the individual prayers and hopes of the people in the crowd. Mariachis with faces painted in playful skeletal expressions trumpeted and serenaded the returning souls and cheered the faithful minions.

Within the crowd, Enrique and Emmie stood together. Their youthful faces shone in the firelight. In his arms Enrique held a framed photo of his beloved grandmother, and whenever he looked down at it tears came into his eyes. He brushed them away. Emmie turned to place a tender kiss upon his cheek, setting him afire so that he became a votive candle in the crowd. As the urn slowly passed, both youths placed prayers into baskets held by attending priests and priestesses.

On this eve of All Souls' Day a perceptive person might observe a slight shift in temperature, a presence filling a room, a breeze moving through a window, lifting the curtain when there was no wind. Across the Old Pueblo spirits flowed from all directions, entering barrio streets and adobes and passing through doors wherever families and friends had constructed an *ofrenda*. These altars were draped in white and honored the memories of their departed with wreaths of golden marigolds, images of their loved ones, sparkling sugar skulls, platters of *pan de muerto*—the bread of the dead—and candles to guide the departed home. In any given house one might find a pair of glasses, a pocket watch, a pack of cigarettes and matches, or a favorite wine or whiskey, each item lovingly placed for returning spirits on this one special night when those departed and those present were reunited.

A discerning ear might catch a favorite tune played by a once-animated musician strumming on his guitar. Other ghosts sat by children's beds or whispered advice into grown children's ears, chastising them for poor behavior or making suggestions for how they could do this or that.

And many spirits swigged shots of tequila to bolster themselves against the gravity of earthbound existence, not only its literal weightiness, but also that physical yearning and confusion that tortures the flesh.

Not far away, Daniel, Ed, and Carla held up a framed photo of Bonnie as the drummers and the spectacle of ghosts passed by. For Ed the memory of Bonnie would remain an old wound, never to be healed but always cherished. And for Daniel the whole night symbolized the end of sorrow and the beginning of an exciting future that lay just ahead. Now with a new family forming and a baby on the way, Daniel would remember his mother as that sturdy trunk from which his life had blossomed forth. He shed no more tears but was filled with an awe at the mystery of life that only youth can know—that good medicine that unfortunately fades with adulthood but that returns just before death. Suddenly he understood the gift of death, and then in a flash he forgot it again.

Luna Lopez stood near the procession with her aunt and uncle among other Tohono O'odham and Pascua Yaqui families that were there to honor the dead. They too tossed their prayers into the passing Urn of Hope. For native people the night was not really different from any other, except for its splendor and pomp. The bones of their people had accumulated under their feet for more than four thousand years—a continuum in time. Luna felt stronger than before, aware of something like a muscle deep inside that had always been there supporting her, but of which she'd had no awareness until this night. The feeling quickened in her as the urn passed and the drums reverberated through her.

Luna looked up at the moon and was sure she saw something move across it, something with wings, a dragonfly perhaps, a strand of iridescent gossamer in rainbow colors.

ABOUT THE AUTHOR

Susan Feathers is a writer and educator with 30 years of experience in communicating science to the public. She served as the Director of Education at the Arizona-Sonora Desert Museum and as Education Liaison to K-12 Schools for the Center for Environmental Studies at Arizona State University. Susan is a graduate of the Aldo Leopold Foundation's Land Ethic Leader program. She facilitates book-club readings focused on land ethic issues. Her essays are available in *Paean to the Earth,* on WalkEarth.org, and in the anthologies *Hope Beneath Our Feet, Restoring Out Place in the Natural World* (North Atlantic Press, 2011) and *Songs of Ourselves* (Blue Heron Press, 2015). *Threshold* is Susan's first novel. Go to WalkEarth.org to join discussions, find links to information about Tucson and the Sonoran Desert, or to arrange a reading or book-club discussion.

DISCUSSION QUESTIONS

Threshold contains themes and characters that are intended to evoke conversations about the role of place in forming the character and destiny of people, plants, and animals. Climate change is altering the landscape under our feet. What does that mean for each community of people that inhabits a place, a region, or a country?

Use any of the questions below to spark a discussion with your book club, classroom, or community reading group and facilitate the exploration of thoughts and the sharing of ideas with each other.

DUMA, THE GHOST CAT

By including an animal character, the story is broadened to encompass the natural world and other perspectives about events and circumstances.

1. In what ways did Duma's story contribute to the overall story and your understanding of the region? Why do you think the author included the jaguar? How does the author weave Duma's story into the other characters' narratives?
2. How do attitudes and regulations about threatened or endangered species differ among countries, regions, and/or people? What particular issues did the story explore regarding the fate of wild animals in human settlements? About captive animals and the role of zoos?
3. How do you think climate change might alter attitudes and regulations regarding the fates of animals?

LUIS AND KIM

In Chapter 2 the reader learns about the condition of Sonoran Desert plants and animals, and the role of the natural history museum in encouraging the public to conserve the biodiversity of the desert.

1. What are Luis and Kim's concerns?
2. What is the tension that zoo scientists and educators have to balance?
3. If you were in Luis and Kim's position, what would you have done to protect Duma? The museum's animals? What are the problems with releasing captive animals?
4. Is your local zoo or aquarium making plans for climate change?
5. Some zoos have made the decision not to replace endangered megafauna like lions or elephants, but to allow such animals in their displays to pass away naturally without being replaced with others. What do you think about that?

CARLA AND ED

These two characters begin as polar opposites in their attitudes and beliefs about climate change.
1. How do they change as the story progresses?
2. Are they believable characters or not? What makes you think so?
3. Can people change rapidly? Why or why not? What forces acted upon Carla and Ed that might have led to their radical actions?
4. What were Carla's concerns about her pregnancy?

DOLORES AND ROBERTO

Dolores and Roberto return to Tucson, their birthplace.
1. What are the reasons for their return to Tucson? How do they think about community, and what cultural traditions do they draw upon?
2. Dolores is a rare kind of teacher. What makes her so? Have you had a rare teacher?
3. What did you learn about Tucson's history and

culture through these characters?

DANIEL, ENRIQUE, AND LUNA

As climate change alters landscapes, the human community will have to adapt and make critical decisions that will affect generations to come. Daniel, Enrique, and Luna are teenagers who each face particular challenges.

1. How does the quote from Albert Schweitzer at the beginning of the book inform you about the author's intent in creating these characters? What do you think the author was saying through them?
2. How are the circumstances for each teen different from those of the others? How are they similar?
3. How do the adults in each teen's life help him or her mature? How do they hinder maturation?
4. Each teen is dealing with loss. Can you describe these losses? How are all of us dealing with loss in relation to climate change?
5. In *Threshold*, each child is assisted through certain kinds of ceremonies. What are they? What is the role of ceremony in meeting the challenges of life?

SONYA, SAMANTHA, AND BOB

Nogales and Tucson—and the Tohono O'odham Nation—are subject to the crimes of the cartels and Mexican mafia at the border between Mexico and the United States. The desire for drugs in the United States continues to fuel the fires of the dark world that the author sketches in *Threshold*. Not only animals get caught up in border conflict, but children and families as well. It is an ongoing tragedy in which both countries and their citizens are complicit.

1. What circumstances and forces form Sonya's character and career choice? Would you respond to them as Sonya did? Why or why not?
2. Rape is a common war crime across the world, and

in times past, when women were considered little more than chattel, it was commonly accepted. Today it is used as a form of intimidation. How does this problem affect your state, your community?

3. Sonya and Sam form a partnership early in their friendship to fight sex crimes against children and women. What examples of similar leadership do you have in your community?

THE COMMUNITY

The author has strong views about the potential of community to solve problems.

1. What are some examples of these views in the story?
2. How does the author regard government? Give some examples. Does this viewpoint resonate with the current national mood or not? In what ways can government play a key role in protecting the rights and welfare of communities?

THE LAND ETHIC

Aldo Leopold, regarded one of America's most important conservation leaders, believed that the idea of community must extend to include the plants, animals, soil, waters—collectively, *the land*—in places where people live.

1. In what ways are people and the land where they live connected? Give examples from *Threshold*. How does the condition of each influence the other? Give some examples from your own community or region.
2. Leopold wrote that people must learn to "live on a piece of land without ruining it." What are some ways that people can learn to do that? Give a few examples from *Threshold* of instances in which characters think or act in ways that relate to land.

GENERAL QUESTIONS

1. Do you feel that this book changed your views on climate change? Why or why not? Pick a scene in which you would have acted differently than one of the characters.
2. If you could change something about this book, what would it be and why?
3. In chapter 4, as Sonya reflects on the plight of illegal immigrants struggling in this country for economic freedom, she thinks that El Norte (the US) is no El Dorado. What seems most true to you?

OTHER RESOURCES TO EXPLORE

The author's website, www.walkearth.org, includes links to sites and organizations whose subjects and mission relate to *Threshold*'s themes and characters. Questions and/or comments for the author can be submitted on the same site.

Join a discussion about the Land Ethic—developed by Aldo Leopold in the early 20th century and even more relevant today.

Submit ideas for a sequel—say, something that takes place twenty years later. What will happen to the characters? To the community? What new technologies, and/or human practices and policies, might define the experience of people and animals living then?

OTHER TITLES FROM
FIRESHIP PRESS / CORTERO

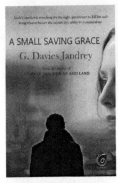

A SMALL SAVING GRACE
G. Davies Jandrey

Set in Tucson, Arizona, *A Small Saving Grace*, is a tale of suspense with wry sensibilities, offbeat characters and just enough menace to make the reader wince and say, "No, don't go there."

Life is in turmoil, yet against the odds, Andy, and those who love her, make slow, but steady progress. All the while, Andy's attacker is stalking the entire household, searching for the right opportunity to kill his only living witness before she regains her ability to communicate.

A Small Saving Grace is full of suspense, but at its heart, this is a story of love, resilience, perseverance and healing.

CHARLATAN
Kate Braithwaite

How do you keep the love of the King of France?

1676. In a hovel in the centre of Paris, the fortune-teller La Voisin holds a black mass, summoning the devil to help an unnamed client keep the love of the King of France, Louis XIV.

Three years later, Athénaïs, Madame de Montespan, the King's glamorous mistress, is nearly forty. She has borne Louis seven children but now seethes with rage as he falls for eighteen-year-old, Angélique de Fontanges. Athénaïs must do something to keep the King's love and secure her children's future, but how? And at what length is she willing to go?

At the same time, police chief La Reynie and his young assistant Bezons have uncovered a network of fortune-tellers and poisoners operating in the city. Athénaïs does not know it, but she is about to named as a favoured client of the infamous La Voisin.